CAJUN RULES

COLD WEST PUBLISHING

Cajun Rules
The Blue Line: Book 2
By Martin Brown

Published by Cold West Publishing,
An imprint of Creative Texts Publishers, LLC
PO Box 50
Barto, PA 19504
www.coldwest.com

"Cold West" is a Registered Trademark of the Cold West Detective Agency and Creative Texts Publishers, LLC

ISBN: 978-1-64738-050-2

CAJUN RULES

by

Martin Brown

Contents

PART ONE
The Hour of the Wolf

"The hour of the wolf is the hour between night and dawn ... when most people die, sleep is deepest, nightmares are most real. It is the hour when the sleepless are haunted by their worst anguish, when ghosts and demons are most powerful." Ingmar Bergman

CHAPTER 1

The sound of a telephone ringing in the middle of the night is never good. Any news that can't wait until a decent hour is just bound to be bad news. It often means someone is dead...or dying. When you are the detective responsible for the investigation of death in a suburban police department, it usually means your night is over and your day is starting. So, with stinging eyes and a dry mouth, you grope around for the telephone receiver and try to sound alert. My wife, Kay, told me once that when the phone rings in the middle of the night, I always sit straight up in bed and say "shit!" I had not known that. I guess this was no exception because I could hear her softly laughing against her pillow.

Creekwood was one of several suburban cities that lay in the sprawl of the Dallas/Fort Worth Metroplex. By 1972, it had reached a population of around 35,000. Had it been uprooted and placed in the middle of west Texas, it would have been a respectable-sized town, but it was comparatively insignificant against the urban giants that surrounded it now. It was what was called a "bedroom community" meaning that it was where the legions of workers from the city came home to in the evenings, relaxed with their families, and rested up for another day in the city. "Bucolic...peaceful" are terms used to describe Creekwood. As one of the Creekwood Police Department's three detectives I intended that it stay bucolic and peaceful. But Oscar Wilde once pointed out that it is with the best of intentions that the worst work is done.

"This is Bryant," I managed to choke out of my dry throat, waiting for the usual glib and irritating greetings by the night dispatcher, like "Wakey Wakey," or the all-time favorite, "Were you asleep?" The edge in his voice was enough to bring me out of the last of my haze and put me on full alert.

"We've got a dead body on the side of the Trinity River at the bridge. Coleman is at the scene and said that the body is tied up, so it looks like homicide. You want me to call the captain?"

1

"Oh, hell no, don't call him yet. Let me get out there and look around first before he comes out and screws things up. Have someone pick up the camera in the darkroom and bring it to me at the scene. I'm on the way."

It was that slow period between Christmas and New Years when the kids were beginning to tire of the gifts that Santa had worked his butt off all year to pay for while Kay was busily looking around for a New Year's Eve party to drag me to.

The last of the bed warmth had left my body when I walked out to my car. I was surprised to see that the sun was just breaking over the horizon and realized it was later than I thought. Suddenly, I didn't feel quite so deprived of my rest. I drove through quiet, placid suburbia thinking that normal people were just getting up, having a cup of coffee, reading the paper and easing into their day while I was on my way to survey some human wreckage that had the bad form to find itself dead in my little town.

Creekwood PD had three detectives, including the captain, which in reality meant that we only had two detectives. Captain R.J. Copeland was the "Peter Principle" in perfect symmetry. He had supervised patrol officers from sergeant to lieutenant to captain. With no room at the top of the tiny hierarchy at Creekwood PD, the only logical move was to make him Captain of the Detective Division. Never mind that there were only two detectives in the division and that he had absolutely no experience investigating crime. To disguise his ineptness, he stayed moored to his desk and only ventured out when he thought there was a big enough case to get his name in the papers. He spent most of his time coming to our office doors and asking what we were working on or making suggestive remarks to the blonde receptionist at the front desk. Barbie Morris was both pretty and smart. She was able to deflect the captain's lurid comments like a matador caping a charging bull.

I arrived to find that parked cars already crowded the approach to the Trinity River bridge on Waycross Road. Since this was ordinarily a somewhat secluded area, I suddenly had a sense of dread about the condition of my crime scene. A dirt road, so infrequently used that grass grew thick between the wheel ruts, angled to the right off of Waycross Road and down toward the river bank. I was familiar with the area, as was most other officers since we would often roust nighttime lovers in dark cars that were hidden just off the road. Among a few of the officers, it was a competition as to who would find some young girl in the least amount of clothing when they shined their spotlight into the dark cars. As the father of two girls, I didn't find the bragging very funny.

I blocked off the dirt road at the edge of Waycross and started walking. After a short distance, I could see a patrol sergeant standing solemnly over something in the knee-deep grass. I was relieved to see that Officer Jerry Coleman had kept a few of the bystanders away from the immediate area. My relief was short lived when I realized that there were two patrol cars and another civilian car parked next to the scene; all three having driven over any chance I might have had to get a decent tire print in the dirt.

I walked over to the patrol sergeant, being careful about where I stepped. As I approached, the sergeant glanced up and said "Looks like he was shot several times in the head."

"Well, let's not disturb anything until the medical examiner gets here. Have the dispatcher put in the call. Oh, and have the oncoming shift send a couple of their guys down here since we are going to start having problems keeping people away from the area." Sergeant Don Berry was an old time cop and a damn good one. Although he had years of seniority on me, he always deferred to me at a crime scene. I had tried several times to recruit him into the detective division, but he liked to go home at the end of an eight hour shift and not look back.

"First, let me tell you what we've got. There is a young couple up there in that car that came down here to watch the sunrise over the river," he said. When I laughed, he said; "Yea, well, that's their story and they are sticking to it. Anyway, as it got lighter, they could see something in the grass and decided have a look. When they realized what it was, they drove over to the brick factory across the river and had the night watchman call us. Coleman made the call and they led him back down here. I made them wait until you got here."

"Thanks, Don!" I had caught a break already in having a pro like Sgt. Berry as one of the initial officers at the scene. It was one of the few I was going to get in this case.

As I approached the side of the car where the young couple was now sitting discretely across from each other, the male decided to exert a little bravado, maybe to cover an earlier quaking fear at finding a dead body.

"It's about time someone got here. We've been waiting over an hour. She needs to go home. That other cop could have taken our goddamn phone number and let us go."

I reached the driver's window as he appeared to be taking a breath in preparation of renewing his tirade. As I did, my eyes fell on a switchblade knife that was lying on the console next to the gear shift. His eyes followed mine and I could hear the air rush out of him like a slashed tire. He sat silently as I reached inside and picked it up, hefting it in my hand. As I pushed the button, the blade sprang out with such force the knife nearly jumped out of my hand.

"Nice," I said; "illegal…but nice. Italian?"

Before he could answer, Sgt. Berry walked up and said, "Can I talk to you a second?" As we stepped aside, he said: "They checked out okay. They don't have any local record. We're waiting for the State to reply to our teletype request, but she's 18, and their story seems tight. I'm just saying…"

"Okay, the sergeant has your names and numbers. I would like to get a formal statement from both of you, but that can wait. Possession of this knife is a crime. What I want for you to do is bring her to the police station in the next couple of days and sit down for a formal interview and statement. When you do, I'll give you your knife back. I have two years to file this case on you, so when I call I strongly advise that you show up. Deal?" He readily agreed and I told Jerry Coleman to let them pass and drive back up to Waycross Road and leave.

As that problem resolved itself, two more came. While the couple was leaving, Captain Copeland's car pulled up to the edge of the roadway. He had Chief Clendon Rogers with him. "Well, so much for loyalty from the night dispatcher," I thought to myself. As they were walking down the dirt road toward me, I heard Sgt. Berry shout from behind me.

"Hey, here's another one…quick."

He had taken the initiative to widen the search around the scene now that I had arrived and his diligence paid off...in a way, I guess. A second body was lying in the tall grass about 30 yards away from the first. It was on a slight downhill slope going toward the river bank.

"Try to keep the captain and the chief from stomping all over my crime scene," I whispered to him. I then turned my attention to the newcomer at our roadside drama.

Both bodies were of young Caucasian males who appeared to be in their early to mid-20's. Both had their hands tied behind their backs with neckties. Both were face down. Similarities stopped there. The first man was not wearing a coat, which was odd considering how cold it had been that night. This led me to believe he had probably been abducted indoors. The second man was wearing a heavy coat. The first man had several wounds to his head and face. The second body had only one apparent wound, a head shot that could have been made from a large caliber weapon. Blood had sprayed from the wound to the surrounding grass, indicating that the shot had been administered while he was on the ground. It was an execution.

As I looked around the area of the second body, I noticed that Chief Rogers seemed to be walking off measurements from the side of the river up to where I was examining the second body. I first thought that maybe he was going to pitch in and help by making a diagram of the scene, but he wasn't taking notes. I leaned over toward Capt. Copeland and asked: "What the hell is the Chief doing?"

"He told me that the river and a portion on either side is actually the jurisdiction of the State of Texas. He's probably trying to see if this could be someone else's responsibility." I should have known better than to think he might be doing something useful.

Three officers from the oncoming shift arrived and I had two of them completely block off the dirt road from the edge of Waycross Road. The third joined us at the scene and I had those with me start a slow zone search of the entire area. Just as I had started them in their slow walk examination, I noticed a plain Ford sedan pull up to the shoulder of the road and three men climb out, showing badges to the officers at the roadway. Finally, my luck was starting to turn. One I immediately recognized as Deputy Johnny Flynn of the Dallas County Sheriff's Department: arguably one of the finest detectives in North Texas. My father was a sheriff's deputy, and I had known Johnny since I was a teenager. Even back then, he was a well-known investigator. Having him on the scene brought my anxiety level down considerably. The other two deputies were experienced investigators, as well. I felt as though the cavalry had just ridden over the hill.

As they started their walk down toward me, Flynn turned and said something to one of the other investigators who then opened the trunk of their car and removed a large roll of colored construction tape. As they cautiously entered the scene of the crime, Flynn stopped and watched as Chief Rogers continued his useless measurements.

"Hey Marc, we aren't here to get in your way. The sheriff heard the dispatch office trying to locate one of the field agents with the Medical Examiner's Office and figured you might need some additional help. By the way, what is your Chief of Police doing? He looks like a football ref marching off penalty yardage."

When I explained the chief's theory of making the State of Texas responsible for the investigation, Flynn ducked his head and chuckled. "What's he going to do, call Parks and Wildlife?"

"Well, at least he out of my hair, for the time being," I whispered.

As one of the deputies began to string orange construction tape from tree to tree along the area where we were standing, I finally began to feel like I had a proper crime scene with experienced investigators inside of it. Now I could start my investigation. Flynn said that the sheriff cautioned him not to butt in but to offer what assistance he could. I was anxious for him to butt in as much as he wanted to.

Capt. Copeland handed me the camera from the department darkroom. He said that the dispatcher told him that I had requested it brought to me and he stopped and picked it up on the way to get Chief Rogers. I made a mental note to have a little talk with the night dispatcher. But having the camera gave me an opportunity to start recording the scene while the others were carefully combing the tall grass. Little, if anything, was found. The place was littered

6

with trash that had blown in from the road, and it was impossible to tell if any of it had a connection to my crime. However, one piece of evidence told a lot about what may have occurred. Lying on the ground next to the first body was a brown button that we realized had come from the jacket that was worn by the second body. Evidently, it was pulled off while the two deceased men were standing next to each other. As I was processing this thought, the field agent for the Dallas County Medical Examiner arrived. He then began his careful examination of the two bodies.

Eventually, we all huddled and began to talk out what we were seeing. The field agent had removed identification from the first body. He was Richard Allen Littleton, age 25, with a Dallas address. He had received multiple gunshot wounds in the head and face. The examination by the field agent indicated that the shots were of different calibers and, it appeared, more than one person had fired into him. His hands had been cinched together using men's neckties. The knots had been so tight as to have caused pain while he was alive.

The second body was Terry Don Ryan, age 22, also with a Dallas address. His hands were also cinched behind his back with neckties. He had one single bullet wound in the back of his head. As I had suspected, it appeared to the agent that he was shot while lying face down on the ground. The button from his coat was found next to Littleton, telling us that when Littleton was shot, Ryan probably bolted and ran, managing to break the grip someone had on his jacket. The fact that he was running downhill with his hands tied behind his back made him easy prey, and whoever killed him simply ran him down or approached him after he had stumbled and fallen. He was dispatched with a single shot to the head. The agent felt that the wound was from a large caliber weapon, possibly a .38 or .357. Once we felt we had done all we could at this scene, we cleared the bodies for removal. The field agent radioed for a private hearse. Once the bodies were bagged and loaded, I headed for the police station.

-

I was cold and in dire need of a cup of coffee. I would even be glad to have the abysmal coffee that was waiting in the lounge back at the station. I had reluctantly driven away from the crime scene, racked by feelings that I hadn't done all I could or should have done there. I was encouraged by Deputy Johnny Flynn that we had done all we could, but that somehow didn't diminish my uncertainty. My thoughts were interrupted by a prolonged rumbling growl from my empty stomach, reminding me that I hadn't eaten anything since dinner the night before. Contrary to everyone's favorite police lore, I don't like donuts. At that moment, all I could think of was the baklava that the Greek bakery in town no doubt had sitting on their counter at that very moment. I had too much to do. Maybe I could get one of the patrol officers to bring me a couple. We all got along well.

I had mentioned earlier in my story that we had three detectives at Creekwood PD. Two you have already met; Capt. R.J. Copeland and me, Detective Marc Anthony Bryant. The third was my sometimes partner and close friend, Detective Alan West. Capt. Copeland had divided up responsibilities between Al and me. Al caught all cases involving property, such as burglary and theft. I caught all cases involving people, such as murder, assault and rape. Armed robbery cases were sort of a toss ball. Whoever was handy was responsible. Although we carried different cases, we worked together on whatever was on the front burner at the time. Al was older and, I believed, wiser than I. He had a calm manner and was very easy to work with and around. He had been a detective at a police department in Louisiana and had decided to move his family to Texas where he thought it was safer and the pay was better. He brought a lot of experience with him. I was relieved to walk into the station and find him at his desk.

"I decided to just wait here and hold down the fort in case you needed something while you were at the scene," he said as I slumped down in one of his chairs.

"I tell you what would help me a lot," I said. "Would you go out and locate the families of our two vics and find out what you can about when they last saw them? If they have wives, bring them here if you can. Better still, take the captain with you. It'd be nice to have a couple of hours without him. I'll call the ME's office and tell them not to make notifications. We're handling it. Okay?"

CAJUN RULES

I hated to pass such an unpleasant task to someone else, but I was sort of relieved not to have to face these families with such tragic news. I hated making death notifications. I recall once in my rookie days when an elderly man in town was on his way to meet his usual breakfast companions at a neighborhood café. He had a heart attack while driving and was dead before his car had plowed through a wooden fence and into a backyard shed. I was sent to his home to notify someone of his death. I was met at the door by a lady who was everyone's vision of a sweet grandmother. She saw my uniform and, I think, immediately knew why I was there. When I asked if I could come in and talk to her about something, she began to filibuster. "Can I get you some coffee, officer? I just had some but there is still more in the pot. Please sit down. Can I get you anything?" She was speaking faster and more frantically as if she was trying to forestall hearing this bad news as long as she could. Maybe she thought that as long as I hadn't spoken, the tragedy had not officially happened. After a few minutes, she finally stopped talking and slumped into a chair and cried. It was one of the hardest moments of my life and one I painfully look back on sometimes.

As I was filling Al in on the identities of my two victims, the morning shift sergeant stopped at the office door. "The state just sent back teletype confirmation that the two people who found the body have no criminal records." At least that stone had been rolled out of my path. I suddenly recalled the switchblade knife in my pocket. I now regretted my promise to give it back, but I was stuck with it.

"Okay, we're on the way," said Al. "I'll grab the captain. Some outside air might do him good." Al was a true friend.

When I called the medical examiner's office, they confirmed the receipt the bodies of Littleton and Ryan. I asked that they not attempt to contact families until we had a chance to locate and talk to them ourselves.

"We'll handle notification," I told the clerk in the field agent's office. "Any idea when the docs might do the posts on those guys?" Normally, autopsies started early in the morning, but followed no discernable schedule. It didn't seem to be "first come, first served," as best I could tell.

9

"Nope. You'll just have to come early tomorrow and avail yourself of our accommodating lounge and gourmet coffee until your case comes up." Waiting in the medical examiner's office was like spending eternity in the waiting room of hell. It meant sitting in a glass-walled office adjacent to the autopsy tables, watching three pathologists systematically dissemble human bodies while they murmur into microphones that hang from the ceiling above. Warm water constantly runs along the edges of the tables to wash the blood into stainless steel sinks along the wall. The warm steam brings the coppery odor of blood up and into the room. Although there was a ventilation system on the ceiling, it didn't stop the humid, fetid air from reaching every part of large space, or maybe it was mostly my imagination. I hated that place and had nightmares about it for years.

I quickly typed up the names, dates of birth, and addresses for the two victims. I had operated a radio teletype in the Army for a couple of years and could type as fast as I could write out something in longhand. My request for a typewriter in my office had been turned down by Chief Rogers until I purposely made my handwriting illegible enough that he ultimately gave in. I got an old office reject, but it was all I needed to keep up my notes and write out memos.

I gave the names to the morning dispatcher and asked him to teletype the Department of Public Safety in Austin for any criminal records that they might have on Littleton and Ryan. I then returned to the office and called the Identification Division of the Dallas Sheriff's Office. The deputy there responded with a list of criminal cases that he read from Richard Littleton's rap sheet. Most were "investigation" cases, meaning that he was held for investigation of a crime without being formally charged. They included robbery, burglary and one interesting case: "Investigation of Illegal Dog Fighting." He also had several "vagrancy" cases, which was telling.

Vagrancy meant that he was found under suspicious circumstances in a place where he had no business and had no visible means of support...like a job. It was a handy charge that was used by officers to hold onto someone that the officer was suspicious of but didn't have enough information to jail them on investigation. It was also a way to harass known criminal offenders by inconveniencing them with an overnight stay in lockup. Multiple vagrancy raps meant that the police had reason to keep an eye on someone. One well-known Dallas hoodlum had the all-time record of 138 vagrancy raps in one calendar year. Most learned to live in the suburbs, Creekwood being one, and only venture into Dallas when they had a good reason. Vagrancy would soon meet its demise at the hands of appeal court judges.

The deputy also had a copy of Littleton's FBI rap sheet. It listed a charge of shoplifting in Cleveland, Ohio, as well as a burglary charge that was filed there but never tried. He had skipped out on his bond and was listed as a fugitive. He had been on the run for four years. Terry Ryan had one aggravated assault case. It was withdrawn by the Dallas District Attorney. The deputy assured me that he would copy the rap sheets and the fingerprint cards and have them brought to me by the first patrol deputy that was headed out my way. I thanked him and then dialed the number of the Identification Section of the Dallas Police Department.

A female records clerk at Dallas PD answered with a mezzo-soprano voice that was as sweet as honey and about as thick. She could read a grocery list over the phone and make your heart skip. I was so mesmerized by the silky voice that I kept missing items she was reading from the records, or maybe I was doing it on purpose so that I could get her to repeat. She told me to stand by and I could hear a brief muffled conversation she was having with someone else in the office. She came back on and told me that I should talk to the sergeant in the Intelligence Section about Littleton. "I think they might have a lot you would be interested to hear, Detective Bryant," she teased.

"Dead! Are you shittin' me?" Sergeant Walter Wood seemed barely able to contain his excitement. "Who killed him? You got any leads? We got a file on him down here as thick as Manhattan Yellow Pages."

I kept trying to steer him back to my inquiry, but he began to shout the news to the others in the office while he held the receiver a few inches from his mouth. Finally: "Okay, sorry. You need to come down to here and sit down with us. We've been hearing about some bad blood developing between him and some of the crew he runs with. You know he's one of the crew for Randall Donovan."

11

I knew the name. He was an old time Dallas hoodlum who was on every "Known Offender" list in the county. He was even brought in and questioned about the assassination of President John Kennedy that occurred in Dallas seven years earlier.

"What kind of bad blood," I asked.

"Who knows with those people," Wood replied. "We heard a couple of stories. One was that Littleton held out on some piece of expensive jewelry that came from a home invasion over in Highland Park. We also heard that it had something to do with someone stealing a pit bull puppy. Ran Donovan and Littleton were into pit dog fighting. Anyway, get your ass down here and we need to pow-wow. Okay?"

"I've got to be in Dallas for the autopsies tomorrow morning, so I'll try to get there when they are finished."

"Great!" Wood responded. "I'll treat to lunch. Later."

Lunch. Suddenly my stomach growled. Almost as if they heard the complaint from my empty stomach, the "steak boys" came through the front door and stopped to flirt with Barbie at the reception desk. The steak boys were the CEO and the Chief Financial Officer for Wellington's, a popular steakhouse chain with its international headquarters in Creekwood. Their steaks were expensive but worth every penny. They also had one of the new concepts in dining that was becoming popular: a large salad bar with cold selections of salad toppings and dressings. Kay loved the salad bar and would often make that her dinner. Being an ardent carnivore, I preferred the Wellington filet mignon and a nicely aged bourbon from their bar. It was a rare treat for Kay and me and one I could hardly afford on a cop's salary. That's where the steak boys came in. Whenever Wellington's opened another restaurant in a different state, the corporate officers had to submit their fingerprints to that states' liquor control offices in order to get a license to serve alcohol. They always came to me to take the prints and certify their fingerprint cards with my signature and badge number. For this small service, they would always give free dinner passes for me, Kay, and the girls.

As I rolled the prints on to the card, I tried to calculate how many states I had left when the CEO, Dan Tyson, glanced around and in a low voice said;

"When are you going to give this up and join our corporate security staff. You are exactly what we need."

"What…and give up these free meals?" I laughed.

"It'd be steak every day for you," Tyson smiled.

"Ah, I'd just eat so much I'd blow up like a poisoned toad, drop dead of a cardiac. I'm probably better off here where I can't afford such temptations."

"Well, I tried," he laughed as I handed him the signed cards. "Enjoy your meal with the family, Marc. You're a good man."

CHAPTER 2

My mother named me Marc Anthony. I never really got a straight answer why. She once told me that she loved to read Shakespeare when she was in school and always liked the name. Another time, she told me that it was the name of an old boyfriend. She liked the name a lot better than the old boyfriend, she said. I always avoided using my middle name because it brought on the inevitable "Friends, Romans, Countrymen, lend me your ears" from kids in school. My father was a Dallas County deputy sheriff. Although I grew up among the various deputies, jailers and trustees, I never considered becoming a police officer myself. I wanted to be a newspaper reporter. I went college with that future goal in mind only to drop out after a year with a bad case of wanderlust. It wasn't long before Uncle Sam scooped me up in the draft. I had taken a typing class in high school to fill credit hours that I needed and found that I had a knack for it. Because of that skill, I was trained as a radio teletype operator and that kept me safely out of the action. When I got out, I had a wife and daughter. I needed a job that had good health insurance and a steady income until I could get back to college. With my father's connections, I knew I could get a police job and even continue my education at the same time. The sheriff made a couple of phone calls and I was immediately hired by Creekwood PD. So far, I have not darkened the door of a single classroom.

I glanced up from my office to the lobby where Al and Capt. Copeland were coming in the front door, leading two young women. Both had their heads down and were crying. The wives, I figured. The contrast between the two immediately caught my attention. One was small, slightly stout with dark shoulder-length curly hair. She wore blue jeans that looked to be a size too small making her midriff spill over a leather belt with a rodeo buckle. She would raise her head, glance around the lobby and then glare menacingly at anyone who looked her way. The other was a complete polar opposite. She was tall, really very tall with a slender waist and long legs. She wore jeans as well, but that's where the comparison stopped. Her jeans fit snugly on her narrow frame, hugging her hips. They flared out to bell-bottoms at her feet where she wore thin leather sandals. She had a waist-length buckskin jacket with a fleece collar that was turned up to frame her face. Her hair was blonde and was worn straight down, disappearing under her collar. Despite her obvious grief, she was elegant. She was a Hollywood director's idea of the perfect hippy chick, straight out of central casting. She didn't look around like the other one. She just kept her head down as she passed out of my sight, no doubt being escorted to the officer's lounge in back.

Al came into my office and sat down. "How did it go?" I asked.

"That's Mary Beth Ryan and Lynne Littleton. Ryan was at the address you gave me. It's her parent's house in the south end of Dallas. The apartment address for Littleton was vacant. Mary Beth knew where she was living and led us there. She and Richard were staying in an old white clapboard house on a gravel road near Mesquite. I started not to get out of the car since there were some very angry-looking dogs chained to metal stakes in the yard. She came out and climbed into the back seat with Mary Beth. She didn't seem particularly surprised to see us. When I told her why we were there, she just said 'Yea, I know' and hasn't spoken another word since. There was a lot of staring back and forth between the two on our way back, but they didn't talk."

"I saw them coming through the lobby. Which one is which?" I asked.

"Lynne Littleton is the tall drink of water with the hippy jeans. Mary Beth is the chunky cowgirl."

"Well, let's get this over with." I'll interview Lynne Littleton, if you don't mind. Walter Wood at DPD gave me some information on the phone about Richard Littleton that I want to run at her."

Al smiled; "Don't blame you. She's a hell of a lot easier to look at, that's for sure."

Lynne Littleton still had the head-down pose as she was led into the office by our receptionist. She no longer wore her jacket and I could see that her hair was long and straight and ending at the middle of her back. She sat down and then looked up, focusing on my face. She had ice-blue eyes that were so arresting that I fumbled for something to say. Before I could start, I noticed Al standing at the door, motioning me to come outside. He quietly told me that as the receptionist was asking Lynne to follow her, Mary Beth whispered to her "Keep your mouth shut."

"Now that's interesting. Thanks!" I said and returned to my desk.

"Mrs. Littleton, there isn't anything I can say to make this better for you, so I'll just try to make it as short as I can so we can get it over with and you can go home. First, you told the officers who picked you up that you already knew about your husband's death. How did you know?"

"Mary Beth's mother called me before they got to my house. I guess they told her when they picked Mary Beth up."

"When was the last time you saw your husband?"

"He left the house last night around seven. He said he was going to meet some friends."

"Did he tell you who? I asked.

"No."

"How did he leave? Did he have a car?"

"He has a black '69 Bronco. Did you find it?"

"No, no car," I said. "Do you have the license number?"

"The title is at home. I can get it later."

Alarm bells were going off in my head like a building on fire. She was scared. It was more than shock and grief, which I would expect. She was holding something inside and it was causing her to tremble slightly. She wrapped her arms around herself to keep me from noticing.

"Let's get something out in the open, Mrs. Littleton, before we go on," I began.

"Please, just call me Lynne. That missus thing makes me think of my mother."

"Okay, Lynne," I continued, "Mary Beth Ryan told you to keep your mouth shut just before you came into my office. I want to know why. What is it that you need to keep your mouth shut about? I'm trying to understand why your husbands were murdered, why they were taken from you. I would think you would want to tell me everything you know to help us find the truth."

Lynne looked over her shoulder in the direction of the lounge, as if she was trying to see if Mary Beth was standing behind her. She then turned, lowered her head again and I could see tears as big as raindrops falling to her lap.

"Lynne, talk to me. I can't do anything unless I know more about what happened. Do you know where Richard and Terry were going? Do you know what friends they were meeting? I know you're scared of something; I can see it all over you. Just help me out here, okay?"

"I can't go back home. By now they know I'm here. They'll think I talked to you and that would be the…the end."

"Who are you talking about;" I asked. There was silence.

"Okay, let me go about this another way. Are you talking about Randall Donovan?"

Her reaction was startling. She stood quickly, grabbed her stomach and said she was sick and needed to go to the restroom. I asked the receptionist to take her into the lobby restroom, telling her to stay with her and not let her out of sight. In a few minutes, they returned to the office. Lynne was pale and holding a paper towel to her mouth. The receptionist told me that she had thrown up into the toilet. Now the shaking was obvious.

"Lynne, talk to me. If you are worried about Ran Donovan I can protect you. But, the only way I can is for me to know everything you know. I can't help you unless you help me."

"I can't do anything to help Rick now. I have to look out for myself from here on. If I tell you what you want to know, I can't go back. They'll know I talked and they will find me and they will kill me too'. She trailed off and seemed to just be whispering to herself. Then, she was quiet.

"Look Lynne, I'll do everything I can…"

Her head jerked up and again, she fixed her blue-eyed gaze straight into my eyes. "Okay, here goes: I knew something was wrong before Mary Beth's mother called me. I got a call early this morning from Maurice Cox. He has a place over near Irving. He has a big barn behind his house with a pit and bleachers. They fight roosters there and sometimes dogs. He told me that Rick was there with Terry. Ran Donovan was also there. Around midnight, Ran went into Maurice's bedroom and came out with some neckties. A few minutes later, he said he saw Rick and Terry walking toward Rick's car. They had their hands tied behind their backs with the neckties and were walking ahead of Ran and two other guys. Ran had a gun in his hand. They put Rick and Terry in the back seat and two of the guys got in with them. Ran drove out behind them in a different car. Maurice said he had never seen the other two guys before. After a while, Maurice got scared and called to see if I had heard from Rick. I knew then I would never hear from him again. There! I've done it."

"Did you tell Mary Beth Ryan any of this? Is that why she told you to keep your mouth shut?"

"No, she doesn't know any of this. She doesn't know much of anything about Rick and Ran Donovan. She just doesn't trust cops. Terry just liked to hang around Rick. Ran didn't like him. He never got involved in any of their business."

"What exactly was their business?"

"I'm so tired. I just don't want to get into this now. I want to just lie down for a while."

"Well, let me prime the pump a little. Did this have something to do with Rick holding out some stolen jewelry from Ran?"

"No, no that's not right. Who are you talking to? The owner claimed that the jewelry was stolen to collect on his insurance. He owned money to some Dallas bookie. That wasn't a problem between Ran and Rick. Where did you hear that? I want to know." Suddenly she didn't look so scared. She looked angry.

"We have a lot more to talk about, but let's not get into that yet. I need to pay Maurice Cox a visit and see what he has to tell me first. I don't know how long I'll be, so I can have someone take you home or I can get you a cab."

"You don't understand. I can't go home now. Can I just wait here for you? Can you put me in a cell? They are probably looking for me right now."

"How about going home with Mary Beth?"

"No, that's the last person I want to be around. Just leave me here."

"Okay, hang on a minute."

18

I walked to Al's office door and could see that he was talking to Mary Beth Ryan. From the look of things, there wasn't much conversation. I motioned for Al to come outside to the hall.

"What does she say?"

"Precious little," Al smiled. "She doesn't know who would want to kill her husband. She said that he was a good man until he started running around with Richard Littleton, and she blames Littleton for his death. She doesn't like cops and finally told me that she didn't want to talk anymore and wanted to go home. I let her call her mother who is on her way now to get her."

"Good! Let's put her in the lobby until her mother gets here. Let's put Lynne Littleton in the lounge and we need to go pay a visit to the place where the vics were abducted from last night. I'll fill you in on the way."

The directions that Lynne gave us for Maurice Cox's place led us to a semi-rural section in western Dallas County that time had forgotten. Old farm-style houses sat on small acreage, many having wooden barns in back that were as dilapidated as the houses. Highways and warehouses were encroaching from all sides. Cox's place was prominent from the others only by the fact that there were several large metal trash cans sitting along the shallow bar-ditch at the edge of the road in front. As Al and I climbed out of our car, we were immediately hammered by the thick odor of decay from these cans. Not certain what I was going to find, I cautiously went over to one of them and slowly lifted the lid. A squadron of black flies sprang from the can. It took my brain a few seconds to process what I was looking at. Finally, I realized the can was full of dead chickens…roosters actually. I heard Al's voice next to me as he lifted another can lid.

"Jeez, that's dead roosters!"

A screen door in front had been pulled against the eye-hook lock so many times over the years that it sagged away from the top of the jamb. Behind it was a closed wooden door. What wasn't peeling paint was dirt. The screen door was so loose in the jamb that as I knocked, it did a double-slap on the door frame. I figured someone inside would have to be deaf not to hear it…or dead. I was getting no response.

"Let's go out back and have a look around," I told Al. I started to tell him that Lynne Littleton had described a fighting pit in the barn, but decided not to. There was no telling if someone inside was listening to us.

The old barn appeared to have had its last coat of paint during the administration of Grover Cleveland. In fact the only thing that was less than 50 years old on the outside was a hasp with a padlock on the big double doors. The padlock was unlocked and hanging loose in the hasp. I guess that passed for security in that part of the county. I pulled the lock away from the hasp and opened one of the double doors. The only light came from a couple of dirty skylights on the roof making the inside a gloomy collection of shadowy forms and shapes. The air was thick with a moldy odor of decay.

As my eyes became adjusted to the low light, I could make out a circle of wooden bleachers that was raised up on heavy wooden posts. The bleachers surrounded a round pit in the center with wooden walls like large barrel stays. Although the pit would be fully visible from the raised bleachers, the walls were too high for us to see inside. I figured they were about six feet tall. We climbed up the ramp and to the bleachers to get a better look. We could see that the floor of the pit was filled with sand. It had an access door on the side. The inside walls had dark stains and streaks. As I was trying to get my eyes to adjust enough to see if the stains could be blood, I heard a voice from the double doors.

"Hey, you ain't supposed to be in here. This is private property. I'll call the police," only he pronounced it "poe-leese."

"Here, I'll save you the dime," I said as Al and I lifted our badges.

"You got a search warrant?"

He was a little old man who appeared to have dried up and shrunk since he had last put on his clothes. His shirt hung from his skinny frame and his belt seemed to be holding on to his khaki pants for dear life. He had now retreated behind one side of the double door and only his head was visible as he leaned out and spoke.

"Whata ya want, anyway? I ain't done nothin'."

"Well, it's pretty simple," I said. "What I want is for you to step in front of that door so I can see both of your hands. You do that and I'll be happy.

20

You just stay there and we'll come to you and go outside to talk. This place is beginning to give me the willies."

As I approached the old man, I asked him if he was Maurice Cox. When he opened his mouth to speak, the sour smell of whiskey rolled toward me like a storm cloud.

"Yea, that's me. Whata you want and why are you breakin' into my place like this?" He was listing to one side like he was standing in a gale and I wondered if he was going to be able to stand much longer.

"Since the lock wasn't closed, I really wouldn't call it 'breakin'…uh, you want to come and sit down on the porch? You look a little unsteady."

Al held his arm as Cox stumbled to the wooden porch and sat down hard on one of the steps. I asked him if he knew Richard Littleton. He nodded yes. When I asked him the last time he saw Littleton, he said; "He was here last night watching the chicken fights. He had his little toady with him."

"When did he leave?"

"I dunno. I didn't see him leave."

"Did you see Ran Donovan here last night?"

"No, I don't see him around much."

"Did you see Littleton and Ran Donovan leave together?"

"I tell you, I didn't see anybody leave."

"Maurice, I'm going to need you to come with us to Creekwood PD and give us a statement. Let's lock your house up and go. Is there anyone else inside?" We watched as Cox locked his back door and we walked him to our car and drove back to the station.

"You know, it's funny, Maurice. You haven't asked me why we're talking about Richard Littleton. Aren't you curious?"

"I just figured you wanted him for something. He's gets in a lot of trouble I hear."

"He's dead. Did you hear THAT about him?" No reply.

Once we arrived and got out of the car, I told Al: "Let's walk him in the back door and through the lounge. I want him to see Lynne Littleton. Maybe that might jog his memory some."

Lynne was sitting on a couch in the lounge watching television. As we entered, she stared hard at Maurice Cox. Cox didn't utter a sound, ducked his head and walked past her. Maybe he wasn't that drunk after all.

We steered him into Al's office and he collapsed into a chair and hung his head down, his chin against his chest. "Come on, Maurice. I need your full attention here," I told him as we pulled our chairs up next to him. After a minute, he began to snore loudly. I couldn't tell if he was faking it or was actually that drunk. He did reek of whiskey fumes.

"Let's just put him in one of the cells for the night and see if he's any better in the morning."

"You think we're legal to do that," Al asked with a smile.

"Let's just call him a material witness and he's under our protection. I doubt that he'll complain. Hell, as drunk as he is, he'll probably think he's in a Holiday Inn." Can you try to get something out of him in the morning? I've got to be at the medical examiner's office early and then I promised Walter Woods at DPD Intelligence that I would fill him in on what we have. Besides, I'm too hungry and tired to go on much longer. I just want to go home, eat some dinner, and see my kids."

"Sure, I'll handle it tomorrow morning," Al agreed. "But, what are you going to do about Lynne Littleton? You going to leave her in the lounge for the night?"

CAJUN RULES

"Oh shit, I forgot about her. I'll go see if there is anyone she trusts enough to stay with until we can get back together tomorrow. She's pretty scared."

When I got to the lounge, I saw Lynne and our receptionist Barbie talking quietly. Lynne looked like she had been crying. Before I could say anything, Barbie jumped up, grabbed me by my arm and pulled me into the hallway.

"That kid's scared to go home and she's got no place else to go and nobody to go to. It's just me and my little boy at home and I've got an extra bedroom. Is it okay if she comes home with me? I'll bring her with me when I come to work in the morning. She seems very nice. Whata ya say?"

"Look, Barbie, you don't really know her…oh, well, if you don't mind, it would sure take a load off of my shoulders for the time being. I need to be in Dallas in the morning but I'll try to get here by early afternoon. Thanks, Barb. You're a good person."

I sat down next to Lynne on the couch and was immediately transfixed by those deep blue eyes. "Barbie's going to take you home with her tonight. I've got something to do in Dallas tomorrow morning but I'll get back as soon as I can and then we'll see if we can find something more permanent for you. You might be able to help Al out by confronting Maurice Cox in the morning. He's availing himself to our hospitality for the night. He's not admitting to anything so far. Anyway, that will be Al's call. He's going to handle Cox while I'm gone."

"I know he saw me when he came through that door. He's scared, just like I am. I don't want to get that old man hurt. I don't know what to do. I just want to go someplace, get a shower and sleep. That lady Barbie is an angel for letting me stay with her. But, I'm going to need to find a place of my own and not put anyone else in danger. Okay, see you in the morning."

It was dark when I pulled into my driveway at home. It had been dark when I pulled out of it this morning. I was like a vampire returning to his native soil.

"Daddy…daddy!" My girls rushed me at the door. "Daddy's home," my youngest announced proudly to my wife as she came in from the kitchen. The three-way hug I got was exactly what I needed at that moment.

23

"I kept some food warm for you," said Kay as she handed me a bourbon and water on ice, my favorite. I'll get it ready for you if you'll put the kids to bed. They should have been in bed an hour ago, but they wanted to wait on you."

"You got a deal," I said.

"Read us a story, Daddy," my oldest said as we piled up together in her bed. She already had her favorite book in her hand.

My day had gone from blasted bodies to a mysterious beautiful widow to a blood-splashed cock-fighting pit and was now being rounded out with Dr. Seuss's "Wickersham Monkeys." It was like slamming on the brakes at 100 miles an hour. But, it was a great way to end the day.

CHAPTER 3

I could feel a presence hovering over me, pressing near my face. I struggled to wake, trying to pull myself out of a paralyzing sleep to confront the threat. A voice whispered from somewhere at the edge of my dream.

"You awake?"

"Yea!"

"Your eyes are still closed."

"I'm awake, I'm awake. Who you gonna believe, me or your lying eyes?"

I could feel Kay's face inches from mine. I bet she was smiling that devilish smile that always made her look like a mischievous child. It never failed to melt my heart.

"Good news! I have us a New Years Eve party to go to tonight. Tom's company is throwing a party at Winfrey Point on White Rock Lake. He invited us. There's going to be a band, dancing…everything. Mom said she would keep the girls tonight. Come on, Detective Bryant, give the criminals a break and take a night off."

"Your old boyfriend, Tom?"

"You took me away from him, didn't you? So, who's the better man? Come on, you told me to get you up at six. It's six. You still haven't opened your eyes. What about the party?"

"Yea, okay…okay. I've got to get up and get going. I need to be at the medical examiner's office before seven."

"Oh great. An autopsy is really going to put you in a party mood. I know how much you hate those things," she said, losing her smile.

"It's important that I be there in case the pathologist has any questions. I'm sure I'll have a few. Tell you what. I'll watch with just one eye open so maybe it won't be so bad."

The traffic was light on the drive into town at that time of the morning. It was just shy of seven as I pulled into the parking lot of the Dallas County Crime Lab, officially known as the Institute of Forensic Sciences. It was in a three-story building on the same campus as Parkland Memorial Hospital.

Parkland had picked up the "Memorial" part of its name after President John F. Kennedy was pronounced dead in one of its trauma rooms seven years before. That room was just a short walk away from where I parked my car and entered the building.

The offices for the Dallas County Medical Examiner were in the basement. I always had a sense of dread every time I stepped into that elevator and pushed the "B" for Basement. It meant that I was about to stack yet more nightmare material on what was already burned into my subconscious. I thought I could already smell the blood-tinged steamy air as I stepped out of the elevator and walked to the field agent's office. A couple of Dallas detectives that I recognized were already there. Looked like it was going to be a busy morning.

"Well, we got a full house today folks," came a cheerful voice over my shoulder. It was one of the field agents, Tony Simms. His chirpy manner just served to make the whole process that much more macabre. "It's standing room only today, so the doc's have already started. Must have been a full moon. Did anyone look?"

"Have they started on my guys, Littleton and Ryan?" I asked, ignoring his dumb question.

"No, but they're in line. Just make yourself comfortable."

"Yea, right…comfortable," I grumbled as I sat down in a lobby chair. There was seating in one of the glass-walled offices inside the autopsy area, but this morning I decided that tubular metal furniture and blank walls were more to my liking. "Hey, Tony, let me know when they bring my guys in, will ya?"

"Will do, Marc," he chirped.

After nearly an hour, the Chief Pathologist Dr. Carl Pittman came into the lobby and motioned for me to follow. "I had a look at your guys earlier this morning. The gunshot wounds on Littleton were unusual enough that I waited for Dan James to come in so he could look at them as I do the post. Sorry you had to wait."

Dan James was a nationally recognized firearms and ballistics expert. We were lucky to have him in Dallas County. His books had been used in some of my in-service training. I was anxious to hear what he had to say.

CAJUN RULES

As we entered the autopsy area, that old sense of dread came crashing back. Three pathologists were busily about their grim tasks of cutting, probing, weighing, and describing what had only hours earlier been living, breathing people. I followed Dr. Pittman to a table where the chalk-white body of Richard Littleton lay bare. Dan James was already there, gingerly probing Littleton's head and face with a gloved hand. Dr. Pittman joined him.

"Looks like what we have is a large caliber bullet wound that is through and through from the back to the front. Judging from the size of that exit wound, this may have been a dum-dum type round, like a wad cutter hollow point. It didn't expand much if it was. The other two wounds appear to be one shot each of maybe a .22 round and a load of bird-shot from a shotgun, probably a .410. They were on the side of his face and head, so I figured he was face down on the ground when they were fired, probably after the shot to the back of his head had already put him down." Dan finally looked up and smiled when he saw me.

"Hey Marc, how's the country cop?" he smiled. "Got yourself a regular old gangster-style rubout going here, looks like."

"Let me ask you this, Dan, if the shot to the back of his head was enough to knock him down and do all that damage, I wonder why the extra shots? I mean, how dead do you need to make somebody?"

"I'll know more once we get into this, but I have a theory. I think that three guys had him. One guy put a large caliber pistol to the back of his head and shot him. Then the other two fired into the body as sort of a bonding thing…to bond them each to the murder. Don't let the light calibers fool you. A .410 shotgun is very lethal and can be cut down to be easily concealed. A .22 pistol is deadly up close and the rounds usually shatter when they hit bone, making a ballistic examination difficult. I suspect that's probably what we will find here. You may have some very experienced pros at work here, but then I'm getting into your area."

As Dr. Pittman began to start his autopsy of Littleton, Dan James walked over to the gurney where Ryan was covered with a green sheet. He lifted it and began to probe the area of Ryan's head. "Hey Marc, come over here and look. You may have caught a break on this one. Looks like there isn't an exit

27

wound. The round is probably still in his head. Might give us something to go on."

"How long before you know?" I asked.

"It's going to be a while before Doc Pittman finishes that one. He wants to do the posts on both. I think you've seen enough to know what you are dealing with. Why don't you just let us finish and I'll get you a preliminary report and lots of photographs? I don't see any real need for you to hang around here. Besides, you are looking a little green around the gills."

"Thanks, Dan. I really hate this place. Besides, I promised Walter Wood over at DPD that I would fill him on what we have. So, I'm out of here. Let me know what you find with that round in Ryan's head."

I walked out into the parking lot breathing in a much fresh air as I could. I felt like I was trying to purge that bloody humid air out of my lungs. I started my drive up Harry Hines Boulevard into downtown Dallas.

For visiting police officers, parking at the Dallas Police Department was in a small, cramped basement that was accessible from Main Street. Large concrete support pillars made navigating around inside the basement parking garage a real challenge. I don't think that there was a detective in the whole county that didn't have a least a couple of dents in the fenders of his car compliments of the Dallas PD parking garage. I finally maneuvered into a space and headed toward the entrance to the building. It was at that spot were presidential assassin Lee Harvey Oswald was gunned down by nightclub owner Jack Ruby just seven years before.

CAJUN RULES

Dallas Police Intelligence had offices on the second floor of the police building. "Intelligence" was printed in block letters on the frosted glass panel at the top half of the door. The office consisted of two rows of desks in a bullpen arrangement. At one side was the supervisor's office behind glass panels. On the other side was a small interrogation room. The desks were all occupied and every face turned up toward me as I walked through the door. "Detective Marc Bryant, I presume," came a booming voice from the back of the room. "Come on in, we were just talking about you." Sgt. Walter Wood stepped forward. He was a tall man with a sturdy build and graying hair that he combed straight back from a receding hairline. From his appearance, he could have been a banker or a car salesman. One could believe on first sight that he could be anything he said he was. I guess that's the general idea of intelligence.

"Go grab a cup of coffee over there in the corner. We just made a pot... hey, Harvey, what day did we make this pot?"

I decided that maybe it wasn't a joke after all when I saw that the coffee had the consistency of well-used crankcase oil. I poured a cup, laced it with plenty of powdered creamer and sat next to Wood's desk.

"I can't believe that Richard Littleton is dead," he began.

"Well, you can believe it because I watched Doc Pittman lift the top of his skull off less than an hour ago. If he wasn't dead before, he sure as hell is now." There was laughter around the office. Cops have a dark sense of humor.

"We've been talking about this all morning. First of all, you are dealing with some very bad people. Randall Donovan is an old time Dallas hoodlum. He goes back to the gang wars of the late forties and early fifties. When Benny Binion left town, those old gangsters just grabbed what action they could. Ran worked down in Cuba for Lansky for a while but when Castro took over, he came back up here and started running his own crew."

"What kind of stuff were he and his crew into?" I asked.

"They started out knocking over high dollar poker games until the gamblers got wise and started putting armed guards in the rooms. From there, they got into juice enforcing for some of the local books and just general strong-arm stuff for New Orleans mob guys. A couple of years ago, they started doing takeover robberies of wealthy homes in Texas and Louisiana.

Donovan seems to have good inside information about who has what and where they were keeping it. His crew would dress as deliverymen in a truck and would slip scarves over their faces when someone would come to the door. They seemed to know what they were looking for because they were always in and out in less than thirty minutes. Usually it was jewelry and cash, sometimes collectable stuff like coins, art, whatever. We understand Littleton was a real up and comer in the crew and was getting to be one of Donovan's favorites."

"Evidently they had some kind of falling out" I told Woods. "Littleton's wife got a call from a guy who saw Donovan and a couple other guys walk Littleton and the other dead guy, Ryan, at gunpoint out of a cock-fight over in the west county the night before we found them. The guy's name is Maurice Cox. The chicken fights were at his place. We have him in our jail, but he's denying it all now. Something must have changed. You told me about some stolen jewelry and a stolen puppy over the phone. What's that all about?"

"Here's what we are hearing from our sources: A year ago, Ran Donovan was tipped that Gaylord Dillard III had high dollar jewelry at his home in Highland Park. He's a degenerate gambler and ran up some big debts to a sports book here in town. Dillard has some family money, but most of his wealth is from his wife's family. She is related to old Mexican royalty. His wife, Charlotte, has an old and very expensive necklace that has been passed down through her family. It is usually in a bank box, but she wanted to get it out to wear to the Idlewild Club Ball last year. Somehow Donovan knew that and sent his crew to the house, posing as deliverymen. They took over a hundred thousand dollars worth of jewelry, not including the necklace. That alone was priceless. It was worth more than a million. Dillard had it insured and reported it stolen right along with everything else."

"At first, Donovan thought one of the crew had the necklace and was holding out on him. Richard Littleton had found most of the jewelry in an unlocked safe in a bedroom closet, so suspicion fell on him. He took a good beating, I'm told and tried to convince Donovan that it wasn't part of the jewelry in the safe and he didn't see it. The rest of Donovan's crew wasn't so easily convinced and things were pretty tense for a while for Littleton.

Eventually, word got back that Dillard had probably fenced the necklace for cash to settle his gambling debts and collected on the insurance. It was enough to convince Donovan and Littleton was off the hook.

"But I think your best motive was a fight over a pit bull puppy," Woods continued. "Donovan is a big time fan of pit dog fighting. He has money behind several pedigreed pit bulls around the state and regularly attends the fights and bets big money. That's how he met Richard Littleton, so we're told. Littleton is from Ohio and had pit dogs there. He came here after a burglary bust in Cleveland and got into the local dog fighting scene. He sank a bunch of money into an expensive puppy with some champion fighters in its lineage. One day, the puppy turned up missing and Littleton heard that it was taken by another dog fighter named Otto Sack, also known as "Sad." Evidently he lived up to his nickname when Littleton caught up to him. He lured Sad and his wife to his house one day, held them at gunpoint while a friend tied them up. Littleton and his friend spent the next twenty-four hours beating Sad and sexually abusing his wife. Eventually, Sad admitted to taking the puppy and told Littleton where to find it. Everyone decided to call it even, but the problem was that Sad Sack is related to Ran Donovan...sort of a distant cousin. Some think that Donovan may have put Sack up to stealing the puppy in the first place. It got back to us that Donovan was heard saying that Sad got what was coming to him, but we also hear that Donovan was not happy. He's not someone you want to make mad. I think he was just waiting until the right time to take Littleton out."

I spent an hour filling Walter Wood in on what I had heard from Lynne Littleton and our trip to the fighting pit inside Maurice Cox's barn. I told him that Lynne Littleton was convinced that they would come after her next. I finished by telling him that I had Littleton somewhere safe and Cox locked in a jail cell.

"I don't blame Littleton's wife for thinking that. You need to make sure that Donovan and his crew doesn't know where she is. I'd also keep an eye on that Cox guy if he admits to you what he told Littleton's wife."

"Anything you can find out from your sources will be a big help," I told him.

31

"Be careful, though," he cautioned. "Back in the old days, local hoodlums like Donovan were tolerated to a great extent because they kept criminals from other places, like New York and Chicago, from coming in and taking over. Some in law enforcement back then believed that it was better the devil you know than the devil you don't know. Some strange allegiances were formed that are still around today. Be careful of some of the people at the district attorney's office and at the sheriff's department. Hell, you might be careful of cutting anything up with some of the old timers here. I've said enough about that. Just be careful."

The drive back to Creekwood gave me some time to go over everything I had learned that morning. I wondered why three killers would want to bond themselves to one kill. I thought about the warning that Walter Woods had given me about Ran Donovan. If he has old friends among prosecutors and cops, how is that going to impact my investigation? I knew that I needed to get Lynne Littleton and Maurice Cox someplace safe, but now that had taken on more urgency.

When I arrived at the station, I checked the lounge to see if Lynne Littleton was waiting. It was empty. I found Barbie Morris at the front desk. "Where's Lynne Littleton?" I could hear an edge of panic in my voice as I spoke. It caught Barbie's attention.

"What's the matter? Something happen? She's at my house. She wanted to stay and use my phone to find a place to move to, a permanent place. I told her she could stay with me as long as she wanted to, but she said that she doesn't want to put me in danger. Do you think I'm in danger, Marc?"

"No, but it's probably a good idea for her to find another place to stay. Is Al in his office?"

"He was talking to that old man, Cox, earlier. It didn't last long and Al took him back to the jail."

As I walked to the door of Al's office, he looked up and said: "You need to call Johnny Flynn at the sheriff's office. He's been trying to find you."

Walter Wood's warning was playing over and over in my mind as I sat down at my desk and reached for the phone. I've known Flynn since I was a teenager. He was one of my father's best friends. There's no way that he's connected to anyone like Ran Donovan, I reasoned. I was still trying to decide how much to tell him when his extension answered "Flynn" in his booming, no-nonsense voice.

"Johnny, it's Marc Bryant."

Before I could say anything else, he started in: "I was hoping this was you. I've tried to find you all morning. We found Littleton's black Chevy Blazer. Someone called our dispatcher early this morning reporting a car on fire just off of Old Seagoville Road. It was pretty much completely gone by the time deputies got out there. They found that the license plates were gone, but were finally able to read the identification number once the car cooled down enough. It's registered to Littleton."

"What are you going to do with it?" I asked.

"I figured you would want to have our ID guys look it over, what's left of it, that is. It's still smoldering, but once it's cooled down enough, I'm going to have it taken to our impound lot and put under a shed. You do want our ID guys to do the work, right?"

"Yea, sure, Johnny, I'd appreciate that. They would have a lot more experience with something like that than we would here."

I took a big breath. "I talked to Dallas Intelligence earlier and found out that Littleton was part of Randall Donovan's crew. It may be that Donovan is involved in this. Do you know much about him?" There was a long unnerving pause on his end.

He finally spoke: "Yea, I saw Littleton's rap sheet when I came in this morning. I didn't know he was one of Ran Donovan's guys. Look Marc, you need to be careful with this one. Play it close to your vest. I'll help you where I can, but you need to know that he's big time and has lots of friends. You understand what I'm telling you?"

"Do you feel like getting involved in this with me?" I felt timid in asking.

"Oh hell yes," he responded with a laugh. "Nothing I'd rather do than put that old bastard in the joint where he belongs. There's an FBI agent in town that has been on Donovan's trail for a couple of years. He's agent Jim Griggs. If I call him, he's going to jump right in the middle of your case, so I can hold off until you get to a place where you can let him in. In fact, why don't I just give you his number and you can call him when you're ready. But I wouldn't wait long. He's going to find out eventually, especially if you've talked to someone at DPD."

As I hung up the phone, Al came in and sat down. "I couldn't get anywhere with Cox. He's claiming we abducted him for no reason. I finally confronted him with the call to Lynne Littleton. He said he never called her, doesn't even have her phone number. He still says he saw Littleton and Ryan that night, but didn't see Ran Donovan. He's scared, and I don't think he's going to be any help."

"Can you take him back home, Al? I need to talk more to Lynne. She's at Barbie's house, and I'm going to go over there.

"Sure, Marc. I'll catch up with you when you get back." My friend Al... takes another dirty job and never complains.

Barbie Morris and her six year-old son, Andy, lived in a brick ranch-style house in an upper-middle class section of Creekwood near the back nine of the Creekwood Country Club. She got the house as part of a divorce settlement from her husband, a Dallas lawyer. Because of the quality of the local schools, she struggled to keep the payments current so her son could take advantage of a better education. Her ex-husband fought every request for additional child support and, because of his legal experience, almost always got his way. He had been controlling and abusive during the marriage and continued to be threatening toward her afterward. Many of the officers at Creekwood PD hoped that one day he would show up at the house and try to cause her trouble. They wanted to see how his idea of justice matched theirs. Evidently he was too smart for that.

Lynne apparently had been watching me walk up to the porch because she opened the door before I could knock. She looked up and down the street and then told me to come in, hurriedly closing the door behind me. "There isn't anyone out there, Lynne. I checked before I parked. I even checked to see if I was followed. Don't worry, you're safe."

"I found an apartment that I can afford. It's in Richardson. It's furnished already and has a new mattress. I can move in tomorrow. I'm using my maiden name. No one here knows me by that name. I need my own place and time to figure out what I'm going to do next."

A sense of relief washed over me. Maybe getting her to a safe place may not be as hard as I was afraid it would be. This sounded like a good plan.

"Can you drive me to my house and let me pick up some things? I just need my clothes and some household things. We can get it in your car. Oh…car! Did you ever find Rick's Blazer?"

"Well, bad news about that" I told her. "The sheriff's department found it burned over near Seagoville."

"No matter," she shrugged. "I couldn't have used it anyway. Everyone knew it that black Blazer. Ran Donovan has been in it several times. Maybe I could have used it for a trade-in, but now…,"

"Tomorrow's New Years Day. I'm off, anyway. I'll go with you to get the apartment rented and then drive you to get your stuff. We'll worry about a car later on, once I know you are in a safe place. I'll be here in the morning to get you. Maybe not real early, though. My wife is dragging me to a party tonight and I might sleep in."

Lynne seemed to be appraising me as she stared into my face. I could almost see her mind working. In the low light of Barbie's living room, Lynne's eyes were the color of cobalt crystal.

"What's she like, your wife? I bet she's pretty." The gaze got deeper.

Breaking the spell, I hurriedly said; "Yea, she's real pretty. Look, I gotta go. I'll be here in the morning. Barbie's off tomorrow, also, so I'll see you both when I get here."

By the time I got home, changed, took the kids to their grandmother's house, it was after nine when Kay and I arrived at Winfrey Point. The party was underway and we could hear a small combo inside slaughtering their rendition of "Sweet Caroline." I knew that somewhere in the world, Neil Diamond must be weeping. I hadn't even set foot in the place and I was already miserable.

"Come on! It'll be fun," Kay smiled and tugged on my arm and pulled me through the door. I was immediately assaulted by thick cigarette smoke and, somewhere in the air, the unmistakable smell of burning marijuana.

"Come on in, you guys. What can I get you to drink?" I guess "old boyfriend Tom" was talking to both of us, but he didn't take his eyes off of Kay. "Let me guess, white wine for Kay and Budweiser beer for Officer Bryant," he said over his shoulder as he disappeared into the crowd. Before long, he returned with our drinks.

"Hey Marc, how many speeding tickets did you write today?" He said it loud enough for those around us to hear. Heads turned my way. I figured somewhere in the place, someone was dropping and smashing a marijuana joint under their foot. Kay jumped to my rescue: "You know very well that Marc is a detective and doesn't write traffic tickets. Tom, you can be a real shit." Good girl!

It wasn't long before my lungs had absorbed as much smoky air as they could and my ears were ringing from the sound of out-of-tune guitars. I stepped on to the wooden deck at the back of the clubhouse and closed the door behind me. My solitude didn't last long. As I stared out toward White Rock Lake, I heard the door open and felt Tom walk up and stand beside me.

"Look out at the curb. I just bought that." He pointed to a sleek red sports car that glimmered from the lights of the clubhouse. Before I could respond, he continued as if he had memorized a script ahead of time. "That's an E-Type Jaguar. Finest sports car on the road. It will go from zero to sixty in just over six seconds."

"Why would you want to do that?" I asked.

"He turned his gaze away from his car and faced me. "Do what?"

"Go from zero to sixty in just over six seconds. You planning on running from someone?"

Old boyfriend Tom gave a forced laugh and fumbled for something to say. Finally, "Well...no, not really" seemed to be all he could come up with. I was suddenly aware that Kay had walked out and was standing behind him. Tom brushed past Kay as he hurried inside.

"Hey, you wanna go home and have our own party?" She was smiling that heart-melting mischievous smile. "We got no kids, remember? Just the two of us."

"I thought you'd never ask. You want to tell Tom we're leaving?" I asked.

CAJUN RULES

"Nah, we're already outside. Let's just go. I'll send him a thank-you card."

CHAPTER 4

I had already showered and shaved by the time Kay woke up. "Lover boy, it's a holiday, remember? Why don't you jump back in this nice warm bed and let's continue what we had going last night."

"Can't. I gotta go in today" I said as I pulled on a pair of canvas sneakers. "I've got something to do that's related to that murder investigation. I'll try to get home early."

I got a suspicious look from Kay. "Jeans and a sweatshirt? I thought the official uniform was coat and tie?"

"I promised Littleton's wife...widow, whatever, that I would help her relocate. She's been staying at Barbie's. I'm going to stand guard while she picks up her personal belongings at her house and then take her to an apartment that she has arranged for over the phone. She's an important witness and I need...we need to protect her."

"Is Al going with you?" There was a concern in her face that made me wonder if I was doing the right thing. "No, I couldn't do that to him. He's done enough for me in this case. I didn't want him to give up his holiday, as well. Besides, the less people who know where she is, the better. She's giving me information on some very dangerous and well-connected people."

"If they are that well connected, won't they find her anyway?" The import of that simple question made me pause. She noticed it, too.

"You've got me and the girls to worry about, too. You need to tell Chief Rogers what you're doing. You don't need to go at this by yourself. Please, just stop and think this through."

Kay was right and, in my heart, I knew it. Walter Wood's warning for me to "be careful" kept nagging from the edges of my mind.

"Take me with you, then," Kay said as she started grabbing clothes from her closet.

"Hell no," I said. "You're the last person I want to pull into this thing. Look, let me just get her in a safe place today and then I can take some time to think all this through. I need to find out more about the people she's afraid of

38

and how much of a threat they really are. I'll check in with you before five this afternoon. If I don't, call Al. He knows Lynne Littleton's address. Okay?"

Lynne came outside and met me at the curb in front of Barbie Morris' house. Evidently she had been watching for me from the window. She still wore her bell-bottom jeans and the buckskin jacket. The jeans appeared to have been recently washed and pressed. Before I could stop her, she folded her arms around me and buried her head into my shoulder. Her hair smelled like orange blossom shampoo. I recognized the scent as one that I faintly detected on Barbie a few times as I passed her at the front desk. I even had the courage to comment on it once. She said that the orange blossom shampoo was her favorite. On Lynne, it seemed exotic.

"Thank you! I feel so much safer with you here," she said as she breathed into the side of my neck. Her warm breath felt good. As she spoke, Barbie stepped out on the front porch wearing a bulky terrycloth robe.

"Marc, you take good care of her, okay?"

Lynne turned loose of me and then walked back to Barbie, who had joined us on the sidewalk. She hugged Barbie tightly and said: "Thank you for everything, Barbie. I don't know what I would have done..." and then she began to cry. She then turned around and gave me another hug. As she did, Barbie rolled her eyes at me and winked. "Okay, let's go," I said, trying to break up this soap-opera scene. Lynne climbed into the front seat of my car and as I went around opening my door, I could see Barbie grinning and winking at me from the sidewalk.

For some reason, I felt awkward and fumbled for something to say as we drove away from the curb. "Al told me that you had some dogs at your place. What are you going to do about them?"

"They're pit bulldogs, bred to fight other dogs. You have to be careful with them. Rick has...had a friend who helped him with their training and conditioning. He's big into pit dog fighting, much more than Rick. I called him yesterday and he was going over to pick them up for me."

"You need to tell me who he is. I'll want to talk to him."

"His name is Gipson Tuttle. Everyone calls him "Gip." I'll give you his number and address, but you can't tell him where I am. He asked me yesterday and I told him that I was on my way out of town to move back with my parents in Ohio. He knows Ran Donovan. He doesn't like Ran, but they have a lot of the same friends. I like Gip, but I don't trust him."

"Is one of the dogs he picked up the puppy that was stolen by Otto Sack?" The question caught Lynne off guard and she quickly turned and faced me.

"Where did you hear that?"

"Look, Lynne, I probably know a hell of a lot more than you think I do. Were you there when Rick tied up Sack and his wife and tortured them for hours?"

"You make it sound worse than it was," she shot back, angry now. "Of course I was there. Where else could I go? I just tried to stay away from them. I finally left, went to a movie. I hoped it would all be over when I got back, but they were still there."

"Who was doing the torturing with Rick?" She stayed silent for a while, staring out of the window at the passing landscape. Finally, she turned toward me.

"It was Terry Ryan. Look, Sad and his wife got what they deserved. They weren't tortured. Rick just threatened them, gave them a good scare. They stole that puppy from Rick. He paid over two thousand for it. Terry threatened to rape Sad's wife, but he didn't. Rick wouldn't let him do that. He just convinced Sad that he would. Maybe he slapped Sad in the face a few times, but it wasn't like torture. Sad finally admitted that he took it and promised to take them to it. He had it hidden in an abandoned shack near his house. When Rick got the puppy back, he let them go. That's all there was to it."

"What did Ran Donovan think about all of that? I hear that Sad is Ran's cousin or something. Is that why Rick and Terry were both killed, do you think?"

"I don't think so. I don't know." Lynne turned and began staring out of the window. After a moment of silence, she said; "Rick told me that Ran was cool with it. He told Rick that if it had been his dog, he would have put a bullet in Sad and his wife, both. But…I don't know. You never know about Ran Donovan. Maybe he had second thoughts."

Eventually we pulled into the gravel driveway of the old wooden house. It looked almost in as bad a shape as Maurice Cox's barn. I noticed three short metal culverts or "tin-horns" in front that had been cut in half and apparently served as shelters for the dogs. There were empty chains in front of each that were affixed to metal stakes in the ground. As we approached, we saw that the front door was standing open.

I told Lynne to go back to the car, lock herself in, and if I didn't come out in a few minutes, to get on the radio and call for help. She didn't hesitate and quickly climbed back in the car. I heard her press the door locks as I approached the porch, pistol in hand. I stood against the wall next to the door and listened. I didn't hear a sound. I yelled through the open door: "Police officer! If you are in there, you'd better show yourself now. I don't like surprises, so if I come in and find you, I'm probably gonna just shoot you. You hear me?" Still nothing. I cautiously eased around the edge of the door and looked around. Although I could tell that the inside had been nicely furnished, everything was scattered and the furniture was turned over. It looked like someone had done a quick, thorough search of the place and wasn't too careful about how they left it. Cops maybe, I thought. I quickly cleared all the rooms and then went to the front porch and motioned for Lynne to come in.

When Lynne came through the door, she stopped and surveyed the disarray. I could hear her breath catch in her throat. Without saying a word, she walked quickly toward the bedroom that was just off the living room. She went straight to a small old-style wooden dresser and looked at the items scattered around on top. I could feel that she was relieved and smiled faintly to herself. As she started to gather up her clothes and stack them on the bed, I walked over to the dresser and looked to see why she seemed so relieved when she saw what was there. There was nothing out of the ordinary. Maybe I was wrong.

Lynne stuffed clothes, sheets and towels into two large suitcases, then gathered the items on the wooden dresser. She had a lot of makeup, creams and other beauty items. Why would a woman who is as naturally beautiful as

Lynne care about having all those beauty preparations. Maybe there is some insecurity in her that I hadn't yet realized.

Before she closed the last suitcase, she walked over to the window, then turned toward me and said; "Turn your back, okay?"

"What are you going to do, make a break for it out the window?" I laughed.

She didn't smile. "I need to get something and I don't feel like doing a lot of explaining right now. I just want to get this over with and get out of here." With that, she reached down and pulled up one of the floorboards next to the window sill. She removed a plastic-wrapped bundle and dropped it into the open suitcase. It was obviously a bundle of currency.

"We'll need to talk about that later, you know," I said. She nodded, then grabbed one of the suitcases and started toward the living room. I grabbed the other and fell in behind her. "You sure you don't want to take anything else? You don't need any kitchen stuff?"

"I just want out of here. I got everything I need. The old lady who rented this place to us can have the rest. Please, let's go."

The trip to Richardson was done mostly in silence. What questions I asked were answered with one or two words. "I hate to bring this up, but what are you going to do about Rick's body," I asked.

"I called his parents from Barbie's phone. They're taking him back to Ohio."

"Are you going to go back for the funeral?"

"No."

Still more silence. I could see tears in her eyes as she stared straight ahead. I decided to just let her have a few moments of peace.

I was pleased to see that the apartment complex that she had contacted was very nice. Most of the cars in the parking lot were less than two years old and appeared well maintained. The grounds were landscaped, and the complex was next to a small lake that was part of a nearby public golf course. There was only one person in the office, a 30-ish looking blonde woman who smiled and stood behind her desk as we entered. I started looking around while Lynne extended her hand.

42

CAJUN RULES

"Hi, I'm Lynne Nilsen. Thank you so much for meeting me on New Year's Day. It was a big help to me." It was the first time I had heard her maiden name.

As they talked and Lynne filled out the paperwork, I walked around the office and the attached meeting rooms. There was a small gym with two exercise bikes and a treadmill that was accessible from the office and from an outside door. As I walked along the wall, I could see a large swimming pool just outside with poolside furniture, now stacked against the wrought-iron fence.

Behind me, I could hear Lynne say; "I can pay the deposit and next two months in cash, if that's okay."

"We normally like to have that in a check, so we have a banking reference, but I guess it's okay." The woman said.

"My parents gave me cash to get started until I can open a bank account. As soon as I do, I'll start paying by check."

"You said by phone that you will be attending the University of Texas at Dallas?"

"Yes. My father used to work for Texas Instruments before he took another job out of state. He wanted me to attend UTD and maybe work at TI." I was amazed at how smoothly Lynne could lie, and I had to suppress a laugh.

"Well, anyway, welcome," the woman beamed as she stood and handed Lynne two rings of keys. "These are two sets of keys to your apartment, the laundry room and the outside door to the gym. You're welcome to use them at any time. Please let me know if you need anything. There is a new mattress on the bed and the walls have been freshly painted. I hope you enjoy living here. Come by and visit once you get settled in, okay."

I was relieved to find that Lynne's apartment was on a corner of the first floor. It offered a good view of the parking lots on both sides. The apartment itself was compact, but arranged well. There was a living room that had a small dining nook to one side. The kitchen was separated from the dining nook by a table-top bar. There was a small round Danish-style table in the dining nook with four chairs. Two stools stood next to the bar. A door on the wall between the kitchen and living room opened to the bedroom. The mattress had

43

a clean new smell. A small nightstand with a ginger-jar lamp stood next to the bed. On one side of the bedroom were sliding glass doors that opened to a small concrete patio, surrounded by a six-foot wooden fence. On the other side of the room was a large walk-in type closet. I thought how spare the few clothes that Lynne brought with her would look hanging on the opposing rows. It made me feel sad for her. Here she was on her own in a cold, lifeless apartment with nothing but a few changes of clothes. Oh, and a stack of what could be hundreds of dollars in her suitcase. I really needed to ask her about that.

"Let's bring your stuff in and then go out and find a store that's open today. You're going to need a few things until you can see about getting a car."

"I called a place yesterday. I can lease a new Volkswagen. They said that they would come and pick me up, but I want you to take me, okay?" Her eyes seemed to be studying me, exploring me, trying to see into my thoughts. This was the first time since I had met her in my office that I allowed myself to really take her in completely. She was beautiful, angelic. I began to realize that she had strongly Nordic features. Aside from those incredible blue eyes, she had smooth fine skin, long straight ash blonde hair and a long graceful neck. She was tall, straight and slender with shoulders like a swimmer.

"So your maiden name is Nilsen?" I finally managed to stammer.

"My family is from Norway. My grandparents immigrated here together and settled in Ohio. That's my father's parents. My mother's family was already living here in a Norwegian community on Lake Erie. That's where they met."

"Explains those blue eyes, I guess." I surprised myself at being so forward and backed off by saying; "Sorry, forget I said that. It wasn't very polite."

"Don't apologize. It's nice that you noticed. A lot of people comment on them. Rick told me that was the first thing he noticed about me." She seemed then to break her almost trance-like gaze into my face and then glanced down. "I can't believe he's gone" she whispered.

"Come on, let's go," I hurriedly said. I led us away from this awkward moment and out the front door of Lynne's new apartment.

We found a grocery store a few blocks away that was open on the holiday. As we shopped and talked, I noticed that the few men we passed would glance at Lynne when they thought my back was turned. I had to admit that I felt good walking around beside her, talking about the things on the shelves like we were a real couple. Suddenly my mind turned back to Kay and the girls and I felt ashamed. Lynne noticed the sudden change.

"You okay?" she asked, squeezing my arm.

"Yea, sure." I tried to sound convincing.

Lynne loaded up her shopping cart with frozen dinners, fruit, an electric coffee percolator and, as not to betray her hippy-chick persona, a set of melamine dinnerware in bright "psychedelic" colors. The thought of cooked food against those bright splashy colors made my stomach lurch. As we approached the check stand, Lynne opened her shoulder bag and pulled out several large bills. Again, I was reminded that we needed to talk about that stack of cash.

We stopped for take-out sandwiches on the way back to her apartment. Once we got back and had unloaded her purchases, we sat down at her dining table and she had her first official meal in her new home. I didn't want to ruin the moment, but I had a million questions that I wanted to ask her.

"Tell me about that cash you had hidden under the floorboard." That was my opening line to what I hoped was going to be a revealing conversation with this mysterious girl.

"It's our money...my money, I guess. We didn't steal it, if that's what you're asking. Rick had been stashing money away for a long time. Most of it he won betting on his dogs. There's a lot of money bet at those dog shows...,fights, whatever you want to call them. It was our get-away money. If something happened, we had enough money to get away and start over someplace else."

"Turned out to be a good idea, I suppose," I replied.

"Are you going to be able to do anything to Ran Donovan for this?" she asked hopefully. "I'll do anything, tell you anything I can so that you can get him. I know a lot, but I don't know what would help you. You're just going to have to ask me questions so I'll know."

"How did you and Rick get involved with Donovan to start with?"

"I met Rick when he came to work in my father's warehouse. My dad owns a beer and liquor distributing company in Cleveland. His foreman hired Rick to load trucks. During the summer, I worked in dad's office, doing filing and stuff like that. I would talk to Rick sometimes when he was in the break-room. I was seventeen and Rick was twenty. He seemed so tough and worldly. Anyway, I started meeting him after work at a club near the warehouse. Dad found out and had the foreman fire Rick. A week later, Rick was caught breaking into the warehouse office."

"Is that the burglary charge that he jumped bond on?" I asked.

"Yea. I tried to talk my dad out of filing charges, but dad hated him. Rick's father had gotten him out on bond. I went to Rick and told him I was sorry but my dad was going to prosecute him. Rick said he was going to leave town and never come back. He wanted me to go with him. At that point I hated my father for pressing charges on Rick, so I just decided to go with him."

"How did you wind up down here?" I asked.

"Rick and his father raised fighting dogs. They took their dogs to shows all over the place. His dad knew Gip Tuttle. Rick knew him too. Rick called Gip and told him the trouble he was in. He said that he would put Rick up until he could find someplace else to stay. Dallas was a long way from Cleveland, so Rick thought it would be safe. We came here and stayed with Gip for a couple of weeks. Rick told Gip we were married."

"Did Gip know your maiden name?"

"I don't think so. I never used it when I got down here. Rick and I went up to Rockwall County and got a marriage license. That way, the law would never think to look there for marriage license for us. A Justice of the Peace married us a week later."

"So what about Ran Donovan?"

"Gip had some puppies with good lineage. Ran Donovan came one day and wanted to buy one of them. Gip didn't like Donovan, but was just mostly afraid of him. He's a big scary guy, even though he's an old man. Donovan and Rick started talking and he offered to show Rick some of his dogs. I started to go with them, but Gip whispered for me to stay back with him. Later, he told me that Donovan was dangerous and to try and keep Rick away from him. But, when Rick got back later that day, Donovan was all he could talk about. After that, Rick started to hang around Donovan and his buddies."

"I know that Donovan and his crew were doing some home invasion robberies. Was Rick involved in that? Did you know what they were doing?"

Lynne got up and began to walk around the living room, but continued to talk. "We moved into an apartment for a while. I stayed there mostly by myself. Rick would go off with Ran and his friends and stay for days at a time. When Rick would come back, he always had money. We finally decided to find a place where Rick could start working with dogs again. We moved into the house you saw. Donovan would hang around sometimes. Although I was scared of him, he always treated me nice. He would tell Rick how lucky he was to have me, but he never made a pass at me or anything. He was a gentleman, like he was my dad or something. But I was still scared of him; not because of what Gip said about him, but because he was just a scary guy."

"Do you know of anything that Donovan did that was illegal? I mean anything that you can help me prove that was illegal. I need something to use to pick Donovan up. So far, all I have is your word that you got a phone call from Maurice Cox saying that Donovan was involved in Rick's murder, but Cox denies making the call. I don't have anything."

"Rick never talked about what they were doing, although I knew it was something bad. He said they were betting on those dog fights and he was winning money that way, but I'm not stupid. I know they were doing illegal stuff. It wasn't until Ran accused Rick of stealing a piece of jewelry that Rick finally told me the truth. He was scared to death and he talked about leaving town. He admitted to me that they were robbing houses of rich people and stealing money and jewelry."

"Tell me more about the piece of jewelry that Ran thought Rick had stolen."

"Ran told Rick that some Highland Park rich guy had some jewelry and cash in his house. He told Rick that there was a really valuable necklace that had been in a bank box but that the guy's wife had taken it out to wear to some big party. Rick and a couple of Ran's friends got a box truck with a stolen license plate, then dressed up like deliverymen, and when the maid opened the door, they pulled on masks and went inside. Rick went to the master bedroom and found a safe in the closet. It was unlocked and there was jewelry inside of it. He got all that was there and gave it to Ran Donovan later. He told Ran that he didn't see the necklace that Ran told him about. It was supposed to be yellow gold with diamonds and emeralds. No one else saw it, either, they said. The newspaper said that an expensive heirloom necklace was stolen, and there was a picture of it. Donovan's guys accused Rick of finding it and holding it back and they beat Rick up, trying to get him to admit it. Finally, Donovan said he heard from someone he knew that the rich guy had probably sold the necklace earlier to settle up with some Dallas gamblers and reported it as stolen along with the other stuff. It was insured for a lot of money. Donovan told Rick that it was likely those gamblers who passed the word down about the jewelry being in the house to start with. It was a setup. Donovan told Rick that he knew Rick didn't take the necklace and that was the end of it."

"Why come back later and kill him? Are you sure Rick didn't keep the necklace and lie to Ran and you both? Maybe Ran found out he lied?"

"It doesn't make any sense," she sighed. "There is one reason why I don't think Rick had the necklace. Gip had heard about the trouble with Ran and told Rick that he knew a guy in Miami, a jeweler, who followed the dogs and bet heavily. Gip said that the guy was a fence for stolen goods, especially jewelry. The guy was from Spain and had connections in Europe that could move stolen jewelry. Gip said the guy was a trusted friend and offered to put Rick in contact with him."

"What did Rick say?" I asked.

"Rick said that he didn't need the help because he didn't take the necklace. I think that if Rick had it and it was worth as much money as they say it was, Rick would have taken the name and we wouldn't have been here. We would have taken the money for the necklace and disappeared. But, he didn't. That's why I know he didn't take it. Like I said, Ran heard that the rich guy actually sold it himself so he could get out from under his gambling debts."

"Then, maybe we're back to the deal with Sad Sack and the stolen puppy. Maybe Donovan thought it over and decided he needed to do something about it after all. Both Rick and Terry Ryan were in on the deal with Sack and both of them were killed."

"I just don't know," she said as she slumped down on the couch. "With Ran Donovan, you just don't know what he's going to do. I don't want to think about it anymore right now." She suddenly sprang to her feet. "Hey, would you help me put sheets on my new bed?"

"Uh, I'm not sure that's a good idea," I mumbled mostly to myself. Before I could say more, she said with a laugh; "What's the matter with you. You're blushing. Don't worry. Tucking the corners of a sheet under a mattress is not a commitment. You'll still have your virtue after we're finished. You're such a Boy Scout."

"I never was a Boy Scout," I answered defensively. "I was a Cub Scout, though," I quickly added, trying not to sound so serious.

"A Cub Scout! I bet you were so cute in your little blue uniform. Okay, Cubby, will you please do your good deed for the day and help me with the sheets?"

"What time is it?" I blurted out, forgetting that I was wearing a watch; one that Kay had given me for by birthday.

"Why, are you taking medicine or something?" Lynne teased. Her smile was radiant.

"Okay, let's get the sheets on your bed, then I need to leave. I have to make a phone call before five."

While we, stretched the sheet across her bed, she asked; "Are you going to take me to lease that car tomorrow? I know they said they would pick me up, but I'm afraid to get in the car with someone I don't know. Ran has so many friends around. Please say you'll take me. I'll try not to keep you long. Please?"

I couldn't say no, although I knew I needed to be back at work. Given the seriousness of the investigation, it was going to look strange if I wasn't in my office first thing the next morning. "Okay, but I'll be here early, probably around eight. You will need to be ready so I can drive you over and leave you to handle the lease arrangements. That's the best I can do."

THE BLUE LINE

I finally found a pay phone at a 7-11 store near Lynne's apartment and stopped to call Kay. "Hey, I'm all finished. You don't need to call Al. I'm on my way home. See you in about thirty minutes."

"You were just about out of time. I was getting worried. Mom dropped the girls off. They want Colonel Sanders for dinner. Will you pick up some on the way home?"

Instead of Dr. Seuss, the girls wanted me to read "Sleeping Beauty" for their bedtime story. The drawings of tall willowy Princess Aurora kept reminding me of Lynne with her long straight blonde hair and blue eyes. It was hard to keep reading because my mind kept wandering. I kept thinking of Sleeping Beauty lying asleep on a bed with freshly tucked sheets. "I think daddy's going to sleep," I heard my oldest daughter tell her sister.

CHAPTER 5

"Crestwood Police. How can I help you?" The voice of the morning dispatcher sounded stiff and official. Evidently, our receptionist, Barbie, hadn't come in yet. I waited until Kay got into the shower before I made my call.

"Hey, this is Bryant. I've got a family thing this morning at my daughter's kindergarten. I'll be a little late. Would you leave a note for Captain Copeland?" It was the first of many lies that I would eventually tell during this investigation. It tasted bad in my mouth.

"Sure, Marc, will do. Everything okay?"

"Everything's fine, Fred, thanks. I'll be in later. I'm following Kay up there, so I'll be in my car. You can reach me on my radio if you need to."

As I pulled into the parking lot of Lynne's building, she walked out of her door and waved. She must have been watching from the front window. She seemed to spend a lot of time watching out of windows. Probably a good practice, considering all that has happened, I guess.

She had a delicate scent that reminded me of vanilla or the talcum powder that we put on the girls when they were babies. I couldn't detect a hint of makeup but she was perfect, beautiful. She wore tan chino slacks and a cyan blue cable-cut turtleneck sweater. Her hair spilled over the turtleneck and down the middle of her back. Against the blue sweater her eyes seemed to radiate a light of their own. She looked like she had stepped off the cover of a fashion magazine.

"Thank you so much for this, Detective Bryant...Marc. Can I call you Marc?"

"Yea, well maybe not if we are around any of the other officers. Cops are notorious gossips."

"I understand. Sorry."

The drive to the dealership in Dallas was done mostly in silence. She seemed to be in a pensive mood and I was worried about not being in my office. Finally, I pulled into the sales lot. She went inside and spoke to one of the

51

salesmen, then came out and waved to me. "Thanks, I'll be okay," she shouted and went back in. I drove quickly to the station.

As I walked toward my office, Barbie waved me over to the front desk. "You've gotten some calls this morning" she said as she handed me several message slips. "An FBI agent named Jim Griggs has called twice. He said that he was coming here around noon to meet with you. He asked that you wait on him. He said it was important."

"With the FBI, it always is. What else?'

"Walter Woods at DPD called once…early. Also Deputy Johnny Flynn from Dallas S.O. called. Both wanted you to call as soon as you came in."

Walter Wood answered on the first ring. "Hey Walter, this is Marc Bryant at Creekwood PD. Sorry, but I just got in. What's up?"

"I wanted to give you a heads up. After we talked the other day, I called Jim Griggs over at the FBI. I hope you don't mind me jumping in on your case, but he has a special interest in Ran Donovan and we keep in touch. He's a good resource for us here. I filled him in on what you've told me. He said he wants to set up a meeting with you, so I thought I'd better give you some warning."

"Yea, I know. He's already called the PD this morning and said he was coming out around noon; wanted me to hang around for him. What's he like? Do you trust him?"

"Completely," Woods answered without hesitation. "I wouldn't give you much for the rest of those guys in the Dallas office, but Woods is one of us. He's a former cop from Philadelphia. You can trust him. He's 'pò-leese."

Cops have their own internal language…call it "shop talk." In the parlance of local cops, when you say "he's 'pò-leese' with the emphasis on the first syllable, that is your way of saying he's a good cop, worthy of your trust and respect. The local bad guys referred to us as "pò-leese" as well, but that's just street jargon. Maybe we picked it up from them. Who knows?

I thanked Walter for the call and then called Johnny Flynn. "Johnny, it's Marc Bryant. You called?"

"Yea, Marc. Gotta couple of things to tell you. First, our ID section didn't get anything useful out of that burned car. They did notice that the driver's seat was pushed back as far as it would go. They figured that whoever drove it to the spot where it was burned must be tall, like well over six feet. Maybe that will help."

"That's good information, Johnny. Thanks," I said.

"Another thing that I need to let you know. The first assistant at the DA's office called me and wanted to know about your case, like what evidence you have on Ran Donovan and his involvement. He said that the DA was interested. He also asked if we knew how to get in touch with the wives of the two dead guys. The DA wants to send some investigators from their organized crime section to interview them."

"So far as I know, Johnny, Terry Ryan's wife, Mary Beth, is with her parents at their house. The last I heard from Lynne Littleton, she was on her way back to Ohio. She said she would give me contact information when she got settled. We didn't have anything to hold her on so I couldn't keep her here."

"Thanks, Marc. I'll let him know." I could almost hear a chuckle in Flynn's voice. I had to sit still for a few minutes and think about this. Already, someone is trying to locate Lynne. Walter Wood had warned me about the district attorney's office and the connection to Ran Donovan. This was beginning to get very serious.

I walked to the door of Al's office, but found it empty and the lights off. I walked over to the door of the dispatcher's office. "Where's Al this morning?"

"Somebody went through the roof of Crite's Pharmacy last night. They found it early this morning. Al's been out there for the last couple of hours. You want me to raise him on the radio?" The dispatcher swung around in his chair and reached for the transmit button on the radio console.

"Nah, don't worry about it. I'll just catch up with him later. If he checks in, though, ask him if he needs anything from me."

"We're right in the middle of a regular ol' crime wave, huh?" the dispatcher said with a laugh. He turned to the radio and answered a patrol officer who was checking out on a traffic violation. "First Street and Stanford, ten-four."

Through the glass walls of the dispatch office, I could see a familiar face coming through the lobby doors. It was the switchblade knife kid, minus his sunrise gazing girlfriend. I had forgotten all about him and walked him into my office. "Thanks for coming. Things have been moving pretty fast on this case. I just haven't had time to call. Where's your girlfriend?"

"Her parents said that they would bring her themselves if you called. I came to get my knife back" he was defiant and had his arms folded over his chest. I had intended to just let him have it since I had promised I would, and I opened the lap drawer of my desk to get it, but the kid just couldn't resist in upping the ante.

"My father's a lawyer. He said you didn't have the legal right to reach into my car and get it. I wasn't under arrest. He said that if you tried to file some kind of criminal case, he would make you look like a fool in court."

"Well, we wouldn't want that, would we?" I answered as I removed the knife from my desk drawer. "Come with me. I'll walk you to your car." I got up and walked toward the lobby, the kid striding behind me. Once I got to the parking lot, I pressed the button and watched the blade spring out. I then bent down, put the blade under the heel of my shoe and pulled up on the handle, snapping the blade off. The kid's eyes shifted back and forth between the empty knife handle and my face, his mouth opened and closed as if he was gasping for air. I reached down, took the blade and threw it on top of the police building. I handed him the handle.

"Here you go. I keep my promises. You can tell your father the lawyer that if he has any problems with any of this, my chief's name is Clendon Rogers." As I walked away, I could hear the kid sputtering behind me as if he couldn't get his mouth to form around any words.

As I got to the front door of the police building, I saw a white Ford Custom with black-wall tires pulling in the parking lot. Behind the wheel was a man wearing a white shirt and tie. That could only be the FBI, I thought as I walked inside. I went to the front desk, turned and waited. He came in after a few minutes.

"Agent Jim Griggs, I presume" I said as he produced FBI credentials. "I'm Marc Bryant. Let's grab some coffee in the lounge and take it back to my office."

Griggs was dressed in the usual FBI uniform, dark suit, starched white shirt and striped tie, secured tightly at the neck. He looked slightly out of place in the suit, however. He wasn't tall, but squarely built and muscular, like a gymnast. He moved with an athlete's grace. He looked like he would be more at home in jeans and a polo shirt.

There were several officers in the lounge when we walked in. Griggs stayed quiet, like he was not comfortable talking around them. He put some powdered creamer in his coffee and followed my back to my office without saying a word. Once I had closed my office door, he sat down, took a sip of coffee, and raised his face to me.

"Walter Woods told me about Maurice Cox's phone call to the wife of one of the victims, Littleton. I drove over this morning to interview Cox. Looks like somebody has worked the old man over good. He has bruises on his face and was so stove up, he could hardly move."

"Did he say who did it?' I asked.

"Yea, he said you did it. He said you and another detective came to his house, kidnapped him and took him to a jail cell and beat him up."

"That's bullshit" I said and started to mount my defense when he raised his hand and interrupted me.

"I know. I asked him if he wanted to file a civil rights complaint against you and the department. He said he didn't and just wanted to be left alone. I got a little out of him, but not much. He's scared to death of someone, probably Randall Donovan. I figured that's who tuned him up like that."

"What did he tell you?"

"He said that he knows Donovan, but didn't see him that night. He said that Donovan uses his barn occasionally to do private dog fights but he hasn't seen him in months. The old man uses it for cockfights when Donovan isn't around. That's about all he would say. I was hoping I would get more out of him, but like I said, he's scared. Someone really put the fear of God into him with that beating."

"He's lying. I don't think Littleton's wife made up that story about Cox's phone call."

"I need to spend some time with Littleton's wife...what's her name?" he asked.

"It's Lynne," I answered, leaving it at that.

"I need to get in touch with her. Where is she now? That house that she and Richard Littleton lived in is empty and standing open. Looks like someone tossed the place and left in a hurry."

"She told me that she was going back home to Ohio. I didn't have any way to keep her here. She was scared and wanted to get out of town. She said she would call me once she got settled somewhere. That's all I know."

One day, it would have to come out that I had lied to the FBI. At the moment though, something just told me to keep her location to myself. There was so much that was coming at me...and fast. I just wasn't sure at this point who I could completely trust. That included Lynne Littleton, as well.

Agent Griggs gave me a long hard stare as if he was trying to read my mind. Finally, he smiled and said; "Of course you will let me know once she does, right? She may be the best link we have to Donovan. We've been looking for him for a long time. We have significant business to discuss with him."

"What business is that?"

"Woods said I could trust you, so here goes: We had a confidential informant that we were trying to work into the Maricone family in New Orleans. He was finally starting to get somewhere with them or at least thought he was. Back in July of '69, the CI got into his car in the parking lot of a bar in Bossier City and the car exploded. It was rigged with composition four, plastic explosives. We understand that's a specialty of Ran Donovan's. We don't have a single lead, but the word on the street is that Donovan's good for it. I would have given my right arm to have had a chance to talk to Richard Littleton. Since that's impossible now, maybe his wife might have heard something that could help."

"She told me that all she knew about her husband and Donovan was that they raised and fought dogs together. She said her husband followed the fights with Donovan and bet a lot of money. She found out more when Donovan accused Rick of holding back some jewelry from a home invasion robbery. He got scared and told her that Donovan was setting up robberies for him and some of Donovan's friends. That's really all she knows."

"Oh yea, the missing necklace from the Empress Carlota of Mexico, I know all about that. Something like that would leave a trail, but we never could pick up on one. We're talking about a very unique and priceless piece of jewelry. That necklace was part of a royal collection from the Hapsburgs of Austria in the early nineteenth century. Archduke Maximilian gave it to his Belgian wife, Charlotte, before they were sent by Napoleon III to rule the French empire in Mexico. The story goes that she passed it down to one of her adopted sons when she returned to Vienna after Napoleon started pulling French troops out of Mexico. It passed down through several generations and wound up in the possession of Gaylord Dillard's wife, who is a direct descendant of that Mexican royalty and is, oddly enough, also named Charlotte. That necklace has emeralds and several matching blue diamonds that, by themselves, are worth a couple of million, to say nothing of the flawless white diamonds that surround them. Trying to move blue diamonds would definitely be noticed. They are very rare and these were exceptional, so I'm told."

"What do you think happened to it? Lynne Littleton is convinced that her husband didn't take it. She said she would know if he did. She said Donovan thought Dillard may have sold it and then reported it stolen along with the other jewelry to collect on the insurance."

"Our only interest in the case was Donovan's possible involvement. From what I hear, Dillard was capable to getting rid of the necklace through some of his gambling connections. The sports book he was dealing with in Dallas was connected with the Maricones in New Orleans. They wouldn't have any trouble moving something like that, probably internationally."

"It's a cinch that Richard Littleton couldn't have moved it. His best chance would have been Ran Donovan. That makes me believe even more that Littleton didn't find the necklace in the house that day," I reasoned.

"If Donovan was involved in killing Littleton and that other guy, your best motive is going to be that beating they gave Donovan's nephew, Otto Sack. Donovan is an old timer. He has his family honor to uphold."

"Lynne Littleton told me that Donovan didn't have any problem with it and told Rick that he would have put a bullet in Sack and his wife for stealing that puppy."

"Well, maybe he had a change of heart," Griggs smiled.

"You said 'if' Donovan was involved. What do you mean? Do you think there may be a chance Donovan wasn't involved?"

Well," he paused for effect, then added: "all you have is Lynne Littleton's word that Cox called her and said Donovan was involved. Cox denies he saw Donovan. Could be his wife found someone else. Maybe set them up. How much do you know about her, anyway?"

This landed on me like ton of bricks. Had I let her beauty and seeming helplessness cloud my judgment? Just how much DO I know about her, anyway? I guess I waited too long to reply because Griggs stood up and said; "I'm sure your instincts are good about her, detective. Here's my card. Once you hear from her, please give me a call. I can fly up to wherever she is and do an interview. You'd be welcome to come along. Keep me in touch, okay."

I walked Agent Griggs to the lobby. "I'll call you when I hear something." He waved over his shoulder and walked out.

As I was walking back to my office, Captain Copeland came into the hallway and motioned me into his office. "Close the door and sit down," he said quietly. "Do you have that Littleton girl someplace safe?"

"Yea, I think so for now, anyway. I'm not sure if she's in any danger or not, but I'm telling anyone who asks that she's out of state."

"I don't need to know where she is right now, Marc. I trust your judgment on that. I just wanted to let you know that Chief Rogers got a call from someone at the DA's office wanting to know where she is. The chief doesn't want to know, either. He just wanted me to let you know that he's getting questions about her."

"She probably should just leave town, but she wants to stay around and help us get Donovan for killing her husband. I think she knows a lot more than what she has told me already. It's just going to take some time. She's pretty shook up...and scared."

"Did that FBI agent have any idea where we can find Donovan?"

"No, he was hoping he could talk to Lynne Littleton and get some leads from her." I took a deep breath and continued "Captain, I lied to him and said that she had gone back home to Ohio. At this point, I just don't know who to trust. I've probably gotten myself and the department in a lot of trouble for telling him that. I just felt that was the right thing to do when he asked."

"We'll just have to deal with it when and if it comes up later. But, for what it's worth, I think you made the right decision. Let's just get a little further down the road with this before we decide who we can trust and who we can't. Okay?"

I felt better after I talked to Copeland. Maybe he wasn't the greatest detective but he was a good supervisor. I guess that's what really counts.

As I was going into my office, my intercom line rang. "You have a call on line three. It's Lynne. She sounds happy. You must make her that way," Barbie said with a tease in her voice.

"Where are you?"

"I'm at a phone booth around the corner from my apartment. I've got a new Volkswagen. Come over and see it. I think you will like it." She sounded happier and more at ease than any time since I first saw her.

"If you like it, I'm sure it's nice. I do need to talk to you, anyway. I'll try to get there before five."

"I bought some beer so they will be nice and cold when you get here. You do drink beer, don't you Cubby?"

"I'll see you later" I said, then hung up.

I spent the rest of the afternoon catching up on my case notes. As I was leaving my office, I ran into Al coming in.

"How are you doing on that pharmacy burglary, Al?" I asked as I followed him into his office.

Al sat down hard on his office chair and heaved a large sigh. "They cut through a ventilator shaft on the roof and walked out the back door. They took a whole shit-load of Schedule II drugs with them when they went. They knew exactly what they wanted and got all the good stuff. They were pros. The Bureau of Narcotics and Dangerous Drugs is interested in the case. It fits an M.O. that they are familiar with. I'm meeting with them in the morning. How's your case going?"

"Donovan's involvement has the FBI interested. I got a visit from an Agent Jim Griggs a few hours ago. He wants to interview Lynne Littleton. In fact, someone from the DA's office is also trying to find her, as well. I've been telling everyone that she has gone out of state, back home to Ohio."

"Is she someplace safe?"

"For the time being, she's in an apartment in…"

Al suddenly raised his hand and interrupted me; "I don't want to know. If the DA and the FBI are looking for her, they're going to pull out all stops to find her. I don't want to know anything about it."

Again, Al gave an exasperated sigh and said; "Sorry. It's been a long day. Look, if I can help, I will. Maybe the fewer people who know where she is, the better. Doesn't mean I won't help you if you need it. You know what I'm saying?"

"Sure, Al, and I appreciate it. She gave me the name of a dog fighter who knows a lot about Littleton and Donovan both. I'm going over in the morning to interview him. I was going to take you with me, but looks like you got a full plate."

"Take the captain with you," he said with a chuckle.

"Sometimes I think maybe he's not such a bad guy after all. But, no, I think I'll just run at this guy by myself. I'll be alright, unless he feeds me to his dogs."

On the way over to Lynne's apartment, I tried to make sure I wasn't being followed. I pulled into a couple of large parking lots then watched to see who came in behind me. When I was satisfied that I didn't have anyone tailing me, I drove to the lot beside her apartment building and parked. Sitting in the lot was a bright yellow Volkswagen "beetle" with a paper dealer's tag. She could have picked something a little more subtle, I thought to myself as I walked toward her door.

Lynne met me at her door, holding out a can of Budweiser beer. "Thought you might like this after a long day," she smiled. Her face showed both affection and concern. It was disarming, and suddenly I felt ashamed of myself for being suspicious of her. I decided to charge ahead, anyway.

"Lynne, let's sit down and talk for a few minutes. I have questions about some things that are bothering me." A slight change came over her face. The concern was still there, but the affection was gone.

"Okay," she said, wrapping her arms around herself as she sat down on the edge of the couch and avoided my eyes.

"When we went inside your house yesterday, you acted as though you were looking for something on that dresser table. I want to know what you saw...or didn't see. I could see in your face that you were relieved about something."

"It was nothing. I was afraid that whoever was in the house found the money we had under the floor board. I saw that the board hadn't been moved, but I didn't want to go over to it or stare at it. I wasn't sure how to explain it to you. I just turned away from it once I knew it was okay. Maybe I was looking in the direction of the dresser. I don't know. Why are you asking me this?" Tears started to well up in her eyes and she hugged herself harder.

"Okay, maybe I was wrong about what I thought I saw. Just forget it." I felt bad for bringing it up but her answer still didn't seem right.

"Are you sure you don't know more about what Rick and Ran Donovan were doing? I can't believe that he would leave for days at a time and then come home with a pocket full of money and you weren't more suspicious. I mean, I don't know anything about betting on dog fights, but I don't think it would generate that much cash money. That house had a lot of nice things in it, expensive furniture. Then there's that bundle of cash that you have stashed away. I just think there is a lot you aren't telling me."

"Please don't do this," she suddenly pleaded. "Please trust me. I want to do everything I can to get Donovan and you're the only person I can trust. Don't start doubting me...being suspicious." She moved her arms from around her waist and put her hands together in a prayerful pose. Her eyes began to fill with tears. It made the blue in her irises shimmer. Her chin began to tremble. It reminded me of my daughters when they began to cry. It never failed to make me give in.

"You are the only person I have now," her voice began to crack. "If you can't trust me, then I've lost you. I don't have anyone." She began to sob.

"You've got your parents, don't you?" I reasoned.

"My dad hates me now," she managed to say, her throat tight. "Because I ran away with Rick after he broke into dad's office; it's like I betrayed him. I talked to my mom on the phone. She said she loves me and wants to help me but she's afraid to go up against my dad."

"Look, Lynne, you haven't lost me. I'm with you. Never doubt that. I'll be here for you." I stood up and walked to the door. I felt like I needed to be home with my family.

"Listen to me. There is an FBI agent who wants to talk to you about Donovan. Also, someone from the district attorney's office is asking around about where you are. He called my chief today. I'm telling everyone that you have gone back to Ohio. Right now, I'm not sure you're safe. Just be careful and look out at the parking lot every once in a while. You need to get a phone."

"The apartment manager came by earlier and said that the phone company will hook up my line tomorrow. The man will bring a phone to me."

"I'm going over and talk to Gip Tuttle tomorrow. I'll stop by on the way back and get your telephone number if you have one by then."

As I started to turn the knob on the door, she rushed from the couch and threw her arms around me, burying her head in the curve of my neck. Her breath was hot and wet. She turned her face up to me and kissed me. Her tongue flicked gently across my lips. Her mouth tasted yeasty from the beer and salty from her tears. It was earthy and exciting. I turned toward the door, but she grabbed my shoulders and turned me around to face her.

"I lied to you" she gasped. "I'm so sorry, but I lied to you and I want to get it straight so you'll trust me." My breath caught in my throat.

"It was marijuana. I thought Rick had left a couple of joints on the dresser. I suddenly remembered them when we went into the house. I didn't want you to see them, but they weren't there. I guess Rick took them. I didn't want you to get the wrong impression of me. I'm so sorry." She began to cry again.

"Hey, don't worry about it. I'm glad you told me, though. I just felt like you weren't being truthful with me. Now I understand. I'll see you tomorrow afternoon." I turned and walked away. She closed the door behind me.

Kay met me at the front door with a bourbon and water. It made me think of Lynne and the beer. I could hardly look Kay in the eye.

"Go sit down and relax a minute. Dinner is just about done," she said as she kissed me. "Whoa, I may be pouring gasoline on a fire. You smell like you've been drinking beer. This bourbon may not go down well."

"Just one. I stopped at that bar in the Holiday Inn and had a quick one with a couple of the cops." Lying was starting to come easy.

CHAPTER 6

Gipson Tuttle lived in a rural section of northwest Dallas County. His white wood-frame house sat at the intersection of two tar and gravel roads. It was the only house within a quarter mile of any others. This was probably a good thing since the large lot in front was pock-marked with small wooden A-frame style dog houses. Each had a bored and generally miserable-looking pit bull dog chained to a metal stake that was driven into the ground at one end of each enclosure. Even on this cold morning, the odor permeated the air.

A man whom I presumed to be Gip Tuttle, himself, stood on the front porch with his arms akimbo. He was tall, skinny, wearing canvas bib-overalls and looked about as friendly as his dogs. It was obvious that he was not going to walk out to the roadway where I had parked my car and was going to make me run the gauntlet of the scarred and battle-worn dogs that stood between me and the porch. Eerily, every dog was silent as I passed by. Some gave me a malevolent stare. Others seemed mildly bored with my presence.

"Are you Gipson Tuttle?" I asked as I reached in my coat pocket for my badge case.

"Why?" he asked.

"Why what?" I asked back.

"Why are you looking for Gipson Tuttle?" He wasn't going to make this easy.

"I'm Detective Marc Bryant. I'm with the Creekwood Police Department," I said as I held my badge up where he could see it. "I'm investigating the murders of Richard Littleton and Terry Ryan." By that point, I was standing at the foot of his front steps, looking up at him.

"Oh sure! Come on in." Suddenly his stern face broke into a smile that was so broad and friendly that it made it impossible for me not to smile back. "Lynne called me and told me about Rick and Terry." His smile then faded to a more composed sadness as he held open a screen door for me to pass. "Man, that's just terrible."

His house was neat and clean. The furnishings were dated, but well kept. I realized why as I entered when I saw a stocky built woman who was wearing a large apron and holding an old style feather duster.

"That's my wife, Judy" he gestured broadly with his hand as if he was introducing a stage act. "Judy, this man is a detective working on Rick's case. Do we still have some coffee on? Detective, can we fix you some coffee?"

She smiled and left the room, returning in a few seconds with an unplugged electric percolator and two coffee mugs. As she handed one of the mugs to me, she asked "How is Lynne? I feel so bad for her. She is such a sweet girl. Have you talked to her lately?"

"Not since she left to go home." I felt bad about lying to her. She seemed genuinely concerned. "She went back to Ohio with Rick's body. She promised to contact me once she gets settled." I turned to Gip. "She told me before she left that you are a good friend, and she thought you would help me with my investigation."

"I will if I can," Gip said as he motioned me toward a well-worn recliner. He and Judy sat opposite of me on the couch. She put her arm over his shoulders and they sat close to each other. "I loved those two kids. I've known Rick and his dad for years. We met at some of the dog shows. Rick was just a teenager when I first saw him."

"When you say 'dog shows' you mean fights, don't you? I mean, why don't you just say 'dog fights'? It's not like it's the Westminster Kennel Club or something." There was an edge to my words, but Gip seemed not to be bothered by it.

"You can understand, can't you?" he answered patiently. "As an officer of the law, you know very well that organized dog fighting is illegal in most states. People perk their ears up when they hear the word 'fight'. It brings on a lot of unwelcomed notice. We call them 'shows'. Are you here to talk about Rick's death or you here to talk about dog fights?"

I felt that my opening gambit was a little strong and I decided to back off some. "My only interest is to find the persons who killed Rick Littleton and Terry Ryan. I will accept any and all help you can give me. The dog fights...shows, whatever, aren't my concern. Unless, of course, this involves dog fighting. Such as: I have been told that Littleton abducted and beat up a man and his wife over a stolen pit bull dog. Anything that you know about that would be of interest to me."

"Yea, I know about that. I was the one who sold the puppy to Rick to start with. That pup was from a champion bloodline, an American Pit Bull Terrier from a line that was known for gameness. He was valuable, and Rick paid a lot of money for him. Otto Sack is a sack, alright. He's a sack of shit. He came to Rick's house when he was gone and took the puppy out of a pen on the porch. He and his wife hid the puppy and denied they knew anything about it. Rick and his friend, Terry Ryan, grabbed Sack and his wife, roughed them up a little and got them to admit to it."

"Do you think that Sack was the one who killed them?" I asked.

"Otto Sack is scared of his own shadow. He's a sleazy little coward. When there's trouble, he hides behind his wife's brother. His name is Willard Green. He looks like Bigfoot, stands about six foot five. Of course, Willard's as dumb as a bag of rocks, but he can be dangerous. I think he does some muscle work for Randall Donovan occasionally. I guess you know about Randall Donovan, right?"

"Lynne told me that Donovan and two other guys took Rick and Terry away from a place that belongs to Maurice Cox. She said Cox called her and told her. We brought Cox in but he denies that he has seen Donovan lately and said he never called Lynne. Do you know Cox?"

"Yea, I know about him. I've never been to his place. They fight chickens there, I know that. I also know that Ran Donovan uses his place occasionally for private dog shows. I understand that they fight the dogs to the death there. People like Donovan don't belong in this sport. We take care of our dogs and would never let one die if we can help it. Hell, we have a lot of money and time tied up in them. They're like athletes." Somehow, I couldn't equate the menacing-looking dogs I had encountered in Gip's yard with hurdlers and pole-vaulters.

I decided to change directions: "Let's talk about Randall Donovan," I began.

"I'd rather not," Gip came back. Judy mumbled an agreement under her breath. "He's a very bad man" Gip continued. "Most of what I know about Donovan is what I have heard. He comes here every once in a while, but we're not friends. I don't like him, but I'm not going to cross him, either. He's dangerous and he will hurt you, or one of his minions will, if you piss him off."

"Was Rick one of his 'minions?'" I asked.

"He was becoming one, I think. I wish he had never met Donovan that day they were here. I tried to warn Lynne about him, but she couldn't convince Rick. Rick seemed to make a lot of money hanging around Donovan. He claimed it was from betting on the dogs, but I know better. They were into stuff...illegal stuff."

"What kind of stuff are you talking about?"

"Look, I don't want to get into this about Donovan. Tell the truth, I'm scared of him." Gip suddenly became very uneasy and started averting his eyes from me.

"Do you ever see Donovan at any of those shows?" I asked.

"He comes to some of them, but you never know when. I don't know where he stays. I don't think he even lives around here. He just shows up at them sometimes."

"How do you get the word out that there will be a show? Do you send out a schedule or something? Can you start calling me whenever there is going to be one?"

Gip laughed out loud. "Schedule? Are you kidding me? No, we don't send out a schedule and, no, I'm not going to tell you when there's going to be a show."

"Look," I said; "all I want to do is grab up Donovan and question him. I'm not looking to bust a bunch of dog fighters. I just want a shot at Donovan. That's all."

"Like I said, you never know when he's going to show up. It ain't that often. The cops start showing up and there won't be no shows...and I'm going to be in deep shit for even talking to you about this to begin with." Gip started to stir like he was getting up from the couch. I could sense my time was limited with him today. I decided to cut to the chase.

THE BLUE LINE

"Well then I suppose that you must use that covered trailer that I saw next to your house out there to transport your dogs to those shows. I could set up surveillance on your place here and just follow you the next time I see you hook the trailer up. The FBI and the Dallas Police are also interested in Donovan. I shouldn't have any problems getting plenty of help. Hell, we could go twenty-four hours a day. Whata ya say, Gip. You want lots of company, or do you want to help me out here?"

Gip was up and pacing around his living room. He would stop and stare out of the front door and then go back to pacing. I decided to just let him be the next one to speak. Finally; "So what the hell you gonna do, approach him right there, put handcuffs on him…all that by yourself? He usually ain't alone."

"At least, I'll know who he's with and what he driving. I'll have more than I have now."

"Does he know you on sight?" I could see the wheels turning in his head. "Would he know you are a cop if he saw you?"

"No. I've never seen him either, except for mug-shots. Why, you got a plan?"

Gip stared at me long and hard and I could almost feel his brain thrumming. He seemed to be appraising me, thinking about me. He put his hand up to his chin and cupped it like an archeologist studying a fossilized skull. "I could maybe take you to a couple of shows myself, as long as no one knows you're a cop. If you are with me, I think it will be okay. I could pass you off as an old friend. No one will ask but they will be plenty suspicious. You just can't go in carrying a badge in your pocket. If someone saw it, my ass would be in serious trouble."

"What about a gun?" I asked, almost joking.

"Oh sure, no problem. Everyone carries a gun at those things. You'd be strange if you didn't have a lump under your shirt."

"Well, that's comforting to know. What are they afraid of, the dogs or each other?"

"There's a lot of money being bet, being passed back and forth during the fights. People are just cautious. I've never seen anyone use one. Occasionally

68

if one of the dogs is injured beyond help, they will use it to put the dog out of its misery. Look, Detective Bryant, I might consider taking you with me when the next show is set up. Should be one soon. If you promise me that you will never tell anyone that you are a cop and if you will not use any information you get against me or any of the people at the show, I'll call you and you can meet me and go with me. I don't want you sitting outside my house and watching who comes and goes. This way, I can help you get what you need on Donovan and then, well excuse me sir, but hopefully that's the last I will ever see of you."

"Okay, deal!" I could tell Gip felt like he was being forced to make a deal with the devil, but this seemed to be the best way to get close to Ran Donovan. I had worked some undercover assignments and felt confident I could pull it off. We agreed that he would call when the next show was being set up. I thanked him and started out toward my car. "Here, let me walk you out," he laughed. "Wouldn't want you to get bit in the ass."

I had promised Lynne that I would stop by her apartment on my way back from Gip Tuttle's house. As I approached, I saw the bright yellow VW bug in the parking lot. I could feel a sense of excitement when I realized she was there. I didn't have to knock. She opened the door as I walked up.

"The telephone man just left. I have a brand new yellow phone. It matches my new car. I've decided that yellow is going to be my new favorite color." She was happier than I had ever seen her.

"What was your old favorite color before?" I asked, smiling at her giddiness.

"It used to be blue. Most girls like pink. I always liked blue. I think I may have been a tomboy." She was still talking as she stepped up and hugged me hard. Lynne was much taller than my wife, Kay. Not being accustomed to getting a hug from such a tall woman, I almost lost my balance.

"Whoa, big boy. You alright?

"You just caught me by surprise is all," I said, a little embarrassed. "Good. I'm glad you have a phone. That makes you safer here. Write down the number so I'll have it."

Lynne tore a corner off of the magazine that was lying open on the coffee table and scribbled the number on it. She then folded it and pushed it into my shirt pocket as she looked into my eyes. I could just wander into those beautiful blue eyes and get lost, but I didn't need to go there. "Thanks. Let me tell you about my conversation with Gip Tuttle."

"Did you meet Judy? She's such a nice person. I just love her." I gathered that Lynne was excited to have someone to talk to because she was chattering like a chipmunk. I finally had to break in: "Yea, she's nice. She is very concerned about you."

Suddenly Lynne stopped talking for a second. Then; "You didn't tell her where I am, did you?" "No, of course not, Lynne. I told her and Gip that you went back to Ohio. They didn't ask anything further about you." She looked relieved.

"Actually, Tuttle didn't tell me anything that you haven't already told me. He said that he doesn't know where Ran Donovan is but that he occasionally comes to some of the dog shows…dog fights…whatever they are calling them."

"Is he going to call you if he sees Ran?" she asked. "I would be surprised that he would do that."

"No, but he is going to take me with him to a couple of them in case Donovan shows up. That way, I can see what he's driving, maybe who he's with, stuff like that."

"He said he would do that?" She seemed surprised. "I would have never thought he would do that. He must really trust you. If anyone knew that he brought a cop around to one of those shows, he would be in big trouble."

"Well, we'll see. At least he agreed to as long as I don't use anything I see or find out against him or any of the other people at the fight and never tell anyone I am a cop. He doesn't even want me to bring my badge with me. I don't know how that's going to go down with my chief."

"You need to be very…very careful," she cautioned. "There are some really bad people that go to those things. I think everyone that goes has a gun."

"Yea, that's what Gip told me," I laughed. "But I'll have a gun too, you know."

CAJUN RULES

"I'm serious. I'll worry about you. I don't want anything to happen to you." She seemed so sincere that it was unsettling.

"Look, I'm a cop. I'm supposed to take risks. I'm working on your husband's murder. All you need to worry about is if I do a good job."

She lowered her eyes. "I'm sorry, I didn't mean to be so… If I lose you, I won't have anyone to protect me." She suddenly looked up and smiled. "Oh well, why should I worry. I bet you can be a tough guy in a tight spot…Cubby." She laughed, then grabbed my head between her hands and kissed me hard. I let my hands drop down the small of her back and then slide over her hips. I put my hands behind her and pressed her against me. She groaned and kissed me more urgently. She turned suddenly and pushed me backward on to the couch, falling down on top of me. She wedged her hips between my legs and thighs and then pinned my shoulders to the couch. She straightened her arms and looked down into my face. She turned her gaze from my eyes down to my mouth and began to move in close for another kiss. I caught her shoulders and pushed her back.

"We can't do this," I finally managed to say. "I mean…you can't imagine how bad I want to. It's all I've thought about ever since the day I saw you in the office. You're beautiful, Lynne, and I'm crazy to turn you down, but this is not headed in a good direction. You're the wife of a murder victim. An FBI agent thinks you may even be a suspect. I'd lose my job, my wife and kids. I'm sorry. It would be so easy to just let go right now." I was arguing with myself…and I was losing. I stared up at her soft sweet face and could see the passion and lust in her eyes. We stayed that way for at a few seconds. Finally she climbed off of me and stood beside the couch, holding out her hand to help me up.

"I don't want you to get into trouble. I just want you…period. You're my handsome knight on the white charger like in the fairy tales. I've always dreamed about you, even before I ever saw you. But, it's not good until we both want each other. I can wait." She smiled that beautiful angelic smile, turned and walked to the door, opening it and standing aside.

"You look like you're ready to leave. I know you'll be back. Just make it soon, okay. You have my number now. Call me when you have a minute

71

during the day. Don't look so scared, Cubby. I'm sure I'm not the first girl who's thrown themselves at you."

"I'll call you and let you know how things are going with the case," I said as I stopped and turned toward her in the doorway.

"Does that mean you aren't coming back?" she asked.

"No. I'll be back. You know I'll be back."

"Yes." She smiled as she reached out and touched my lips. "I know you'll be back."

Barbie Morris had several call back messages waiting for me as I walked into the lobby of the station. "Nothing urgent," she said. "That FBI agent said to try and call him before the end of the day. Dan James at the crime lab wanted you to call him, no hurry on that one. Walter Woods at DPD said to call him when you get in. A Douglas McMillan with the DA's office has called twice. He said he's with the organized crime section. Said it was important."

I walked back to my desk and took a deep breath, trying to collect my thoughts. My better judgment told me to turn this case over to Al and stay away from Lynne Littleton. It was bad enough that she was obviously attracted to me and was trying to start a romantic relationship. What was really bad was that I felt like being a willing party to it. I knew then I wasn't strong enough to resist her, and she knew it too when she told me that I would be back. Maybe I could figure out a way to have both: to give in to her and keep my investigation, as well. My thoughts were interrupted by the intercom. "Deputy Johnny Flynn on line five."

"Johnny, I was going to call you. I might have a lead."

"Oh yea?" Johnny said eagerly. "I was just checking in to see how the investigation was going."

"Here's what I have so far. I know that there was bad blood between a guy named Otto Sack and the victims over a beating that Sack and his wife got for stealing a pit dog puppy. Walter Woods told me that in the beginning, and Littleton's wife confirmed it. I talked to a dog fighting friend of Littleton's today and he told me the same thing. Although Maurice Cox denies he called Lynne Littleton, she says that he told her that Donovan and two other guys took Littleton and Ryan away from Cox's place that night. This guy said that

Sack has a brother-in-law named Willard Green who is well over six feet tall. That would match with the front seat of Littleton's car being push back as far as it would go. I think that Donovan, Sack and this Willard Green are our shooters and the motive was the beating of Sack and his wife. You think I would have enough to get a judge to issue warrants?"

"I know Sack and Green. They live down on the south side of the county just before you get to the Ellis County line. We've handled Sack several times for burglary and theft. He has an old house that sits way off the road. He keeps a bunch of Guinea hens around the place that put up a big squawk whenever we come to the house. The deputies down there call it the "Sack Early Warning System." His wife, Ethelene, and her brother have been stealing from neighbors in that area since they were kids. Willard, her brother, is kind of feeble-minded, but big as a bus. He has a child's mind in a giant's body. He would definitely hurt you if you got in his way. They are always out and about down there. We could sit up on them and pick them up for investigation when we see them. That way, you won't have to get warrants."

"I would really appreciate that, Johnny."

"Sure, Marc. I'll get some deputies on it right away. I'll let you know when we have them down here in jail."

I then called Agent Jim Griggs. He came on the line as soon as I asked for him. "Glad you called. I got good news. The Assistant U.S. Attorney in the Western District of Louisiana has green-lighted us to go after Ran Donovan on that bombing. He stopped short of having a warrant issued at this time, but wanted us to locate Donovan and try to interview him. He said they are going to present a case to a federal grand jury once we locate him and talk to him. So, any leads you have will sure be a big help to us."

"I may have something that will help," I told him. "I talked to a guy this morning who knows my victim Littleton and Ran Donovan, both. Donovan and Littleton frequented the dog fights. The guy I talked to, Gipson Tuttle, has several dogs that he takes to these fights. He said that Donovan sometimes goes to these fights; they call them "shows" by the way...dog shows. He agreed to let me go with him to some of these shows and, if I see Donovan, get what information I can like what he's driving, who he's with, whatever I can."

73

"You're not going to approach him, are you? I hear he can be pretty salty."

"No, I agreed that no one would know I am a cop. I won't use anything I see or hear against any of the other people there and will just get what intelligence I can on Donovan and leave it at that."

"That might be a lot more then we know right now," Griggs said. "We've tried to get a line on his current whereabouts and have come up blank. We were going to start rattling the cages of some of his buddies in town, but maybe we'll just hold off and see if your plan bears any fruit. Just be careful, amigo. If they sniff out the fact that you're a cop, they might turn you into dog food."

"As soon as I hear from Tuttle, I'll let you know, Agent Griggs."

He laughed. "Anyone who has balls as big as yours can call me Jim."

My next call was to Dan James at the crime lab. He seemed rushed, as usual.

"Marc, I've got a ballistics report on your shooting. I'll drop it in the mail or you can come by and pick it up. I think I can save you the trip because it's short and sweet. Both died of gunshot wounds to the head. Littleton was shot by three weapons, only one being fatal. That was a through and through gunshot from the back of his head to the front. Based on the size of the entrance and exit wounds and the trace evidence around the wounds, it was a lead .38 caliber semi-wad cutter hollow point round. The stippling and scorching around the wound indicated that the muzzle was about six inches from the back of his head. The other wounds were from number four buckshot. It was fired from a .410 shotgun, judging from the pattern. The barrel was about two feet away from the victim's face. The wounds would not have been fatal. The third shot that hit him was a .22 short, probably fired from a pistol. It was lead and shattered when it hit his upper jawbone. The muzzle was three, maybe four feet from the victim. My guess, he was being led along. The kill shot was fired by someone walking close behind him. Once he fell and was on the ground and, most likely already dead, the other shots were fired by two shooters who were standing upright over him."

"The second victim, Ryan, was also shot in the back of the head with a similar round as Littleton. It was fired after he was on the ground in a prone position. The muzzle was about two feet away from his head. The round entered the upper left side of his skull, spread out and then shattered against the inside of his upper right skull. We removed a mangled round from his brain…or what was left of his brain. It was a lead 158 grain semi-wad cutter hollow point round. There may be enough from the base of the projectile to make a ballistic comparison if you find me something to compare to it. From what was left of the round, I could tell that it had five lands and grooves with a right twist, so you're looking for a Smith & Wesson .38 special, probably a two and a half inch barrel."

"Good work Dan. I'm very impressed. I'll just wait for that report to come by mail." As always, I stopped to think about how lucky we were to have someone like Dan James working at our lab.

My next call was to Walter Woods at Dallas Police. "Woods," he shouted when he answered the call. I wonder if the other officers in the Intelligence office ever get tired of him doing that.

"Walter, it's Marc Bryant at Creekwood PD. I'm returning your call. What's up?"

"Hey Marc! I wanted to let you know that the guys in Vice Control just busted a bookmaking operation in a car lot over on Mockingbird Lane. The bookie is trying to cut a deal with them and was giving up everyone around. I went over to Vice and asked him about Gaylord Dillard and the stolen necklace. He told me that Dillard was in big debt for a while and talk was that he and his wife were both being threatened if he didn't pay up. He finally did, in cash. But, he never heard about Dillard selling a necklace to pay off the debt. He said that if that had happened, he would have probably heard about it. Those guys don't usually take stolen property to settle up a gambling debt. So, that necklace may legitimately be missing. I wanted you to know that Donovan may have it, after all."

"Could Dillard just have sold it to someone else, like a jeweler, to get the cash up to pay off the debt?"

"Sure, I guess that's possible," Woods agreed. "But that necklace, from what I'm told, would be hard to get rid of without it being big talk around the jewelry industry. The cash he used to pay off the debt could have simply come from the insurance settlement. He could have gotten a street loan with big interest to satisfy those bookies then paid it back when the insurance check arrived. Anyway, I thought that was interesting and wanted you to know. Have you got any good leads going?"

I explained to him about Sad Sack and his brother-in-law and told him that the sheriff's office was going to try to grab them up for an interview. "Great, let me know how that comes out," he said as he hung up.

I decided to forget the calls from the district attorney's office for the time being just go home early for a change. I stopped by Al's office on the way out.

"How's your drugstore burglary deal going?"

"Moving along," Al answered. :"The BN&DD asked me to be on standby for the next couple of days. They are putting together a search warrant for a place where these stolen pharmaceutical drugs are being stashed. They want me to come along and see if some of my stuff is there."

"That's good, Al. Let me know if I can help out. Hey, do you have a minute. I need to talk to you about something" I said as I sat down in front of Al's desk.

"Sure, fire away," Al said with a broad smile. It faded when I didn't smile back. "What's up" he then said with concern evident on his face.

"I stopped by to check on Lynne after I talked to Gip Tuttle. As I was leaving, she made a pretty big pass at me."

"How big?" Now Al was smiling broadly again.

"Pushed me down on the couch, laid on top of me and kissed me," I replied. I felt my face getting hot.

"Wow, you lucky dog! That girl is a knockout ."

"I'm serious, Al. I'm not sure if I need you to take over this investigation or what. This could turn into a bad deal."

"Look," Al began; "you really need to discourage that from the get-go with her. Have a talk with her about it. Try to limit your time alone with her, if you can. I'll try to start going with you when I can shake loose. But, you don't need to pass the case to me. You're doing a good job, and it needs to be cleared up. Just try to keep your head…both of them, out of trouble. She's probably still shaken from all that's happened and you're a convenient handle to grab onto. It will probably pass if you don't encourage it. Okay?" I felt better and thanked Al. He's a good friend.

As I walked into my house. I could hear the girls playing in the back yard. I pulled off my coat and pulled my holster and pistol off of my belt and put them on top of my dresser where the girls couldn't reach them.

"Kick off your shoes and relax, Mr. Policeman," Kay said as she started to unbutton my shirt. I'm going to take advantage of your early arrival. I need some adult conversation. As she pulled my shirttail out of my pants, she noticed the torn piece of magazine that was folded in my pocket. "What 'cha got there?" she laughed as she unfolded it. Her face dropped to a frown. I had not looked at what Lynne had written until now. It was her phone number and a big heart next to it.

"Who wrote that," Kay asked, looking into my eyes. "That is definitely a woman's handwriting."

"I stopped at Lynne Littleton's apartment to talk to her about my meeting with Gip Tuttle. She had just gotten a phone installed and gave me the number. Why the heart, I have no idea. Some kind of hippy thing, I guess." I tried desperately to move past it. I could tell that she was turning this over in her mind. Then, she smiled, handed the paper back and said; "Well, she seems grateful for all your help, doesn't she?"

CHAPTER 7

Kay Leanne Carson was what we boys in my high school called a 'fox" and what the adults called a "catch." She was beautiful, smart and came from a wealthy, successful family. Her father owned an accounting firm in Dallas and numbered among his many clients were professional athletes, law firms and oil companies. In our senior year, she was a cheerleader, the Homecoming Queen and voted most beautiful. Although she dated several of the boys in school, mostly football jocks, and some older boys from fraternities at SMU, she spent most of her time with Tom Warner, our local football hero who had a room temperature IQ and was a well-remembered bully from our elementary school days. Like Kay, Tom came from a wealthy family. His father was senior partner of a Dallas law firm that was founded by Tom's grandfather. The Warner & Price Law Firm was a long-time client of Kay's father and his accounting firm. Their families were not only business associates but social friends.

In the pantheon of our high school gods and goddesses, Tom and Kay were Zeus and Hera. To us mere mortals, who watched them sweep along the corridors of our school together as if the triumphal march" from Verdi's "Aida" was playing in the background, they seemed to possess everything that a teenager would want; good looks, money and popularity. But, for the few of us who looked more closely at the pair, and I certainly did because I harbored a huge crush on Kay and had since fourth grade, it certainly wasn't a match made on "Mount Olympus." Kay, who was much smarter and certainly more mature, seemed bored by Tom most of the time. Tom could sense this and it made him grovel and whine around her, much to the delight of the many victims of his relentless bullying. Even when Kay would date one of his friends or humiliate him by showing up at a school dance with one of those SMU frat-boys, Tom was always at her side the next day.

So it came to pass that Bryant and Carson were seated side by side at our graduation ceremony, thrown together by fate of alphabetical order. During the endless speeches, Kay and I talked about our future plans. I told her that I was going to attend North Texas State University and study journalism. She said that her parents wanted her to attend Baylor University and study finance. Even way back in the W's, I could feel Tom Warner's eyes boring into the back of my head as I leaned in and chatted with Kay. After the final strains of "Pomp and Circumstance" had drifted away and I stood talking with my parents outside the auditorium, Kay walked up, smiled at my parents, and stuffed a piece of paper into my hand. She hurriedly whispered "Call me" in my ear and then joined an anxious-looking Tom Warner and her parents on the front steps. The only thing on the note was her telephone number. The feminine softness of her handwriting made my heart skip.

Not wanting to appear too anxious, I managed to wait an entire twenty-four hours before I called the number. Before the second ring, Kay answered with a breathless "hello." "Hey, this is Marc. This is the first chance I've had to call you," hoping I sounded like I had a full, busy life. "Can you come to a pool party at my house tomorrow night?" she hurriedly asked.

"If you mean can I come to your pool and watch Tom Warner do jackknives off of the diving board, I'd rather stay home and watch paint peel."

"Oh, he's not invited" she replied, sounding just a little unsure.

"Sure. What time?"

"Come around six. Don't eat. Dad is grilling hamburgers. Oh, and bring a swimming suit," she added as if not being so instructed; I might show up in the buff.

There were only a few other guests at Kay's pool-side party when I arrived, but it was who they were that was the big surprise. A couple of them were on the school's newspaper and yearbook staff. Another I recognized as the President of the school's Thespians Club and well known as the school "nerd." Two girls I recognized as being on the cheerleading squad with Kay and they were with boys from the baseball and track teams. Altogether, the guests represented a motley selection of students from our school and were kids I never would expect to see socializing together. Kay grabbed my arm as I arrived and marched me up to her parents, who were putting out food on a large table. Kay's father warmly shook my hand and welcomed me to his home. When he asked what my father did for a living, I hesitantly told him that he was a deputy sheriff in Dallas.

"The Sheriff is a good friend of mine. So you must be Captain Bryant's son. Well, I've known your dad for years. He is a good man and seems to have raised a good son." I was stunned.

Later in the evening, I sat on the edge of the pool and had a long conversation with the school nerd, finding him to be amazingly bright and very interesting to talk to. Kay came and sat down beside me, stirring the water with her feet. "I want to talk to you about something," she said as she turned face toward me. "I'm not interested in finance and I don't want to go to Baylor. I have thought about taking journalism since my sophomore year and when you said you were going to North Texas next year, I decided to finally confront my parents about it. They agreed, and I'm going to enroll at North Texas as well. Isn't that cool? We won't have to go to a place where we don't know anybody. We'll know each other. I'm so glad I talked to you at graduation. It made me finally set my mind on something I want." I stared back into her beautiful face, taking in those soft brown eyes and waited for the alarm to buzz at the side of my bed, knowing that this must be a dream. It wasn't an alarm clock that brought me back to reality but the sound of Tom Warner's voice as he rounded the corner of her house and marched defiantly toward the pool.

Kay jumped up and ran toward Tom, intercepting him half-way across the lawn. "No wonder I wasn't invited," he said as he glared over at me.

"No, you weren't invited, Tom," Kay calmly replied, "and I would like for you to leave. We don't have to be side by side every day. I have other friends, you know."

"Okay, I'll leave," he said grinning down at her. "But first, I'm going to whip Bryant's ass before I go." As he said this, he shoved Kay aside and charged toward me.

My dad always told me that if a fight was inevitable then make sure you were the first with the most. "Put a quick end to it," he always advised. I stood my ground and waited until Tom had gotten within reach. His fists were balled up and his face was flushed and tight. He was distracted for a split second by stepping from the grass to the concrete walkway beside pool, giving me a chance to strike first. I hit him square in his nose with a downward right-hand punch. Tears sprang into his eyes and blood gushed from his nose. He hurriedly tried to clear his eyes and wipe the blood from his now swelling nose. He threw a wide round-house punch that came nowhere close to me.

"Tom, give it up. Swing at me again and I'm just going to hit you again. Why not just sit down in one of the chairs and let's look at your nose and try to stop the bleeding. I don't want to fight with you anymore." He staggered over to a pool chair and sat down, holding his head back and pinching his nostrils. Kay's mother was suddenly there with a towel and some ice. I guess she'd seen bloody noses before.

"I really wasn't going to whip your ass, Marc," Tom said, his voice muffled through the towel.

"Yea, I know you weren't, Tom." I answered.

Kay and I dated during our freshman year at North Texas. I dropped out after that year and it wasn't long before I got my draft notice. With war raging in Vietnam, a draft notice seemed like a death warrant. Kay wanted to marry before I reported to duty. We had a quick wedding at her parent's house and a brief honeymoon in Galveston. I found out later that she was pregnant when I left for Army Basic Training. She was living with her parents and commuting to the Denton campus while I was away. Tom came around, but seemed resigned to being a friend, even expressing concern at my safety in Vietnam.

After two years, I came home to a wife and one-year-old daughter. Kay had managed not only to continue her studies, but got her Bachelor of Arts degree in Journalism after three years. With her degree and her father's connections, she had a job with a Dallas public relations firm when I came home. My father's connections landed me a job as a rookie officer at Creekwood Police Department. I promised Kay it was temporary until I could return to college and get my own BA degree.

The look of pride and love was always in Kay's eyes when she saw me in my Army uniform and then in my police uniform. As the years passed, there was not only pride and love but trust in those beautiful brown eyes. That is, until this morning. As I came out of the shower to dress for the day, I could see the love but the trust was gone.

"Are you getting anywhere on your murder investigation?" she asked. I could tell she was trying to initiate a conversation that would segue into one about the widow, Lynne Littleton.

"The justice department has given an FBI agent I'm working with the green light to go after Randall Donovan. Right now, my main interest is in finding him."

"How about Lynne Littleton? How is she holding up?" There it was.

"We've got her in a safe place." I managed to say "we" instead of "I," hoping it would allay any further suspicion. I wish I had looked at that note before Lynne stuck it in my pocket. "She knows how to find us if she needs anything. She's not my main concern at the moment." I hoped this would ease Kay's suspicions. It seemed to work and, I got that brilliant smile that she is so capable of giving.

"Should I expect you tonight for dinner?"

"I really don't have anything other than to go in and see what leads I can develop today. Sure! I'll see you this afternoon."

As I entered the back door of the station, I was surprised to see Johnny Flynn and two other deputies drinking coffee and watching the news on the television that we kept in the lounge.

"Hey Marc, glad you finally got here. Guess who we have sitting in your jail?"

"Johnny Cash? Is he looking for inspiration for another prison song?" That got a good laugh from the three deputies.

"Nope! Not even close. We have Otto Sack and his trusty side-kick Willard Green. Patrol grabbed them up last night making their way back home. I figured that our jail was too close to a courthouse full of judges and possible writs of habeas corpus. This way, maybe we can get in some quality conversation time before some red-mouthed lawyer friend of Ran Donovan's shows up and stops the show."

"Good idea," I laughed.

"I wouldn't get too optimistic, though," Flynn warned. "Both of them are surly as hell and I doubt we'll get much out of them. But, it's worth a try, especially with Green. If we separate him from Otto, he might get rattled and give us something. If brains were dynamite, ol' Willard wouldn't have enough to blow his own nose." Another round of laughter followed.

"Did they have any firearms with them when you picked them up?" I was hopeful.

"Nah, I wish! Nothing. Knowing Ran Donovan, he probably had them dumped somewhere when they were finished. He's no dummy, for sure" Flynn laughed.

We put Sad Sack in my office and put Willard Green in our interrogation room. The room had a panel with one-way glass that allowed us to watch from the adjacent office. As big and dumb as Willard Green was, it was decided that giving some other officers a view of the interrogation room might come in handy should things get out of hand.

Sack was at times defiant and condescending and at other times whiney and meek. He admitted having taken Rick Littleton's dog and said that Rick had promised to sell it to him and then reneged. He said he figured he got what he had coming and didn't bear a grudge against Littleton and Ryan. I asked him if he had gone to Ran Donovan hoping to get some revenge for the beating. He said that when he told Donovan what had happened, Donovan told him that he got what he deserved and would have done the same thing to him under the circumstances. When I asked him if he was at the chicken fights that night at Maurice Cox's place, he said that he wasn't there and didn't watch chicken fights because it was "cruelty to dumb animals."

"You fight dogs. Isn't that cruelty to dumb animals?" I asked.

"Pit dogs are bred and trained for fighting. You can't train a chicken. They're dumb!" As it turned out, that was the most profound thing we got out of Otto that morning.

Green wasn't quite so effusive and philosophical. In fact, he refused even to speak. He sat with his arms folded and glared at us as we asked question after question. Occasionally, he would glance over at the door as if he hoped that Otto Sack would appear and do the talking for him.

As we were upping the pressure on Green, there was a knock on the door of the interrogation room. Perhaps one of the greatest sins one can commit in police work is to interrupt an interrogation in progress. Everyone knew that it was a well choreographed dance where you slowly but deliberately moved the suspect in the direction you wanted him to go. Interrupting the process would set you back, often to square one. I knew it had to be important and went to the door. Captain Copeland motioned for me to come outside.

"Sorry, Marc, but there is a lawyer in the lobby who has writs for Sack and Green and is demanding to be taken to them. I'm going to have to bring him back here."

"Yea, okay, captain, thanks" I said as I returned to the interrogation room. I told Johnny Flynn and the other deputies and we brought Otto Sack into the room with Green. Then, we brought the lawyer back to the room, as well. I immediately recognized the lawyer as Lincoln Treadwell, who was well known for defending local gangsters in Dallas. I always thought of him as the personification of the cartoon character Colonel Foghorn Leghorn, the strutting rooster with the southern drawl.

"You boys don't need to say another word to these poe-leese officers," Treadwell said in his best Texas aw-shucks good-ol' boy drawl. "I have writs here that say if they don't have warrants or haven't filed any charges, you can get up and leave with me right now."

As the three walked through the lobby toward the front door, I told the lawyer "Say hello to Ran Donovan when you check in with him and tell him we're coming for him as well."

"Ran who?" he replied, giving me a big Cheshire Cat grin.

"I really don't mind lawyers," Flynn said as the trio walked out of the front door, "just as long as they are back in their coffins when the sun comes up." That broke the tension and I had to sit in one of the lobby chairs and catch my breath from laughing.

"Well, it was a good try, Johnny. Thanks!" I walked the deputies through the lounge and out to the back parking lot.

"I guess someone in our office must have called Donovan and snitched us off," Johnny said as he opened his car door. "I'll let you know if something else comes up."

"Thanks again, Johnny. Tell my dad hello when you see him."

"Will do, amigo," he said as climbed into his car. I watched him and the other deputies drive out of the parking lot, wondering what my next move was going to be. I didn't have to wonder long. As I walked back to my office, Barbie called from the front desk and told me that FBI Agent Jim Griggs was on hold.

"Marc, can you shake loose for a little while? I thought we would go have a talk with one of Donovan's buddies, maybe rattle his cage a little and see if Donovan falls out of the bottom."

"Sure, Jim, just tell me when and where."

"Meet me at The Waffle Shop on Mockingbird Lane and Central. We'll go from there."

Griggs was sipping coffee and flirting with a pretty counter waitress when I entered the restaurant. He motioned to an empty booth and picked up his coffee cup. I asked the waitress for a cup and joined Jim in the booth.

"Donovan has a old-time friend named Jacob Rosenthal, also known as "Jake the Jew." Jake owns Preston Gold and Silver Exchange and has been fencing stolen property for Donovan and his crew for years. He also launders money through Jake, but we've never been able to prove it. I have always wanted to go over and confront Jake but never had a good case to back me up. Now, with Justice being onboard with Donovan, I thought he would be a good place to start. I don't have much but maybe we can bluff him enough with the money laundering charges that he might crack and tell us where we can find Ran. Are you up for doing a little dance with Jake the Jew?"

"Sure, let's do it," I said as I took a big gulp of coffee and climbed out of the booth. Griggs tossed a dollar bill on the table as he stood up. "Those FBI guys are high-rollers," I thought to myself as we headed for the door.

Preston Gold and Silver occupied a spot in a strip-mall on Lovers Lane in University Park. We hung around, looking at used jewelry and gold coins in the display counters as Jake finished up with a customer, eyeing us suspiciously all the while. He was smallish, sixties with a receding hairline and wire-rimmed glasses. He perfectly fit the image of a pawnbroker. When the customer reached the sidewalk outside, we showed Jake our badges. As I explained that I wanted to talk to Ran Donovan about a murder, Agent Griggs was giving him a dizzying list of facts and figures related to possible money laundering. As we spoke, Jake the Jew looked back and forth at our faces as if he was watching a tennis match. As we finally ran out of things to say, a silence fell on the three of us as Jake stared slack-jawed at both of us.

"So you're an FBI agent, huh?" he asked Griggs after a long pause. Turning to me, he then asked; "And you are a police detective? You guys must be pretty smart to have those jobs. So, if you are smart enough to find your way into my shop, then you must be smart enough to find your way back out again, 'cause I don't like cops and I particularly don't like FBI agents. I haven't seen Ran Donovan in years, and I got nothing else to say. Good-bye"

As we got out on the sidewalk, Jim Griggs began to laugh. "Smart enough to find our way back out. That was pretty good. I might have to use that one day myself. Very clever."

"I guess that's that, huh? I asked as he was still chuckling to himself.

"Nah, not by a long shot. I got another trick in my bag for Jake the Jew. He lives in a fancy high-rise condo building over on Turtle Creek Boulevard. Let's take Donovan's mug-shot over there and see if any of those richy-rich residents might have seen him around lately."

We started at the top floor of the seven-story condominium building and worked our way down, knocking on every door. As each resident answered our knock, the questioning was always the same. We showed them Donovan's mug-shot, one where he looked particularly menacing, and asked if the resident had ever seen this man in the building. When each one said that they had never seen him, Griggs would then ask; "Are you sure you haven't seen him in the company of Jacob Rosenthal on the third floor?" Most expressed surprise that "Mr. Rosenthal" would be associated with a criminal and, as we passed out our business cards, expressed their willingness to call us should they see Donovan and Rosenthal together.

"Now, let's go over to the Fandango Club on Northwest Highway," Griggs said as we drove up Turtle Creek Boulevard. "We know that Jake is banging one of the strippers there. Let's see if she knows anything that might help."

As we started to walk past the doorman at Fandango, he stepped in front of us and blocked the way. "That's ten dollars cover for each," he said,

86

spreading his legs as if he was going to break into some karate moves if we didn't comply. When he saw the badges, stepped aside and gave a sweeping gesture with his arm as if he were welcoming us aboard a luxury liner.

"We're looking for April. She here?" Griggs asked.

"Yea, she should be in the dressing room. Go ahead on in. It's behind the curtain at the back."

As we passed the stage in the center of the club, a bored looking girl, who was topless and wearing a skimpy leopard-skin brief, was shuffling back and forth to the ear-splitting sounds of "American Woman" coming from every speaker in the place. She was shifting back and forth with just enough movement that allowed her pendulous breasts to swing back and forth like two hanged men. Of the few patrons that were there at that time of day, none seemed particularly aroused.

We found April sitting at a dressing counter, staring at herself in the lighted mirror. She was adjusting false eyelashes that made her eyes look like they were peering out at us from under two black awnings. When we showed our badges to her reflection in the mirror, she turned in the chair to face us. I found it difficult not to stare at her bare breasts as we explained why we were there. Griggs showed her the mug-shot of Ran Donovan and asked if she had ever seen him and Jake Rosenthal together.

Without making a single reply, she got up, walked over to a telephone and started dialing. In a few seconds, she shouted; "There are two god-damned cops in my dressing room showing me a mug-shot of some asshole I've never seen before and wanting to know if he was one of your friends. Let me tell you something, you little Jew cocksucker, if you get me in trouble with the cops, I'm going to wring your little chicken neck." She then slammed the receiver down, turned to us and said: "I've never seen that prick before in my life." April then sat back down and returned to the job of gluing eye-lashes to her face. We took that as our cue to leave.

"Nice tits" was all Griggs said as we got into his car.

After Griggs dropped me off at my car in the Waffle House parking lot, I contacted the dispatcher. "Any traffic for me," I asked.

"10-4. You've had two calls from Douglas McMillan at the DA's office. You want the number?"

"Negative. I'll pick it up when I get in."

"10-4"

I couldn't continue to ignore that investigator at the DA's office but I was just not ready to face a grilling about Lynne Littleton. I was told not to trust the DA's office, but I knew I had to talk to them at some point. I was surprised that I wasn't getting some heat from the Chief or the Captain about it.

Since I was in Dallas, I decided to run by Lynne's apartment on my way back to Creekwood. I wanted to fill her in on what I had learned, which admittedly wasn't much. It was something I could accomplish on the telephone and I knew it. The truth was I just wanted to see her.

I got that familiar rush as I saw her yellow Volkswagen in the parking lot. As I walked to her door, my mind kept going back to April at Fandango. I was admittedly aroused by her casual nudity and her youthful, jutting breasts. It wasn't a state of mind that I need to be in while visiting someone who obviously wanted to seduce me. I was playing with fire and I knew it.

Lynne opened the door as I approached. The sight of her took my breath away. She was wearing white lounge pants with bell-bottoms and a tie-dyed midriff top that exposed her stomach and stopped just below her breasts. She was braless. As I stepped inside, she closed the door, pushed me against it and kissed me, exploring my lips and mouth with her tongue. I was erect immediately and she grounded her hips into my hardness. I reached down past her shoulders and lifted the flowered top over her head. Her breasts were round and perfect with nipples like small rosebuds. I brought my mouth over one of them and she moaned and pushed my face hard against her chest. She tasted of soap and had that scent of vanilla that I was becoming so familiar with. As she leaned over me, her hair fell forward around my shoulders.

She didn't say a word as she pulled my head up and away from her breasts, stared into my face with those electric blue eyes and then began leading me toward her bedroom. She didn't speak and seemed to just communicate with sighs, moans and her body. We made love urgently at first, then slower and more gently until we collapsed into each other's arms. We lay side by side looking into each other's eyes for what seemed like an hour, or a day, or an eternity. I was lost. At that moment, my love for her was as intense as any I had ever felt.

I told her about the FBI agent and our visit with Jake Rosenthal and the encounter with April at Fandango. She seemed to react to the mention of Agent Griggs and stared up at the ceiling for a few seconds. She then asked; "Why the FBI? Why are they interested in Rick's case?" I explained that Ran Donovan was a prime suspect in the murder of a federal witness and they wanted to work with me to locate him.

"Is that agent wanting to talk to me?" she asked hurriedly. "

"No, he hasn't mentioned that." She then seemed a little more relaxed and laughed at my description of April's eloquent phone call to Rosenthal. "Well, I guess poor Jake won't be seeing those perky tits for a while, unless he works his way back in with some of that gold he has," she laughed.

"You know, I think that was exactly what Griggs had in mind. He seems to be trying to smoke Donovan out by going after his friend," I said. It was the first time I had actually thought about it that way.

Lynne sat on the bed with her legs crossed at her ankles. She seemed as comfortable in her nudity as April had been earlier. It was all I could do to keep my eyes on her face has she talked.

"I'd be careful of Ran. He has a lot of very powerful connections. If you embarrass him in front of his friends, he's going to come at your for it. He has a lot of pride."

Suddenly I realized that I had completely lost track of the time and blurted out "What time is it?"

Lynne laughed and asked; "Why, you taking medicine or something?" Then, she climbed on top of me and began kissing my face. As badly as I wanted to stay, I knew I had promised Kay that I was coming home early and broke away from Lynne, reaching for my clothes that were piled on the floor next to the bed.

"I know, you have to go home to the little wife, huh? Call her and tell her you are working late. I can cook some dinner and we can eat on the patio. I miss you so much when you aren't here." Her bottom lip began to tremble and tears formed at the corners of her eyes. Walking out that front door was one of the hardest things I had ever done. I promised I would be back as soon as I could. I was caught in a whirlpool and it was pulling me down.

On the drive home, I thought of Kay and our relationship over the years. Kay had been a passionate lover and possessed a beauty that would make any man happy to be with her. After our second daughter came, our lovemaking was less passionate and more mechanical. Getting two kids ready for bed and clearing up dinner dishes and picking up toys around the house made our time together in bed less spontaneous and more like a duty that we fulfilled to each other. The kids had taken their toll on Kay's body, as well. She seemed self-conscious of these changes and would often throw her arms over her breasts when I watched her come out of the shower or sometimes she would reflexively cover her pubic area with her hands if I walked in and surprised her in the nude. Lynne was so open in her nudity and seemed to enjoy watching my eyes as they roved over her body. I still loved Kay very much and still saw her as the gorgeous, vivacious girl I went to college with. She still had those soft brown eyes and smooth olive complexion, gifts from her mother's Italian ancestors. She was now comfortable with her life and with our marriage and saw no reason to try and compete for my attention. She felt that she had it.

I arrived to a chorus of "daddy's home" from by girls. This time, there wasn't my usual iced bourbon and questions from Kay about my day. Instead, she was in the kitchen gazing out of the kitchen window. "I thought you would be home early. I was going to suggest that we take the girls out for dinner" she said, still gazing out of the window.

"Sorry, I got tied up with that FBI agent. I was in his car and had to follow his schedule. We went over to the gold and jewelry place…" I could hear myself babbling on about my day and not paying any attention to what I was saying. Finally, I managed to stop my dialog and asked if she wanted me to drive to the Kentucky Fried Chicken place and pick up something for dinner.

Kay came over and hugged me, then stepped back and said; "I can smell perfume on you."

"That's from that dressing room at Fandango. Place smelled like a cathouse."

90

"Sure. Go grab some chicken. Be sure to get mashed potatoes. The girls will eat that, if nothing else. I'll have the table set when you get home."

After dinner, Kay got the girls ready for bed and I went in and asked what book they wanted me to read. "Where the Wild Things Are" was the unanimous choice. While describing the "terrible claws and terrible teeth" I noticed that Kay didn't come in to listen along with the girl something she usually did. I found her in bed reading a book.

"You okay?"

"Yea, just a little tired, that's all" she said, not looking up.

I climbed in beside her, wondering if I could perform sexually with her after the exhausting tryst I had with Lynne earlier. She saved me from having to find out by telling me good-night, turning her back to me and going to sleep.

CHAPTER 8

Saturday mornings are always slow and easy in the Bryant household. That is, when I was lucky enough to be home to enjoy them. Kay and I tried to set Saturdays aside for the girls and to catch up on the attention that we both felt we had neglected to give them during the week.

When I woke, I was alone in bed. I could hear the usual sounds of Saturday morning cartoons on the television in the den. I could hear "What's up doc" from Bugs Bunny, followed by giggles from the girls. My oldest was doing a pretty good imitation of him as my feet hit the floor. I grabbed my robe and headed in to join in on the laughter. I found Kay sitting on the floor with the girls, laughing at my daughter's attempts at the cartoon voice.

"Daddy, daddy…listen: Eeeh, what's up doc." Katy laughed at herself so hard that she sat down hard on the floor. I glanced over at Kay and she seemed relaxed and smiled up at me.

"Hey, guess what I have in my coat pocket," I said to Kay.

"Uh….a million in cash and plane tickets to the Riviera."

"Close," I smiled back. "Dinner passes to Wellington's. Wanna take the girls to dinner tonight?"

Before she could answer, the girls began to shout, "Oh boy, oh boy. Dinner out."

"Well, that sure doesn't say much about your mother's cooking," Kay said as she scowled at the girls; then, winked and smiled and added, "But it sure sounds good to me."

The rest of the weekend was filled with miniature golf, followed by steaks at Wellington's, then church and Sunday dinner with Kay's parents. Looking back, I was lucky to have had those two days of calm because the days coming up were anything but.

~~~~~~~~~

Barbie Morris was waving what looked like a fist full of call messages as I walked toward my office the following Monday morning. "Agent Griggs has called a couple of times and said it is very important. That guy with the DA's office, McMillan, called first thing and accused me of not giving you his messages to call him. He was real pissy and said that he was expecting you to call him back before noon today. And, finally, the Chief called just a few minutes ago and wanted to know if you had come in yet. He told me to tell you to wait around until he got here because he wanted to talk to you."

I grabbed my phone and dialed the Dallas FBI, wondering what had stirred up the villagers while I enjoying my weekend at home. When Griggs got on the line, he started out with "Well the excrement has definitely hit the ventilation device." He sounded almost giddy.

"What excrement?" I asked, almost wishing I didn't have to hear this.

"Jake the Jew called our Agent in Charge and yelled at him in a combination of English and Yiddish, claiming that we harassed him and his girlfriend and is demanding that I be fired. He is coming down today to file a formal complaint. He is also trying to have formal charges filed against both of us for assault....verbal assault, if there is such a thing. He's calling the DA's office here in Dallas." I suddenly realized why Chief Rogers wanted to talk to me when he came in.

"And...I haven't gotten to the best part yet," Griggs continued, sounding more and more excited. "One of our informants contacted his controlling agent over the weekend and said that Randall Donovan is livid at the way we treated his friend and is vowing vengeance against us. As a matter of fact, I'm having a device sent out to my office that I can attach to my car. It will let me start it from my house without having to be in it. Car bombing is one of Donovan's specialties, you know. Do you have something like that at your department?"

"Are you kidding? We had to buy our own god-damn whistles and handcuffs. I've never even seen a device to remotely start a car. I wonder if they sell them over at the fucking Western Auto." I asked rhetorically, feeling myself getting angry. I had suspected that the whole exercise of questioning Jake Rosenthal and his girlfriend was just to draw Donovan out. Griggs had pulled me right into it with him. We've now set Donovan on a path of revenge, and I was afraid that Lynne was right in the middle of that path. All this attention from the FBI and the police would make it more important than ever to get rid of Lynne and anything she could tell us.

"Well, for the time being, have your guys give your home a close patrol. Put some small pieces of folded paper in your car doors and in your hood at night and check to see of they've fallen out the next morning. Better still, just look under your car before you start it. I'll see if I can get another remote starter for you. I'll keep you in touch about what I hear."

I was just about to call McMillan at the DA's office when Captain Copeland came to my door and told me to see Chief Rogers in his office. As I walked in, the Chief motioned me over to a chair as he was finishing up a phone call. "Yea, he just walked in now. I'll see what he has to say and get back with you."

"Well, you sure kicked over the chamber pot…you and that FBI agent. The DA has been getting calls all weekend from several big-deal lawyers in town claiming that you threatened a prominent citizen…a businessman and harassed his girlfriend. He said you purposely tried to humiliate him by insinuating to his neighbors that he associates with known criminals. The DA claims that the verbal abuse you two committed was tantamount to assault and he is considering filing a case. He said that the prominent citizen, Mr. Jacob Rosenthal, is claiming slander and plans to file a suit against the City of Creekwood. Please tell me that this is nothing and will just go away." His last sentence sounded almost pleading.

"It was all legal and above-board, Chief. Rosenthal is a known fence for Ran Donovan. The Justice Department has given Agent Griggs a green-light to track down and interview Donovan regarding the car bombing of a federal witness. He thought we might question Rosenthal and see if he would tell us about Donovan's current whereabouts. He refused to talk to us and pretty-much ran us out of his shop. Thinking that Donovan might be staying with Rosenthal at his condo on Turtle Creek, we went there and showed some of the residents Donovan's mug-shot. Sure, we asked if they had seen him with Rosenthal, but I don't see anything wrong with that. Anyway, when that didn't pan out, we contacted Rosenthal's girlfriend, a stripper over at the Fandango Lounge, and asked her if she has seen Donovan with Rosenthal. When we showed her Donovan's mug-shot, she said that she had never seen him before. It was an exercise in good solid police tactics, Chief. Didn't yield much, but at least we tried. We never threatened Rosenthal. In fact, he told us to get out of his place so quick that we never had a chance. I barely had my badge out of my pocket."

Chief Rogers drummed his fingers on his desk and looked across at me for a few seconds. He then turned in his chair and picked up his telephone receiver. He dialed a number then leaned back in his chair. "This is Chief Rogers over at Crestwood PD. Let me talk to the DA." He then put his feet on his desk and leaned back further in his chair as the DA answered the line, "I've got my officer here, Detective Bryant. His description of events differs from what Mr. Rosenthal told you. In fact, Detective Bryant's version makes a great deal more sense. If you believe you have some sort of criminal case to file on my officer, I say do it. I'd be interested to see what Rosenthal swears to you in the affidavit. But, here is some friendly advice: I'd check into his background first before you embarrass yourself and the DA's office. In the meantime, my officer will carry on his regular duties. If and when you have a warrant for his arrest, let me know and I'll surrender him to the Sheriff myself."

There was a pause as Chief Rogers listened for a few seconds. "Hang on, I'll ask him." He looked across at me and asked; "Why have you not returned the call of one of the DA's investigators, a guy named McMillan? He's complaining that you aren't calling him back."

"I was just about to dial his number when Captain Copeland told me to come into your office. I didn't want to keep you waiting."

"He's going to call your man just as soon as we hang up." Another pause. "Hang on." He cupped his hand over the receiver and said "The DA wants to know where Rick Littleton's wife is. Their organized crime unit wants to interview her and they can't find her."

"She's gone back home to Ohio, as far as I know. I haven't heard from her since my initial interview with her." The Chief winked and then said into the phone "As far as Detective Bryant knows, she is back home with family in

Ohio. No, we don't have their number. They shouldn't be too hard to find for an organized crime unit."

"He hung up," Chief Rogers said with a laugh. "Go right now and call that investigator, McMillan, and get that DA off my neck."

"Detective Bryant, I was beginning to believe you are a myth. I've called several times and haven't heard a thing back from you." Douglas McMillan sounded like a real asshole.

"I'm really sorry about that, Mr. McMillan. I've been running out leads as fast as they come in. I finally had a morning that I could come to the office and return some calls. Please, what can I do for you?"

"I'm the Chief Investigator with the DA's Organized Crime Unit. Randall Donovan has been on our radar for years. I understand he is a suspect in the murder investigation you are conducting. I'd like to work along with you on it. It would be in our mutual interests. We both want to put Donovan away. I think he has valuable information about organized crime here in Dallas and your murder case might be just the incentive he needs to cooperate with us."

"So you want to make him a snitch? What do you intend to do, deal away my murder case when we find him?" I could feel the heat rising in my stomach.

"Well, we have to find him first, don't we?" he said with barely contained sarcasm. "Which brings me around to the point of my many unreturned calls to you: we want to interview Lynne Littleton. We want you to set it up."

"I don't know where she is. So far as I know, she went back home to Ohio with her family. I haven't heard from her since the day she left. So, why don't you just go there and set it up yourself?"

"What's her maiden name? What's the name of her family?" he was sounding more and more angry.

"Hell, I don't know. I don't even think I asked. I'll go review my notes and see if it was mentioned. You might go ask Maurice Cox. He seems to know about her."

"You mean the chicken fighter? You haven't heard? He's dead. See, Detective Bryant, you need our assistance down here at Organized Crime. You don't even know that your main witness is deceased."

CAJUN RULES

The shock made my heart throb and I felt it in my feet. As I tried to process the information and come back with something that didn't make me sound weak and unsure, he continued on: "One of our investigators found him in his bed when he didn't answer a knock at his door. Looks like he'd been dead for a couple of days. So, he's no longer a possible source of information, Detective Bryant, and that brings me back to Lynne Littleton."

"I've told you all I can tell you about Lynne Littleton, Mr. McMillan," I finally managed to say.

"Oh…I'm not so sure about that. I think you might know exactly where she is. I can understand why you would want to protect her. Randall Donovan is a very mean character and she's probably in danger. I can help. My interest is building a case against Donovan, and I think she may be able to do that. You need to put us together."

"You're accusing me of lying?" I felt myself getting angrier at his boldfaced accusation, even though it was true. It was an interesting position to be in.

"Ah, don't get your knickers in a twist, Detective. "I'm just doing my job."

"Let me give you some advice, then" I tried to keep my voice level. "Why don't you go find a nice quite, private place and fuck yourself." I slammed the receiver down just as Al walked in the door.

"That's very sage advice, Marc. Who are you giving it to?"

"Some asshole with the DA's office; an organized crime investigator. Sorry, he just pissed me off."

"Maybe my advice won't be quite as colorful as yours, but I gotta say that going to war with the DA's office isn't such a good idea. You know…just saying."

"He's accusing me of lying when I said I didn't know where Lynne Littleton is; which I am…but he doesn't know that. So, he doesn't have any call to make that accusation." I had to laugh at that point.

"Well, that circular logic has made me dizzy," Al laughed. "I think I'll go sit down at my desk before I fall on my face."

"Oh, hey! He told me that Maurice Cox is dead. Someone from the DA's office found him in his house. Said he had been dead a couple of days. I guess I need to call the medical examiner and find out what's going on."

"From the looks of him, he was mostly dead the day we brought him in. Let me know what you hear."

I called the Dallas County Medical Examiner's office and got Field Agent Tony Simms on the line. He put me on hold as he went to retrieve the paperwork.

"I didn't know this would be of interest to you or I would have called you. We're calling it homicide. He had injuries from a recent beating. Those injuries included bleeding in his brain that, evidently, he wasn't aware of, although he would have had terrible headaches. Anyway, the bleeding eventually caused a stroke and he died in his bed. An investigator with the DA's office found him when he went out to interview him. You want the investigator's name and number?"

"Nah, I just talked to them on the phone. That's how I knew to call. We interviewed him on that Littleton-Ryan murder case. Any indication of recent injuries; maybe something consistent with the time of his death?"

"No. The bruises were fading and appeared to be several days old. There was nothing more recent that we found."

"Who's got the case?" I asked.

"Sheriff's Department."

"Good, I'll give Johnny Flynn a call there. Thanks, Tony!"

Whoever gave Cox that beating managed to kill him in the end. My money was on Willard Green. I doubt he had the presence of mind to think of Cox as a liability on his own. Either Donovan or Sad Sack, maybe both, had probably sent him out to impress on Cox the importance of keeping his mouth shut. It would be like a gorilla tossing around a rag doll. I felt sorry for the little old man. He was in the wrong place at the wrong time.

I called Johnny Flynn next. He checked and found that someone else in the office was carrying the case and didn't connect Cox with our case. It was thought to be natural causes at first, but they had just gotten notification from the medical examiner of the evidence of prior assault and the cause of death.

Flynn said he would assist the investigator and let me know if they developed any leads.

Next, I called Agent Griggs. "He claimed that you beat him up, Marc. Looks like you're the prime suspect." It was his attempt at humor but I wasn't in the mood.

"Given the circumstances, it looks like the intent wasn't to kill him or he would have been dead when they left him. That old guy seemed pretty fragile when I talked to him. I didn't realize he had been beaten so badly. But, it shows you how vicious Donovan and his friends can be. Is there anything we can do down here to help? Griggs asked.

"Would you call Johnny Flynn at the Sheriff's Office and tell him about your visit with Cox the other day? Go ahead and tell him what Cox said about me if you want. You might have something that can help. Otherwise, nothing else I can think of."

"Okay, Marc. I'll call him now."

I went into Captain Copeland's office and explained the events of the morning to him. "What do you need to do, or I should ask what do we need to do?"

"I think I'm going to send Kay and the girls to her parents for the next few days until I get a better handle on things. I would like to have patrol watch my house. I'll probably stay there and just put my car in the garage at night. I'll rig the house so I'll know if someone is trying to get in, although I doubt that will be the way they will come at me." The truth was, I really didn't have much of a plan.

"You probably need to give that Littleton girl some warning that things are heating up. Where ever you have her, make sure her security is good and she's being careful. Then, I would suggest staying away from her for a while in case someone tries to follow you to her."

"I hadn't thought of that," I said, now getting more concerned.

I drove home and explained everything to Kay. "How long are we going to have to stay away?" she asked, tears welling in her eyes.

"I don't know. Not long. At the moment, we don't know where Donovan is and that's the problem. As soon as the FBI can locate him, I'll bring you and the girls back home. It's probably nothing, but I don't want to take the chance."

"Where are you going to be staying?" she asked. "You can't stay here. We're even listed in the phone book. You won't be safe here. Can you just stay with us at mom and dad's?"

"If they try to follow me, I don't want to lead them to you and your parents. Look, this won't be long. I've got the FBI, the Dallas Police and the Sheriff's Department working on this with me.

"What about that Lynne Littleton? You won't be staying there, will you?" There was an edge of hostility in her voice that surprised me.

"Of course not! Why would you even ask that?"

I realized Kay was not only scared and angry; she was suspicious of me and Lynne. Things seemed to be spinning out of control.

I glanced up and down the block as I helped Kay load up suitcases into our Chevrolet station wagon that she called "the tank." I didn't see any cars that I hadn't seen on our street in the past. As I helped her buckle the girls in, I again told her that I would try to get this resolved as soon as I could so that they could come home. She was giving me one-word answers and was very distant. She was stiff and didn't lift her arms when I hugged her goodbye. I watched the tank disappear at the end of our street and felt for the first time that our marriage might not survive.

I started my drive to Lynne's apartment, making sure that I was not being tailed. I drove into a two-story parking garage that I was familiar with in a shopping center along the way. I knew that the entrance and exit were at different ends and waited outside of the exit to see if anyone came out behind me. When no one did, I continued my drive to Richardson.

I parked at the edge of the road leading to Lynne's apartment complex and watched the traffic behind me. I then drove slowly through the parking lot and looked at each car to see if it was occupied. When I was satisfied that I had not been followed or that anyone was watching her apartment building, I got out and walked toward her door. She opened the door as I approached. I felt the passion rising inside me as she smiled, holding her arms out to be hugged. As we did, she breathed in my ear, "God, I am so glad to see you."

We made love slowly and passionately, her lithe beautiful body responding to every touch, every caress, At last, exhausted and satisfied, we lay in each other's arms. I explained the call from Agent Griggs and the attempts by the DA's investigator to locate and interview her. She listened intently, staring into my eyes as I spoke. I could see the fear rising in them. It was when I told her that Maurice Cox had been found dead that they welled with tears and she buried her head into my shoulder; her tears wet against my neck.

"If I hadn't told you about his call, he would still be alive," she said, her voice hoarse from crying. "I feel like I killed him. He was just trying to help Rick and I killed him." She began to sob.

"Lynne, he died because of what he saw that night, not because of you. Donovan and his friends wouldn't have known about his call to you. I've only told a few other people and they are all cops, like me. They wouldn't have told Donovan or anyone who knows him." As I said it, suddenly I wasn't so sure if that was true.

Lynne continued to cry softly as I held her. I pulled her face away from my shoulder and pushed her gently back down on her pillow. I then sat up next to her, stroking her hair as I talked.

"Captain Copeland told me that I needed to warn you about all of this and then told me to stay away from you for a while." As I told her this, she bolted upright and wrapped her arms around me.

"Look, he's afraid that with Donovan's threats and with the DA accusing me of hiding you, someone might follow me over here to find out where you are. I was careful today and I don't believe I was followed. But, the more times I come here, the greater the chance I might miss something. Kay and the kids are staying at her parent's house. Maybe I can come at night, but I'll still be here, one way or the other.

"Are you going to tell the FBI agent where I am?" she asked, looking now more frightened than ever. There was something clearly worrying her about the FBI being involved in my case.

"What is it about the FBI that upsets you so much?" I asked. She suddenly diverted her eyes away from mine and began to stare off as if lost in thought.

"Lynne, listen; If there is something you haven't told me about Rick, something that you are afraid I won't be able to accept or help you with, you need to tell me now. I have to trust you…completely. Lying to me will completely destroy any trust I have in you."

Without speaking, Lynne got up and walked to her closet. She wrapped herself in a robe and then walked into the living room. She sat down at the far end of the couch, pulled her legs up and against her body and wrapped the robe around them. I followed her and sat at the opposite end of the couch. She stayed silent for a few minutes, her gaze moving back and forth between my eyes and the kitchen window. She drew a deep breath, sighed and then spoke:

"Rick killed a guy in Mississippi a year ago. I helped him cover it up."

CHAPTER 9

"It was supposed to be a quick and easy job. Rick said it was drug money that was going to some off-shore bank. A guy from New Orleans knew about the money and when it was going to be loaded on a boat in Bay St. Louis. He wanted a second man to back him up and, he must have called Ran Donovan because Donovan told Rick about it." Lynne spoke in a monotone, never looking up from her hands as she told me her story.

"This guy, Ivan Delacroix, told Rick to fly to the airport in New Orleans. Rick was supposed to rent a car and then drive to the airport in Mobile, Alabama and pick up Delacroix. Then, they would drive to Bay St. Louis. There was a man there who owned a sailboat...a yacht that he kept there in a marina. He had been sailing in and out of Bay St. Louis for years, and everyone knew him. For a couple of years, he had been taking cash money from drug deals in the United States and sailing the money down to some islands near Venezuela. I don't remember the names. He always sailed alone, and no one ever suspected what he was doing. It was a big secret, but somehow this Ivan Delacroix found out and decided to rip him off. The idea was to watch until the money was onboard, then grab it and go. Delacroix needed Rick to cover him and help control the guy until they could take the cash."

"Did Rick know how much money Delacroix was talking about?" I asked.

"No, but Rick told me that the money was in blue Navy duffle bags...two of them. They weighed around fifty pounds each so Rick figured it was maybe three hundred thousand or so. All Delacroix would say about the money was that he would give Rick ten thousand and five for Ran Donovan. Anyway, the man with the boat would always load up with supplies before he sailed and would let the marina know before he left what day he was leaving. He always left early in the morning. Somehow, that was getting back to Delacroix."

"Rick said that they watched the boat all night from a dock nearby. Just before daylight, a car pulled up and two men carried duffle bags onto the boat and then drove off. Delacroix figured that was the money, and they walked along the edge of the marina and just climbed onboard and laid down on the

103

bow of the boat. When the guy came out of the cabin, drinking a cup of coffee, they grabbed him, covered his mouth and took him back down into the cabin. They tied him up, gagged him and then took duffle bags. They walked them to the edge of the dock and threw them over a fence and down on the shore. They walked back to the car, drove over and loaded up the bags and drove away. Rick said it was the easiest score he had ever been on. He said that he should have known it was all too easy."

"What do you mean?"

"Rick said that he had an uneasy feeling about Delacroix from the start. He said that he kept popping pills and would get all jittery and would sweat a lot. Rick said that he thought he was swallowing black mollies…biphetamines. He told Rick that he was accused of murder in Louisiana but was out on bail. He said that he wasn't going to the pen and was going to use the money to disappear. He told Rick that he had a friend in a fishing village in Costa Rica who would hide him out. Rick said that the more pills the guy swallowed, the more he talked."

"They decided to stay overnight in a motel near Gulfport. The idea was that they would put the bags of cash into two locked trunks and then have them shipped to New Orleans. Once Rick helped him with the trunks, he would give Rick fifteen thousand of the cash and Rick could return the rent car at the New Orleans airport and come back to Dallas. But, the next morning, Delacroix seemed different and got mad when Rick brought up the stuff they talked about the day before. Instead of going directly to the Mobile airport, Delacroix wanted to drive down to Biloxi and find some whores. Rick tried to talk him out of it but decided to just play along until he got his money. On the way, Delacroix started talking about an old abandoned plantation in the woods that he had seen as a kid and wanted to show it to Rick. Rick knew then that Delacroix felt he had told Rick too much and was going to find a place to kill him. When they started down a gravel road near a swamp, Delacroix said he wanted to stop and pee. When he stopped the car, Rick pulled his pistol from his belt and shot Delacroix in the chest."

"He said that blood splattered on him and around inside the car. There wasn't a lot and Rick figured he must have hit him in the heart. But, there was still blood on Rick and around the inside of the car. He pulled Delacroix out of the car and hid him in some brush. He said that he pulled off his shirt and tried to wipe up the blood in the car with it, but there was too much and his shirt was getting soaked. He said that they had passed an abandoned wrecking yard earlier. Rick waited until it was dark and then went there and found a couple of tire rims and some wire. He came back, wired the rims on to Delacroix and then pushed him into some water in the swamp. He called me and asked me to fly to New Orleans and bring him some clothes and help him clean up the rent car before he turned it back in. I took a Braniff flight to New Orleans and waited on the curb at the airport for a couple of hours. Finally, Rick came and picked me up."

"We stopped at a store in Kenner and I bought some buckets, bleach, and cleaning stuff. We went to a car wash and washed as much as we could off of the inside doors. We scrubbed the inside of the car until there wasn't any of the blood left that we could see. The seats were leather or naugahyde or something so they were easy to clean. We smoked cigarettes in the car to hide the smell of the bleach. We got some lighter fluid and put it on Rick's clothes at a camp ground we stopped at. We put them in the fire pit and burned them."

"What about the money? What did you do with the duffle bags full of cash?"

"Rick knew that he couldn't take the risk of bringing it back to Dallas and Ran finding out what happened. He knew that the money had to disappear like Delacroix. We took some of it and put it in my suitcase. We were afraid to burn the rest since there was so much and someone might notice the smoke. Finally, we bought a shovel and took them into some woods and buried them. We put leaves and limbs over them so no one would know something was buried there. We threw the shovel off of a bridge."

"So, was that the money you had under the floorboards in your house?" I was beginning to see a side of Lynne that I hadn't seen before. She was capable of lying to me without showing it.

"You can understand why I didn't want to tell you...right? Rick gave Donovan five thousand and told him that his end was ten thousand. Ran was okay with that."

"So, what does that have to do with the FBI?" I asked.

"A few months ago, Ran started questioning Rick about Delacroix, like where was Delacroix when Rick last saw him and what did he say to Rick. Rick told him that they bought two metal trunks, put one bag in each and put locks on them. They took them to a Greyhound Bus terminal in Mobile. He said that he waited in the car while Delacroix made the arrangements with them. Rick told Ran that Delacroix had said he was sending them to New Orleans and he would pick them up when he got back. Rick told Donovan that Delacroix had said he was going to use the money to go to Costa Rica because he was about to go to the pen. He said he last saw Delacroix when he dropped him at the curb in the Mobile airport."

"Ran said that Delacroix hadn't showed up in court in New Orleans and that the cops were putting a lot of pressure on some of Delacroix' friends, particularly some in the Maricone family. These friends were now pressuring Donovan about Delacroix's disappearance."

"Did Donovan buy Rick's story?"

"He seemed to," Lynne answered. "He just told Rick to watch out because the FBI was talking to a lot of people. Donovan told Rick that Delacroix probably did what he said he was going to do and had skipped the country. Rick was scared, though. I've never seen him so scared about anything. He kept expecting Ran to change his mind about the story or the FBI suddenly showing up."

I was too stunned to speak and just sat there and stared at Lynne. She finally looked up. Her blue sapphire eyes were swimming in tears. "I know that what I did was wrong. I know I should have told you when you saw the money. Please believe me, Marc, I didn't have a choice. I couldn't let Rick take a chance of getting caught with blood all over him and all that money. It wasn't his fault. He said it was him or Delacroix. I know you hate me now and I don't blame you if you do. I'm so sorry!" She began to tremble and held her arms tighter around her legs. Seeing her like that was tearing my heart out.

"If I start asking questions about Delacroix, someone like Agent Griggs is going to make the connection between him and my investigation of Rick's murder. I don't know how far I can trust Griggs. I'll try to think of a way to find out if Rick's name has been connected to Delacroix's. Maybe Donovan decided that he didn't believe Rick after all. Maybe they found Delacroix and somehow connected him to the drug money and to Rick and that's why Donovan killed Rick. I don't know." I felt myself getting deeper and deeper into something that I should never have gotten involved in.

I got up from the couch and finished dressing. Lynne followed me into the bedroom and watched me without saying anything. As I started toward the front door, she followed me and said; "Will I see you again?"

"I don't know. Yea…of course. I'll try to come back tonight. We need to be careful, Lynne. If it ever came out that I knew about this and didn't come forward, I would be fired and probably arrested. You, on the other hand, will probably be killed. This is serious stuff."

As I opened the door, I turned to Lynne and asked a question I had wanted to ask earlier: "Did you know what Rick was going to do when he left for New Orleans? Did you know he was going to rob that drug money?"

"No, I swear! He just said he was going to do something with Ran Donovan and that he would be gone for a couple of days. I knew better than to ask questions. I didn't know what had happened until I met Rick in New Orleans."

As I turned to walk out, she wrapped her arms around me and laid her head on the back of my neck. "Please come back. I don't have anyone but you. I love you!"

-

As I walked into my office, Captain Copeland came in and closed the door. "Did you get everyone warned?" he asked.

"Yea. Kay and the girls are staying at her parents. Lynne Littleton is going to let me know if she sees anyone suspicious and will be careful when she goes out. She's scared to death, but I think she's safe where she is for now."

"That's good. Now, you need to stay away from her for a while unless she calls and needs help."

"I agree…and I will," I said, knowing full well that I was lying.

Barbie called on the intercom. "Someone calling himself "Gip" or "The Gip," I didn't understand exactly, wanted you to call him. He said you knew the number."

"Thanks, Barbie. Yea, I know who that is and I have his number."

Gipson Tuttle answered on the second ring with "Yea." "Gip, this is Marc Bryant. What's up?"

"You wanted to go to one of the shows…right? There is one this coming this Saturday. It's out of town. In fact, it's out of state. If you will come here early, like around seven, you can ride with me. We'll put your car in some parking lot so it won't be sitting outside my house. We'll be back that night. You still want to go, don't you?"

"Yea, I still want to…more than ever now. Gip, I appreciate you taking a chance like this to help me out. This thing has really heated up and we need to find Donovan more than ever. I'll be at your place on Saturday morning."

The sergeant in charge of the dispatch office was sitting at the radio console when I walked in. "Hey Sarg, let me ask you a question. If you make an NCIC inquiry and the person is wanted, does any other agency know that you inquired?" The National Crime Information Center was a database maintained by the FBI in Washington DC. Every department had a terminal that could access this database. One had just recently been installed at Creekwood PD.

"Yea, Marc, if there is an outstanding warrant, not only will we get a reply, but the agency that has the warrant will be notified about our inquiry. It's called a "locate." Why, you got a name you want me to run?"

"Nah, not right now. I'll get back with you later." I needed to find out more about Ivan Delacroix but just couldn't think of a way to do it without someone connecting him with my case. I had seen a side of Lynne Littleton that I hadn't seen before and I didn't like it. She was not only able to lie with such ease but seemed willing to lie to me until I called her on it. I wasn't sure that the story she told about Rick and Delacroix was even true to start with. I needed to find out more about it, but couldn't risk the police in New Orleans knowing about Lynne and her whereabouts. I needed to trust someone…maybe Jim Griggs. I'd have to think about it."

In the meantime, I called Kay to see if they were all okay at her parent's house. She was still distant with me, but said they were settled in and that her mother was happy to have them. She said her father was worried about me and wanted me to be careful. For some reason, Ted Carson has liked me ever since I was a teenager. I told Kay that I would be staying at our house tonight and would check in with her in the morning. Before she hung up, she said; "Please be careful." It served only to deepen the wound in my conscience.

I walked into Al's office and sat down. "Whatcha working on?" I asked, trying to sound casual and calm.

"I was just noticing something odd about the recent house burglaries we've had here. They are all the same M.O.; they take small expensive items like jewelry, guns, cameras, stuff like that. And, they always take a bedspread off one of one of the beds.

"I'm sure that they are putting the stuff they are taking on one of the beds, then when they're ready to go, they just fold up the corners of the bedspread and use it like a bag," I answered, knowing that Al already knew that.

"Yea, I figured that part out, but, you know what's weird? They all have Spanish last names." Al pointed to a small stack of case reports sitting in the middle of his desk. "And, believe it or not, these houses have been hit in alphabetical order of the owner's last names. What do you think?"

I couldn't tell if Al just didn't see it or he was testing me. "He's going through the phone book looking for Hispanic names because he's probably Hispanic himself. He's calling and marking off those who answer. When he calls a number that doesn't answer during the day, he checks the place out and hits it if it looks good. Since he's Hispanic, he doesn't look out of place to the neighbors. You might check the phone book and try to get out ahead of him. Maybe bring in some off-duty guys and set up surveillance on a couple of places. You might get lucky."

"Marc, you are a deep thinker." Al laughed and slapped his hand down on the stack of reports.

"Hey, let me ask you something in return. You worked in Louisiana before. Do you know anyone you can trust at New Orleans PD?"

"Those guys were as crooked as a barrel of snakes," Al laughed. "Let me think on it, but I can't think of a cop there who wouldn't turn you around if the price was right. Why, what do you need?"

"Oh, never mind. It was just a name that came up in my investigation. I'll just ask Griggs and see if he knows anyone. Thanks!"

"Let me know if I can help," Al said as he turned his attention back to the alphabetical burglaries.

I sat back at my desk and scratched out a few notes, trying to come up with a plausible cover story for Griggs. I took a deep breath and called the FBI Dallas office.

"Marc Anthony! Have you come to bury Caesar or to praise him?" Griggs laughed as he answered the phone.

"Who told you my middle name?" I asked, trying to sound angry although I was laughing at the same time.

"We're the FBI. We know everything," he came back.

"Good!" I said, "Then I've come to the right place. I need some help with a name that came up in this investigation."

"Fire away, Marc."

"Lynne Littleton finally checked in with me this morning. She didn't tell me where she was, but promised to give me all that once she found a permanent place. Anyway, she said that she has been trying to think of something we could hang on Ran Donovan and remembered a conversation she overheard a year ago between Ran and her husband, Rick. She said that they were talking about a guy from New Orleans who got killed. She didn't know if Donovan had anything to do with his being killed, but he and Rick talked like they knew all about it. She didn't want to get caught eavesdropping on their conversation, but she remembered the guy's name. It was Ivan Delacroix. She asked Rick about it later and he told her to forget that she heard the name and that he was dead. He told her that they would all be dead if she mentioned it to anyone. Do you know anyone in New Orleans who could tell you about this guy? It might be another thing you can hang on Donovan."

"I don't know the name right off hand," Griggs replied. "I could make some inquiries for you."

"Can you make it off-the-record? I would rather not have everyone knowing that Lynne is providing information. Do you know anyone in New Orleans that you can trust?"

"I just might be able to help you," Griggs said. "I worked with an agent in the Philadelphia office a few years ago. We got to be good friends. He's working in the New Orleans office now. They started beefing up that office to work on the Maricone Crime Family. I could ask him to discretely find out what he can and let me know. I trust him. I'll call him and see what he knows about Delacroix and get back."

"Thanks, Jim. Hey, did Jake the Jew come down and file a formal complaint against you like he said he was?"

"We haven't seen him or heard from him since his call. My boss said to just let it lie until he comes forward and makes a formal complaint. I doubt we'll hear anything more from him. Donovan probably told him to keep his mouth shut and stay away from us."

"Yea, I bet he did. Okay, Jim, thanks for the help." I hung up feeling better about having called him. He seemed to understand why I didn't want a formal inquiry to be sent out. For a Fed, he had the instincts of a good street cop.

For the rest of the afternoon, I helped Al compile a list of Hispanic surnames from the Creekwood phone directory. We called each one and noted those that did not answer. Al said he was going out tomorrow and check each house on the finalized list. I told him that I was going to grab some dinner somewhere and go home. As soon as I drove out of the station parking lot, I turned toward Richardson and Lynne's apartment.

I took the same precautions as before, making sure I didn't have a tail. When I was satisfied that I was alone, I pulled into her parking lot and walked to her door, looking around as I walked. She, as always, had the door open before I got to it. There were no lights on behind her in the apartment and in the early twilight, she looked like a beautiful spirit with flowing blonde hair, like an angelic apparition. Her deep blue eyes seemed to burn with some inner-fire. "I was just wishing you would appear and there you are...like magic," she said as she wrapped her arms around me.

For the first time, we had hours to just spend in each other's arms. We made love, then lay on our backs and talked about our lives; about what we were like as kids; about school. She was not the least bit modest around me and was casual about being nude. I, on the other hand, found myself covering up with the sheet whenever she got out of bed. Once, she came in with two cans of beer, sat them down on the nightstand and pulled the sheet completely off of the bed. "Come on, Cubby, I want to look at you. You're such a bashful little Cub Scout!"

It was after midnight when I gently waked her and told her that I needed to leave. She watched me dress and then kissed me goodbye as I leaned over the bed. I let myself out and drove back to Creekwood, pulling my car into the garage. I was asleep as soon as my head touched the pillow.

CHAPTER 10

I was in the throes of a nightmare when the ringing telephone thankfully pulled me out of it. I was in the autopsy room and Dr. Pittman was cutting away at a nude body of a woman. Dan James was standing beside him and motioning me to come to the autopsy table, saying; "Let me show you something interesting here." I don't remember who was on the table and I didn't want to think about it as I groped for the telephone receiver.

"This is Bryant."

"Marc, are you okay? I called late last night because I was worried about you and couldn't sleep." Kay's voice was filled with panic. "I finally fell asleep with the phone next to the bed. I called the dispatcher and he tried to call you on the radio but you didn't answer. Where were you?"

"I met some of the Dallas detectives that I have been working with at their favorite bar and just didn't keep track of the time. I didn't realize it had gotten so late until the bartender started turning off the lights. I checked in service when I left the bar but the dispatcher didn't mention that you had called. I'm sorry. I was going to call you this morning. I was still asleep."

"I'm sorry, Marc, but I was so worried. I called Al at home and asked him if he knew where you were. He said he didn't, but for me not to worry. He said if anything had happened to you, he would know about it." There was relief in her voice, but the suspicion was beginning to return.

I checked the street outside and then unlocked the padlock on my garage door. I felt relief when a folded piece of paper fell to the ground next to my foot. I had put it there when I closed the door earlier. It told me that no one had been in the garage while I was sleeping. I again checked the street as I drove away from the house and to the station.

Al intercepted me as I was about to walk through the back door of the station into the lounge. "Hey, I need to talk to you. Let's grab some coffee before you go to your office." He put his hand on my back and was pushing me toward the lounge kitchen.

"I don't know where you were last night and I don't care. I have a pretty good idea, though, and I'm telling you to watch out. I got a call from Kay wanting to know if I knew where you were. I told her that I didn't, but if there was a problem, I would know. Then, about an hour later, I got a call from the dispatcher. There was a suicide and they couldn't find you, either at home or on the radio. I got up and made the call."

"Al, I'm sorry. I was…"

"Just save it" Al interrupted. "On my way back home, the captain called on the radio and wanted to know if I knew where you were. I told him that I thought you were working with the FBI on that case and were probably away from the radio. I haven't talked to him yet this morning, but I'm sure he's going to be waiting on you in your office."

Just as Al had predicted, Captain Copeland was sitting behind my desk when I came in. "Convince me that I shouldn't take you off this Littleton-Ryan case and give it to Al or someone with the sheriff's department."

"Al just told me about the suicide call I missed last night. I met Walter Wood and some of the guys from DPD Intelligence at the bar that they hang out in next to one of their sub-stations. They wanted me to catch them up on the Donovan investigation. We just let time get away from us and it was around midnight when I left. I checked into service, but the dispatcher didn't say anything about any calls waiting or anyone looking for me."

"Marc, you are a damn good investigator. I know you and Al make jokes about me behind my back and maybe I'm not a cracker-jack detective like you two, but I am smart enough to have good men working under me. I brought you in because you're smart. I hope I didn't make a mistake when I had you moved out of patrol. Hopefully you are smart enough to know not to get involved in something that is as dangerous as getting mixed up with that Littleton woman. I'm going to just leave it at that." He got up and walked out of my office.

Al was back in his office when I went to find him. I sat down at his desk and took one of his note pads. "I'm writing down Lynne Littleton's address and phone number. I want you to keep it in case…I don't know, something happens."

114

"So, you're planning on hanging around there, huh?" I could tell Al was angry with me. "Sure, give it to me" he said as he tore off the page, folded it and put it in his pocket. "I'm going to trust your judgment on this, Marc. It's your case and you know what you should do. You are one of the brightest detectives I've ever worked with. But, let me say, if you are getting romantically involved with her, you are risking everything you have…your job, your family, your reputation, hell, everything. The worst would be to lose Kay. You will never get that lucky again in your life. I know that Littleton girl is a knockout, but she is nowhere near the quality of Kay. I just want you to think about that."

"Lynne is giving me more and more information every time I talk to her. She knows a lot and it's just taking time for her to trust me enough to tell me. She told me about a murder that Rick was involved in a year ago. I'm trying to get some information from Griggs over at the FBI."

"Is that why you asked me if I knew anyone I could trust at New Orleans PD? Did the murder happen there?"

"Yea, close by, anyway. Al, I'm not going to do anything to lose Kay or the girls, or my job, for that matter. You're the only person I can trust completely in this. I have to spend time with Lynne; not only to make sure she's safe but to get as much information out of her as possible. I'm glad you know now where to find her if something bad happens."

"You know I've always got your back, Marc. I'll do what you want, but I'm not sure I want to be dragged into this deal. Well, I'm going to hit the street and start checking on my alphabetical burglaries. If you aren't busy, I could use some help."

"Sure, Al, let me make a few phone calls and I'll meet you somewhere."

I returned to my desk and called the Dallas FBI. Griggs answered with; "Hey I was just about to call you. I have some information on Ivan Delacroix. Seems he's a bad boy, or maybe WAS a bad boy. He's been missing since last year."

"So they don't know for sure, huh?" I was relieved to know that Delacroix's body hadn't been found.

"Delacroix was loosely connected to the Maricone family," Griggs continued. "He was part of what we refer to as the "Dixie Mafia"; not really mafia, but nibbling around the edges. Delacroix and another scumbag robbed a club owner who was living in the French Quarter. Evidently, this owner brought the evening receipts home with him and banked them in the morning. The guy heard Delacroix and his partner coming through a kitchen door and confronted them with a pistol. There was a shootout and the club owner was hit. He lived until the next day. A New Orleans cop just happened to be in the same block and heard the shots. He found Delacroix hiding behind a car a block over. The owner said the robbers wore masks but thought he recognized Delacroix's voice. He told the Orleans detectives that Delacroix came into his club occasionally. He didn't recognize the other guy's voice. That guy got away. They filed murder charges on Delacroix but he wouldn't admit to anything. One of those red-mouth mob lawyers tried to get him out on bond. The cops talked the judge into setting a high bond, five-hundred thousand in cash, hoping they could keep him locked up. Some bail bondsman that does work for the Maricones marched in and put down the five-hundred thousand in big bills. Delacroix walked out and they haven't seen him since. The Orleans detectives came to our office there and asked them to issue a UFAP"

"What the hell is a "you-fap?" I was learning something new.

"Unlawful flight to avoid prosecution; eighteen US code, ten seventy-three. It was written for just that, to allow the FBI to assist local departments whenever they have a fugitive that they believe has left the state or the country. Brings in the awesome powers of the Federal Bureau of Investigation to find the bad boy wherever he may be hiding. However, in the case of Mr. Ivan Delacroix, they haven't found jack-shit in over a year."

"Do they think he's dead?" I asked.

"My friend there said that he didn't leave the country, legally, that is. He doesn't have a passport. He could have left the state and is hiding out. They think he's just hunkered down somewhere around south Louisiana. They shook a few bushes, he told me, but they aren't busting their butts. Actually nobody really much cares, except that poor bail-bond chump who is out five-hundred thousand cash.

116

"What if he never shows up again? Will the bondsman get his money back from the court?"

"Hell, I'm no lawyer" Griggs laughed. "I was an accountant. But, I wouldn't think so unless they found that Delacroix couldn't appear in court because he was dead. Then, maybe he would. Who the hell knows? Who the hell cares?"

"What did you tell your friend about why you were asking?"

"Just what you told me. I told him that you have an informant who overheard the conversation between Ran Donovan and Rick Littleton. Littleton is dead and Donovan is in the wind, so there isn't much to follow up on. The informant only heard the name and talk about his being dead. He just said 'okay'. I really don't think they care all that much."

"Thanks, Jim! I promise if I hear more about it, I'll let you know."

I hung up the phone and immediately called Lynne. She answered with a whisper. I figured it was her way of disguising her voice. "Hey, I just talked to Griggs at the FBI. He has a friend in the New Orleans office. So far as they know, Delacroix has fled to avoid prosecution for murder in New Orleans. The FBI has a warrant for fleeing the prosecution but that is just to help the New Orleans police. They have no idea where he is and aren't really all that serious about looking. They think he's just hiding out."

"Did the agent tell his friend about me?" There was sudden panic in Lynne's voice.

"He just told them that it was an informant who overheard a conversation. I don't think there's anything to worry about. Like I said, they don't seem all that interested in finding him."

"Will I see you tonight" Lynne said, changing the subject.

"I don't know. This is getting very complicated, Lynne."

"Complicated how?"

"I'll try to stop by for a few minutes. I'll explain when I do." I was anxious to get off the line.

"Marc, I love you. I miss you. That's not complicated, at all. Please don't abandon me now."

"Don't worry." I hung up.

I was on my way out of my office to meet Al when Barbie Morris called my intercom. "The Steak Boys are here for fingerprints. Do you have time?"

"Sure, send them back to ID and I'll meet them there." The idea of a free steak dinner brightened my mood a little. Maybe a dinner date with Kay might brighten hers, as well. Dan Tyson, the CEO at Wellington's was getting so used to being fingerprinted that I could probably hand him the cards and he would roll his own prints. As I took his right hand and started to roll his right thumb over the inked marble plate on the print desk, he said; "Well, have you been thinking about my offer?"

"What offer?" I asked, genuinely confused.

"Joining the corporate security staff. I've done everything but beg."

"If I don't watch my step, Dan, I might be taking you up on that offer real soon."

"I won't even ask what that's about" he laughed. As I signed the print cards and handed them to Dan and his chief financial officer, Dan said; "Well, I'll keep the light on for you."

I met Al at a coffee shop and copied some addresses from his list of possible burglary targets. I started checking houses off the list, making note of those that didn't have any indications of the occupants being home in the middle of the day. As I was returning to the station, I stopped at the Radio Shack store on the town square. Tommy, the manager, was what we called in the Army a "wire-head." He was one of those technical types who knew everything about radios and electronics.

"Hey, Tommy, I need some of your expertise," I said as I walked in the door.

"Detective Bryant, long time, no…well, whatever. What can I do you for?"

"I need a radio receiver that will bring in our department frequency. Do you have anything like that; something that won't cost me a month's salary?"

"I am going to make you a deal you won't believe. I have a four-channel radio scanner that belongs to me. It has the crystals for Creekwood Police, Creekwood Fire, Dallas Sheriff's Department and the thirty-seven one-eighty frequency that the Sheriff's Department uses to talk to other departments. I have it here because I listen to it every once-in-a-while. I want a newer model, so I can make you a great deal on it. It's ready to go."

"What's a 'great deal?"

"That Patrolman set originally sold for a hundred without the crystals. I'll take seventy-five. You can't beat a deal like that."

"I'll take it, Tommy. Thanks!"

"Sure, glad to do something for you guys at the PD. I gotta wonder, though: why, after spending all day with this stuff would you want to listen to it at home? Don't you have a radio in your car and a telephone at home?"

"I'm getting it for my father-in-law. He's always interested in what I do every day and I thought he would like to listen to the calls." I found that I was getting as good at lying on the fly as Lynne. "He lives over in Richardson. Will it receive that far away?"

"Yea, it should. It has a telescoping antenna that is built in. Just adjust it until you get a clear signal. If it doesn't, I can get you a high-gain antenna, but I think the one that it has will work." "Hang on and I'll box it up for you. The instructions are still in the original box. You need anything else?"

"What would you suggest for a simple door alarm; something that would ring or buzz if a door is opened like at night?"

"Well, your luck just keeps on happening. We just got these neat devices in that operate off of photo-eyes. You put one of the devices on one side of the door and the other across from it. There is an invisible photo-electric beam that connects them. If that beam is broken, it will ring a bell."

"Sounds perfect. How much for two sets?"

"For you, Detective Bryant, I'm going to give you my employee discount. Thirty bucks for both."

Back at my office, I dialed the number for Kay's parents. Her mother answered. When she recognized who it was, she suddenly seemed as distant as Kay has been. "Hold on, I'll get her" was all the conversation I got out of her.

"I hope you are about to tell me that you've caught this Donovan guy and I can go back to my own bedroom" Kay said as soon as she picked up the receiver.

119

"I wish I could, Kay. I did call to ask you out to dinner. How about steaks at Wellington's? You can meet me there and bring the girls. How does that sound?"

"Sorry, Marc. Dad is taking all of us to the country club tonight for dinner. He has already made reservations."

"Maybe another time then, okay?" I asked.

"Maybe. We'll see" was all she said. She then hung up. I wondered if those rich country club stiffs would look at Kay and wonder why she married beneath her station and then wound up back at home with mom and dad. Gossip spread in that country club like toe fungus in their showers. Stung about Kay's refusal, I called Lynne.

"Hey, why don't I pick you up at six thirty and take you out for a nice steak dinner? We can talk then. How does that sound?"

"That sounds wonderful, Detective Bryant. I'll try to look like a woman who deserves to have such a good-looking dinner date when you get here. Thank you! I love you! I'll see you at six-thirty." The contrast between the last two conversations was sadly amazing.

At home, I experimented with the photo-eye alarms. I found that the beams would reach nearly ten feet. The bell would ring every time I walked between them. I found that the best place was the entrance to the hall outside my bedroom. It would give me time to wake up and grab my pistol if the bell went off. I put the other set in my car along with the radio receiver and drove to Richardson. Lynne was waiting on me as I approached her door. As promised, she was beautiful. She wore white slacks that clung to her narrow frame and, as usual, flared at her feet. A white wool top came down to her waist. She had a jacket that was a deep crimson that she wore over her shoulders. Her blonde hair was spread along her shoulders. As always, she didn't appear to have a spot of makeup. I figured she must spend her days shopping for clothes.

"Let's go eat and then come back here. I'll show you what I brought. I'm hungry and I'm anxious to go out and show you off." When she hugged me, that scent of vanilla that she always has made my head spin.

Once we were seated at Wellington's, Lynne wanted to look at the salad bar. I stayed behind at the table and ordered bourbon. As the waiter was walking away from the table, I became aware of a woman who had walked by and then stopped and stared at me. She looked familiar as she approached the table. Suddenly it occurred to me that she was the mother of a girl who was in the same kindergarten class as my oldest daughter, Katy. I had seen her and Kay talking many times when I went with her to pick Katy up.

"Detective Bryant, how are you?" she asked as she walked up. "I thought that was you. Is Kay here with you? I've been meaning to call her and see if she would like to take the girls to Six Flags...." Her words trailed off as Lynne approached the table and pulled out her chair to sit down.

"This is...I'm sorry, I don't think I remember your name." It was all I could think of to say.

"Margaret. Margaret Layton. Are you a friend of Kay's?" she asked, clearly as embarrassed as I was. In fact, the only one of us that didn't seem embarrassed at this awkward moment was Lynne, who held her hand out to the sputtering Margaret Layton.

"No, I've never met Mrs. Bryant. I know Detective Bryant from the department. My husband and I owed him dinner for a favor he did and we're finally paying our debt tonight." She then turned to me with the same radiant smile.

"I just called his office. He hasn't even left yet. He told us to just go ahead and he will catch up as soon as he can. Is that bourbon you're having? I would just love some white wine, if we're going to wait." Turning again to Margaret Layton, Lynne continued without a pause. "Would you like to join us, Margaret? I could order you some wine."

Margaret stammered around for a few seconds and then smiled broadly at Lynne. "No, but thank you though. You're very kind to offer, but I just finished dinner with some friends and they are waiting on me. Can I say and I hope I don't embarrass you, but, you have the most amazing eyes. Do people often tell you that?"

"Thank you, Margaret. Now, who's being kind?" Lynne never lost that dazzling smile. Margaret hesitated as if she couldn't tear her gaze away from

Lynne's face, then turned and walked toward the door, turning briefly to wave as she passed out of sight.

I was trying to assess the damage that was just inflicted on my life and my marriage when Lynne turned back to me and said; "The salad bar looks yummy. I can't wait to sample it. Let's get our waiter over here. I'm hungry." The preceding moments seem to have passed Lynne by like a cool breeze. I was learning more and more about this mysterious girl.

Over dinner, I explained to Lynne the jeopardy I was getting into with my department. I told her that I was committed to keeping her safe and I would continue to do so until Donovan was behind bars. I told her that my mistake was getting romantically involved with her. It was becoming obvious to Al and to Captain Copeland and was certainly getting obvious to Kay. As I spoke, tears began to cloud Lynne's eyes and she finally blurted out; "But I love you!" This brought a few covert glances our way from surrounding tables. Coming to Wellington's had always been such a happy time in past. It was such a treat for me, Kay and the girls. Tonight, all I could think about was leaving. I knew now that it would never be the same.

Once back at Lynne's apartment, I pulled the radio receiver out of the box and set it up on her dresser near the sliding patio door. I was hoping that the reception would be strongest there. I was immediately rewarded with the distinct voice of the evening dispatcher at Creekwood PD. "This way, when I'm here, I'll know when they are trying to reach me by radio" I told Lynne as I adjusted the antenna.

"So we're going to be making love with that police radio blaring in the background?" she asked, pulling off the last of her clothes and sitting down hard on the bed, folding her arms. "It'll be like screwing in the back seat of a police car. And, no, I don't know from personal experience. It's just how I would imagine it would be." Then, her pout turned into a grin and she said; "Oh, it's alright. I understand. I'll take you any way I can get you, Cubby. Maybe we can just turn it off for a few minutes, anyway. Okay?"

After I switched off the radio receiver, we made love slowly and gently, our heads still spinning a little from the drinks at dinner. In a while, I got up and turned on the receiver again. We lay quietly and listened. Finally Lynne said, "How can you understand what they are saying?" They talk so fast and they use all those numbers."

"Just takes some getting used to it, I guess. I brought something else I want to set up before I leave. It's an alarm that will let you know if someone comes through your front door at night." I got up, dressed and pulled the alarm out of the box. We decided on a place that would cover the front door and front window. I had already put a broom handle in the roller track for the sliding patio door. Now, I felt that someone would have a hard time getting inside at night without Lynne knowing. She had a phone right beside her bed. I was beginning to feel better about leaving her alone.

I held Lynne in my arms before I opened her door to leave. We stayed that way for a few minutes. She pulled back and said; "The manager asked me the other day how my classes were going. I know she was asking because I haven't been leaving much, so I told her that I had dropped out for a semester and was going to go back in a few months. I told her that I was going to find a secretarial job around somewhere. She asked if I would like to work part-time in the leasing office. I could use the money. Mom has been putting money in my account without dad knowing. I still have some cash, but I'm trying not to use that. Anyway, I was wondering what you think about that."

"I think that's a good idea, Lynne. It will give you something to do during the day. Sure, go ahead. Just to make sure, I'll do a little background on the manager to see if she has any connections that might be a problem. But, she seemed nice the day I met her. I say, go for it."

On the way back to Creekwood, all I could think about was the fuse that was lit at Wellington's tonight when I was spotted by Kay's friend, Margaret, and when the explosion would occur…and how much damage it was going to do. I rigged the garage door with the tell-tale folded paper, set the photo-eye alarm and crawled into bed. Saturday and the dog show was just a couple of days away.

PART TWO
Rule 19

"Some men are alive, simply because it's against the law to kill them."
E.W. Howe

CHAPTER 11

The remainder of the week was busy, making it pass by quickly. Al had several houses under surveillance in an attempt to catch his "alphabet burglar," as he was now being called. The FBI still had not found Randall Donovan and seemed no closer to doing so. I had managed to stay away from Lynne Littleton for several days and was home in the evenings. I called and talked to Kay and the girls each night, hoping that Kay hadn't heard from her friend, Margaret Layton. If she had, she didn't mention it. As a matter of fact, she didn't mention much of anything during our conversations. Mostly, I just talked to the girls.

Early in the afternoon on Friday, Barbie called my intercom. "You have a call from Benny Rabalais on line one." When I answered, the caller launched in immediately; "Detective Bryant, my name is Benny Rabalais. I'm a bail bondsman in New Orleans. I understand that you have some information on an absconder that I have a considerable bail posted for. His name is Ivan Delacroix. Ring any bells?" On top of his annoying Cajun accent, I found his sarcasm more than a little irritating.

"No ring-a-ding yet, mister…what was your name again?"

"Rabalais! R-A-B-A-L-A-I-S," he spelled slowly as if he was speaking to a first-grade class.

"Who told you I might have information for you, Mister Rabalais?"

"I have considerable sources within the New Orleans Police Department, Detective Bryant. These sources tell me that you have knowledge concerning the death of Ivan Delacroix; knowledge that, if shared with the judge in his case, could mean that I might get my five hundred thousand cash bond returned to me. You following me, Detective?"

"Well then, Mister Rabalais, if you're wanting me to follow you, then lead me to the source at the New Orleans Police Department who gave you this information to start with. I'll talk to them on an official basis, but not you."

"As the holder of a bail bond I have the authority to pursue and arrest the absconder where ever he may be found. You, as a law enforcement officer, have the obligation to assist me in pursuing the said absconder, Detective Bryant." I felt like I was getting a law school lecture from the Cajun comedian Justin Wilson.

"What I suggest you do then, Mister Rabalais, is go out and arrest your absconder where ever you may find him since you have that authority. You can tell your 'considerable sources within the New Orleans Police Department' that I will assist them in whatever way I can. Just have them call me."

"Detective Bryant, you are hindering the apprehension of a bail jumper and I demand that you tell me right here and now what you know about his current whereabouts." He was now yelling into the receiver. "If you don't, I'll have your job."

"You'll have my job? Sure, go ahead and take it, Mister Rabalais. That's all this department needs is another asshole working here." I hung up.

No more than thirty seconds passed before Barbie called my intercom. "That Benny Rabalais is holding on line two."

"Tell him that I just left. Take down his number for me." A few minutes later, Barbie appeared at my office door. "He told me to transfer his call to the chief. He's talking to the chief now."

"Thanks, Barbie. I'm sure I'll be hearing from the chief in a few minutes."

No sooner than I had said that when my intercom buzzed. Of course, it was Chief Rogers. "Can you come into my office for a minute?" He sounded amused.

"I just got off the phone with some Louisiana bail bondsman who said you called him an asshole. Is he an asshole?"

I gave Chief Rogers the same story of the overhead conversation between Rick Littleton and Ran Donovan that I had given Agent Griggs. I told him that I didn't know Benny Rabalais from Murphy's cat and that I had already shared what I knew with the FBI. When I told the chief about Rabalais' threat to get my job, he laughed and said; "He'd think again if he knew what our salaries looked like." We both laughed. I had put myself further and further out on that limb by hiding the real facts about the demise of Ivan Delacroix.

I returned to my office and called Jim Griggs at the FBI. I filled him in on the call from Rabalais. "I'm sure my friend in the New Orleans office told the case officer at NOPD about my call. I expected that. I'm surprised that NOPD is so cozy with that bail bondsman Rabalais, but that's how it goes down there. If you want me to call my friend again, I will, but I think let's just leave it where it is. If someone from NOPD calls you, you can just tell them what you know. Honestly, though, I doubt you'll hear from anyone there. That will mean some cop will have to admit that they are passing information to a mob-connected bail bondsman."

The dust-up with Rabalais dug deep into my conscience. After all, he was a victim in all this. He was out a half-million dollars. If Delacroix was dead and not able to be in court, Rabalais needed to know and to bring what proof he could before the judge. That proof, unfortunately, involved bringing Lynne into the open, possibly requiring her to travel to New Orleans to testify. She would be an easy target for Donovan. The fact that Rabalais was such an obnoxious ass made it a little easier for me to drop him in the grease, but not much. He was only doing his job. For that matter, I'm only doing my job. I decided to get away from the phone for a while and see if Al needed an extra set of eyes out in the street. I spent the rest of the day trying to stay a few letters ahead of the alphabet burglar.

-

I was glad I had remembered to set the alarm for six the next morning. It was still pitch dark by the time it jangled me out of a sound sleep. I instinctively reached over to stroke Kay's face and found only the cold empty pillow. I was still partially asleep as I groped my way through my dark house to see if, by luck, the morning paper had been thrown. As I stumbled down the hall I was shattered fully awake by the shrill sound of a ringing bell. My first impulse was to reach for the pistol on my hip only to grab a roll of flab, what Kay called my "love handles." Then I realized that I had forgotten to turn off the photo-eye alarm. By now, I was wide awake. I showered, shaved and grabbed a cup of coffee to take with me as I walked out the front door, spilling some of it as I stumbled over the newspaper on the front steps. It was starting out not to be one of my better days.

I was craving another cup of coffee when I arrived outside of Gip Tuttle's house. He was already up, and outside, putting one of his dogs into a small enclosed cage on the trailer that I had seen next to his house the first time I was there. He snapped a padlock on the cage and came to my car. "Fall in behind me and we'll find a place to park that Sergeant Friday-lookin' poe-leese car before we head to Oklahoma." So we were going to Oklahoma. Not only was I going outside of my jurisdiction, I was going outside of my state.

"Oh, and be sure to leave that badge in your car, maybe in your trunk. I ain't taking you around those dogmen if you have that thing in your pocket. If anyone accidently saw it, we'll both be in shallow graves in Oklahoma. I, for one, can think of forty-nine other states I'd rather be buried in." We found a motel on the highway leading north out of Dallas County and I parked it in the lot. On the way to Oklahoma, I got a full lecture on the sport of fighting dogs.

Gip explained that, despite the belief by many, the dogs were not fought to the death. He explained that the fights were conducted under a rigid set of rules that protected the integrity of the contest and the life of the combatants, the dogs. He called them "Cajun Rules." There were nineteen rules and Gip was able to recite each one. The rules seemed to go a long way to prevent someone from poisoning or drugging the opponent's dog. Each dog is washed by a neutral person who is responsible for washing both dogs before the fight and with the same water. That neutral person is searched by the referee before he washes the dogs and has to roll his sleeves up above his elbows before he starts the washing procedure. Sponges and towels were not allowed to come in contact with the dogs and whenever one of the dog handlers gave his dog a drink from a water bottle, he had to first drink from the bottle himself in the presence of the referee. I figured that before these Cajun Rules came along, there must have been some serious skullduggery in the sport of dog fighting.

Forfeit money was put up by each dog owner. If the owner didn't show up at the designated place for the fight, or "show" as Gip called it, the money was forfeited to the would-be opponent. If the owner or handler broke any of the rules, the money was forfeited. A loss was determined by dog's unwillingness to fight or continue the fight once it had started. If one of the dogs turned away from its opponent, the dogs were again separated and allowed to charge into the center of the pit and continue the fight. If a dog refused to approach the other dog, it was like a boxer refusing to answer the bell. The opponent was declared the winner.

It was Cajun Rule number nineteen that was my favorite. It said that if the police were to interfere with the proceedings, it was the job of the referee to choose the next meeting place. Evidently, they weren't going to let the presence of law enforcement rain on their parade. It turned out to be a prophecy.

We were a few miles outside of Ardmore when Gip turned off the highway and onto a dirt road that ran into a wooded area. He waved at a man who was sitting under a tree at the edge of the road and holding a walkie-talkie. Less than a mile further, we came to a large clearing with a dilapidated barn in the background. A big canvas tent with open sides was off in the distance. I counted maybe fifty cars already parked along the edges of the clearing, most with small trailers containing closed cages like that being towed behind Gip's car. "Dogmen" with pit bull dogs on short chain leads were being careful to keep a safe distance from other dog-men with similarly held dogs. Most of the dogs had scars around their muzzles, which were broad and muscular. Their ears were closely cropped. The tent gave the place a sort of carnival atmosphere until I got close enough to see the bleachers inside that surrounded a square, wooden pit.

Gip cautioned me to stick close to him and not to engage in conversations unless he was part of it. I drew some curious looks from many of the people we passed, but no one challenged me. To those who stopped to talk to Gip, I was introduced as "my cousin from out-of-town." Being with Gip was the magic ticket and I was pretty much ignored.

The bleachers filled up fast. I was surprised to see both men and women in the crowd. They all seemed to know each other and conversations were thrown back and forth around me. I tried to scan the crowd as best I could without being obvious. I hoped that I would see Ran Donovan, but so far, he wasn't there.

A dog was being washed just outside of the pit and I could now see the ritual that Gip had explained on the way. I watched as the same man washed off each dog with warm water. The two handlers then led their dogs into the pit and a man I assumed to be the referee stepped to the center. He held a long wooden pole in one hand. On each side of the square pit was a line in the dirt floor. Each handler placed his dog behind their line and then straddled them, turning their heads toward the dog that was on the other side of the pit as the referee said "Face your dogs." Each dog was intently eyeing the other dog and both seemed anxious to engage the other. When the referee said; "Let go," the dogs rushed at each other, colliding in the center of the pit.

I had expected a lot of howling and screaming from the dogs, but they were surprisingly quiet as they went about tearing at each other with their teeth and jaws. There was plenty of growling, but no howling. Some in the crowd seemed as electrified as the dogs thrashed around the pit and were shouting both at the dogs and each other. I began to recognize some of the shouting as bets being placed. One man leaned over me to hand another a stack of twenty-dollar bills. As he did, his shirt opened at the waist and I could see the handle of a small pistol tucked under his belt.

Eventually, it appeared that one of the dogs turned slightly away from the other, as if to say, "If you will excuse me, I think I'd like to leave now." The referee called out "Turn on the white dog" and the handlers picked up their dogs and again set them behind the lines. This continued until finally one of the dogs did not respond to the referee's command to "Let go." Evidently, he had enough. I was glad it was over. During the lull in the action, I was surprised to see a man walking along the bleachers selling soft drinks. Just another Saturday afternoon at the ballpark. I was fanaticizing in my mind about the dogs rising up and attacking the crowd when someone rushed to the edge of the tent and shouted; "Cops on the way." That signaled utter pandemonium. I turned to see what Gip was doing when I felt his hand grasp my shirt sleeve. "Come on, let's get the hell out of here" he said as he dragged me out of the bleachers.

I found myself running toward the woods right along with everyone else. I caught a glimpse of one man tossing a chrome pistol into the brush. I started to assess my situation. I was a police officer, running from other police officers. I was armed but I didn't have a badge. I would have to take the bust for carrying a prohibited weapon for the sake of keeping Gip out of trouble; at least until I could later explain the situation. It would be a tough sell to those Oklahoma cops and an even tougher sell to my department. I was running out of air when Gip said "Let's stop and hunker down here." He pointed at a dry creek bed with brush on both sides. As I hid behind a bush, I thought of the shows I had watched on TV with my daughters about Africa and how the prey animals were protected by sheer numbers. Their chances of being eaten by the lion were lessened by the fact that there were so many other choices. I hoped that this same concept would work for me and that these Oklahoma cops were being occupied by the slower ones among us fleeing criminals.

"What are you laughing at?" Gip whispered, staring wide-eyed at me.

"Rule number nineteen," was all I could think to say.

"Well, get comfortable," he said. "We're going to be here for a while." And, we were.

After a couple of hours had passed, we decided to creep back toward the clearing. From a copse of trees, we watched as a few Oklahoma State Police troopers finished copying the last of the license numbers from the cars in the clearing. A man in a dog-catcher style truck was putting a dog in the metal cage in the back and it appeared that the troopers had several people sitting in the back seats of their cars. Once the last car drove out of sight, Gip and I walked back into the clearing. People were now coming out of the woods all around us. As we walked toward Gip's car, we could see that the door to his cage was standing open. "They got my god-damned dog" he said.

"Let's just get our asses back to Texas, Gip. I'll see if I can pull some strings and get your dog back on Monday."

"Yea and have my name on some police intelligence bulletin and maybe let everyone know that I brought a cop to one of the shows? No way, Jose! Ol' Billy Boy was a good dog, but I'm afraid he's a goner."

As we crossed the over the Red River into Texas, I finally broke the silence by asking Gip if he had seen Ran Donovan in the crowd. "No, and I looked around pretty good before we had to make that dash to the timber. He just wasn't there. He doesn't come real often. But, if you're game, I'll take you a few more times. This deal in Oklahoma has left a lot of forfeit money on the table, so there will be a re-match pretty soon. I'll let you know."

"So you're still willing to help me?" I was surprised.

"Sure. Besides, I'm really helping Lynne. Judy and I love that little girl. I ain't gonna let Ran Donovan do anything to her like he did to Rick. I'll do what it takes."

It was after dark by the time I arrived at Lynne's apartment. She surprised me with a bottle of Weller Special Reserve bourbon. "I knew this was your favorite and I wanted to have it here for you" she said as she poured the golden liquid into two glasses of ice. "I'm going to try it myself and see if I like it" she said as she raised the glass to her lips. After she gasped and coughed for a few seconds, she smiled and said "Pretty good!"

I told her about my day with Gip Tuttle in Oklahoma. When I got to the part about running into the woods from the police, she laughed harder than I had ever seen her laugh before. It was a good deep laugh that caused her to collapse back into the cushions on the couch. I was suddenly reminded of my daughter Katy laughing at her attempt to sound like Bugs Bunny and falling backward on her behind. The memory hurt.

"What did you think about the dog fights? Did you like that?" She seemed to be intently interested in my answer and waited for me to reply.

"Honestly, I thought it was the most needlessly brutal thing I had ever seen." She smiled back and said "Right answer, Cubby."

She got up and surreptitiously poured her bourbon drink into the kitchen sink, thinking that I wasn't looking. At times, I get glimpses like this of what she must have been like as a little girl. It was sad that she and her father were now so estranged. He must have loved her deeply at one time.

"Rick said that the dogs were bred to fight and that it was in their nature. They are bred to bring out aggressiveness and strength. He said that they liked to fight and that they lived for it."

"That's a crock of crap," I said. "I'm sure if that dog had a choice, he would rather be lying on some back porch with a belly full of kibbles and someone scratching his neck than getting chewed up in a wooden pit with no place to hide and with a bunch of rednecks yelling all around it." I felt that I was getting worked up.

"The puppy that Rick bought was so cute. He would crawl up in my lap and wait for me to scratch his belly. If Rick caught me doing that, he would yank the puppy up and take him away from me. He told me that I was taking the fight out of him."

"Can we talk about something else? I finally asked. I had seen and heard enough about fighting dogs for one day. I had reached a saturation point. "I have a better idea. Let's fool around."

"Why Officer Bryant" she said in an exaggerated southern drawl. "I didn't think you were ever going to ask. I was wondering how much more bourbon I needed to ply you with."

Later, when I could hear that her breathing was even, I quietly got up and took my clothes into the living room. I was just putting on my shoes when she came to the bedroom door. "Is there ever going to be a time that we can just wake up in the morning and have coffee and breakfast together? I'll even get up first and bring you breakfast in bed. I don't want you to leave."

"Lynne, you've got to understand something. I still love my wife. I love my kids. I don't want to lose them, but I don't want to give you up, either. I know this isn't fair to you." I didn't know what else to say.

"It's okay. I'll take you any way I can have you." She turned and walked back into her bedroom. I let myself out.

The telephone was ringing when I walked through the front door of my house. It was Kay.

"I haven't heard from you since yesterday. Have you just forgotten that you have a wife and children?" I could tell she was spoiling for an argument. I decided to deflect it by telling her about the trip to Oklahoma with Gip Tuttle. She listened without saying anything. There was a long pause after I had finished my story. With a sigh, she said; "This is getting more and more dangerous, Marc. Can't you get someone else to do some of this; like that FBI agent? Please don't get in so deep."

"I'm going to stick close to the office next week and catch up on my notes." I tried to reassure her. "I have been promising Al I would help on one of his cases. I expect next week to be fairly quiet."

Oh boy was I wrong!

133

CHAPTER 12

I was feeling a little more at peace as I went through my morning garage door ritual. It was a nice sunny morning. After my conversation with Kay the night before, I was feeling better about our situation. Lynne seemed willing to stay the present course with me, even though I had told her that I loved my wife and was not going to lose my family. For the time being, I was managing to keep all the balls in the air. On the way to the station, I took a quick detour by the Greek bakery and grabbed some baklava, making sure I got enough for Al and Barbie. My good mood began to fade as I sat down at my desk and saw the stack of telephone call notes from Benny Rabalais, the New Orleans bail-bondsman. It looked like he had called all weekend. Almost as if I had conjured him up from my thoughts, Barbie called on my intercom to tell me that Rabalais was on line two.

"If you will tell him that I haven't come in yet, I'll give you some baklava from the Greek bakery to go with your coffee," I promised.

"Done!" she said and hung up.

Al came to my office door and waved. "Hey, Al, I brought you some baklava. Let's grab some coffee in the lounge."

"Why don't we bring the coffee and baklava back to my office and talk." His expression was stern. I was wondering what was wrong when Barbie came in the office.

"I covered you with Mr. Benny Rabalais. Now, where's my baklava."

As I smiled and handed the sweet cake to Barbie, I saw the expression on Al's face change from stern to something that looked like surprise, maybe shock. He glanced at the call note that Barbie handed to me and then walked toward the lounge.

As we were filling up our coffee cups, I asked Al if there was anything wrong. "Yea, we need to have a pow-wow." We walked in silence back to his office. He closed the door and sat down behind his desk.

"Kay called me on Sunday. She was asking questions about Lynne Littleton."

"What kind of questions? I asked, feeling a sense of dread rise in my stomach.

"Mainly, she was interested in what Lynne looked like. I told her that she was a tall, thin hippy girl with blonde hair. Then, she specifically asked me about her eyes, like the color. I wondered then if she had seen Lynne somewhere because when I told her that Lynne had very distinct blue eyes, she just said 'Yea I thought so' and hung up. I like Kay and I'm not going to lie to her. You need to take care of your personal business. I don't want to be in the middle of it."

"I took Lynne out to dinner at Wellington's. I had asked Kay to go and she said she had other plans. I just got mad and asked Lynne to go with me out of spite. It was a stupid thing to do. Anyway, we ran into one of Kay's friends. This woman commented on Lynne's eyes. I guess she must have told Kay. I was afraid it would happen. I know I shouldn't have taken her out like that. It was dumb."

"This is getting out of hand, Marc. You need to pull yourself out of this tail-spin because you are headed for the ground really fast. If Chief Rogers finds out that you are squiring her around town like that, he will fire you in a heartbeat."

"Yea, I know" I replied, looking down, not wanting to turn my face to Al's. I knew I had done a stupid thing and it looked like I was going to pay for it. I started to explain that I had talked to Lynne on Saturday about how I didn't want to lose my family when Al interrupted: "What's going on with that New Orleans murder you were talking to the FBI about? Are they investigating it? Have you talked to anyone at New Orleans PD?"

"It was some guy named Ivan Delacroix. New Orleans PD had arrested him for killing some club owner. Griggs told me that the FBI has an unlawful flight warrant for him because he disappeared. Lynne had overheard Ran Donovan and Rick talking about a murder and they mentioned Delacroix's name. That's all that Lynne knows. Griggs said that the New Orleans FBI office didn't seem to be all that interested in the information when he called them. Delacroix was out on a half-million-dollar bond when he vanished.

Someone at the New Orleans FBI must have told the bail bondsman, because he's been calling every day."

Al seemed to reflect on that for a moment, then said, "Do you have anything you need to do today? I would like some help watching those houses for my alphabet burglar. He has hit more on Mondays than any other day of the week."

"Sure, let's go. I owe it to you for being put in the middle of my domestic problems."

As Al walked toward the door, he said; "I'm not going to take sides, either. I like Kay. I think she's about the nicest, sweetest, and I have to say the prettiest girl I have ever known. I'd do just about anything to see that you two don't split up." He turned and walked out.

I spent the morning making the circuit of houses that Al had mapped out, standing by while the surveillance officers grabbed bathroom and coffee breaks. It was just before 11:00 when one of the officers called Al on the radio. "One forty-two, I think I'm getting a nibble over here on Celeste Drive. I've got a Chevy van backed up in the driveway of one of the houses. There is a magnetic sign on the door that reads 'Garcia Cleaning and Restoration'. A guy in white coveralls just got out and went into the back yard."

Al was on the radio immediately; "Hold in a position where you can see the vehicle but they can't see you. One thirty-four, can you cover him? I'm a long way away." Al had called my number. I started in the direction of Celeste Drive. "Ten-four, I'm on the way." Then I called the officer at the location, "Don't crowd him too much. He'll be in there for a few minutes. I'm pretty close. Let's try to wait until he comes out with some evidence in his hands." I turned on Celeste just in time to see that the officer had blocked the driveway with his car and was running toward the back yard with his pistol in his hand. Shit!

As I approached the house, the front door flew open and a man ran toward the Chevy van. As he reached for the door, the van was already moving. The officer hadn't even checked the van before he ran for the back yard. There was a second man in the van and, from the looks of it, was behind the wheel.

136

CAJUN RULES

The van turned and cut across the lawn, throwing sparks as it jumped off the curb and hit the street.

"One thirty-four to Central, I'm in pursuit of a white Chevy van going west on Celeste Drive toward Mesa Drive. Have someone check on the officer at the Celeste Drive residence and I'm going to try and stay with this van."

As the van turned onto Mesa Drive, it slid sideways and side-swiped a car that was sitting at the curb. For a few seconds, it looked like the van was going to flip over on its side, but the driver managed to pull it out of the skid.

It wasn't a matter of catching the van. I could stay with it easily in the Dodge Charger that the department had assigned to me. It had a stronger engine and was much more maneuverable than the Chevy van. The problem was stopping the van. I kept hoping someone would get up ahead of me. Instead, I was leading a parade of flashing red lights by the time we reached the long two-lane highway that led south out of town. I knew that there was a raised railroad grade crossing about a mile further down the road. I decided to try and force a final end to the chase. I pushed the Dodge hard until my front bumper was just a few feet behind the van. I was hoping my aggressive moves would distract the van driver long enough that he wouldn't see the grade crossing coming up before it was too late. I felt like I was just inches behind the van as we were hurtling along at eighty-plus miles an hour. Then, my strategy worked. I saw the crossing coming up and I started to break hard. That must have momentarily caught the van driver's attention because he hit the grade crossing at full speed. Sparks, pieces of pavement and small pieces of the van exploded out from the tracks. The van seemed to float in mid-air for a split second and then came down hard on the pavement. I could tell that the driver was doing all he could to keep the van upright and on the road, but it hit hard, the right front rim digging into the asphalt roadway. This caused the rear of the van to swing and pivot around the now-stopped front end, throwing it on its side. It scattered glass and more sparks as it slid down the roadway and into a ditch several hundred feet from the grade crossing.

No sooner had the van slid to a final stop in the roadside ditch when one of the occupants climbed through the broken windshield and ran for the trees. As the other cars began to stop and officers began running in pursuit of the

137

man in the trees, I decided to take the other guy who was, no doubt, still in the van. I was going to let those eager young, able-bodied officers tear up their uniforms in the briar-choked forest. I went for the low-hanging fruit.

As I leaned in toward the shattered space that had once been the windshield, I saw someone holding their hands up in surrender. "The son-of-a-bitch stepped on my face when he crawled out," he cried.

"Who was that son-of-a-bitch that did that" I asked, smiling.

He just smiled back. "No comprende." I could see blood on his teeth as he grinned.

By now, I was being joined by Al and other officers from my department, along with officers from nearby departments, some deputy sheriffs and even a highway patrolman. In the distance, I could see a fire truck and the fire department ambulance coming full blast with lights and sirens. It's funny how a good old fashioned police chase will stir up so much excitement.

As the paramedics carefully removed "Mr. No Comprende" from the overturned van, Al slapped me on the back. "Good job, Marc!" I was glad to see him in a better mood about me.

"So, are we even now?" I asked.

"In spades!" he laughed as he followed the paramedics to the ambulance. "I'm going to the hospital with this guy" Al called over his shoulder as he helped the paramedics load the gurney. "Will you have someone drive my car to the station?"

"Sure, Al. I'm going to wait here to see if they flush the other guy out of the woods. I'll have a look in the van once the wrecker gets here and pulls it out of the ditch. Then I'll meet you at the hospital."

As I waited for the wrecker, other officers began to arrive to help with the search for the second man. I was happy to see that Deputy Johnny Flynn was among them. "Never a dull moment in Creekwood," he said as he walked up. "What 'cha got?"

I filled Johnny in on the alphabet burglary investigation and today's events. I finished by asking if he could have someone from his identification section come out and fingerprint the van. He walked back to his car and put in the call.

As we watched the wrecker hook up to the overturned van, Johnny asked; "How's the search going for Ran Donovan? Any leads?"

I told him about the dog fight in Oklahoma and my hopes that Donovan might show up. "How did you ever get in with those people, Marc? I would think that they would never let an outsider into one of those fights."

"I have a guy who is trying to help me find Donovan and solve this case. He got me in; claimed that I was his cousin from out-of-town. I promised him that I was only there to find Donovan and was not interested in anyone else or what they were doing. He's taking a big chance with me, but he seems eager to help me."

"I know that some guys in Criminal Intelligence at the DPS have been trying to gain some information on those professional dog fighters. Your information would be a big help. Any chance you might provide some basic intelligence once this thing is over?"

"I promised my source that I wouldn't reveal his name or any other names of people I saw. I'd have to honor that, Johnny. But, as far as just general information, I don't see why not. Don't mention this to anyone for the time being. I want to go a few more times to see if I can spot Donovan before I give up. Okay?"

"Sure, Marc! It's just between us. Let me know when you're ready."

The wrecker finally managed to drag the van out of the ditch and back on its wheels. I was disappointed to find it completely empty. I asked Johnny Flynn to stand by while his identification officer processed the van for prints and other clues. I wanted to check in with Al at the hospital and see what he had learned. Flynn said he would handle it and would let me know what was found. So far, the other officers had no success in locating the man who fled into the woods. Maybe Al was having better luck.

I found Al standing next to a bed in one of the trauma rooms at Creekwood Memorial Hospital. A hospital security guard had been posted at the door. In the bed was a very forlorn looking man who bore the cuts and scrapes from his encounter with the railroad grade crossing. Handcuffs were used to attach him to a rail on the side of the hospital bed. He was, indeed, a sad sight.

Al looked up and smiled. "We're waiting for some x-rays to come back, but he seems to be okay. If there isn't anything broken, they're going to release him to me." We then went outside, asking the security guard to go and stand beside the bed. Al pulled a driver's license from his coat pocket. "His name is Ramon Garcia. He lives in an apartment on Fish Trap Road in Dallas."

"Yea, that's who the van is registered to," I told him. "Did he tell you who the other guy is?"

"Nah, he keeps telling me that he doesn't understand English. Didn't stop him from shouting 'Oh shit' when the x-ray tech pulled on his arm. His English comprehension seems to come and go. I guess they haven't found the other guy, then, huh."

"Not yet, It hasn't been from lack of trying, though. The sheriff's department has sent deputies to help. They'll turn him up sooner or later, I'm sure."

"Anything in the van?" Al asked, hopefully.

"Nothing! It's clean. Johnny Flynn has his ID guy going over it for prints now. It sure would have helped if that officer had let the guy bag up a few items from that house on Celeste before he jumped into the middle of things. Youthful enthusiasm, I guess. I've almost forgotten what it looks like."

"You're such a cynic!" Al laughed as he turned to walk back into the trauma room. As he did, a young doctor came in and announced that there were no broken bones and that they had treated him as best they could. He was free to be released to us. We handcuffed him and took him to my car. He was quiet and calm during his ride to the station, staring out the side window as if he was on a scenic tour.

Once at the station, we booked Ramon Garcia and put him in a cell. We had the dispatcher find our one and only Spanish-speaking officer at Creekwood PD; Ralph Cardenas. The dispatcher found him at home on his day off. He enthusiastically agreed to come in and help. That was probably because he has been trying to get a detective job for the last two years. He's a good cop and his time will come.

Once Cardenas had arrived, we brought Garcia up to Al's office. Al asked Garcia what he was doing in the house on Celeste Drive. As soon as Cardenas translated the question, Garcia began a long stream of Spanish that neither Al nor I could understand. Finally, when he got to a pause, Cardenas said; "He said that he was there to clean some stained carpets. He said that the owners told him to just come through the back door while they were at work. He said that he must have gotten the wrong address. He panicked when he saw the police car. He's been in the pen before and was afraid the officer wouldn't believe his reason for being there."

"Well, he's right about the officer not believing him, that's for sure. Ask him if he's got a work order that has the owner's name and address written on it." As Al was telling Cardenas what to translate, Garcia started to answer, but stopped himself. It was becoming more and more evident that Garcia understood every word we were saying. After the question was asked, Garcia smiled and told Cardenas that he had just memorized the information before he left his apartment.

"Okay, then ask him if he will give us permission to search his apartment."

Once Cardenas had asked the question and got Garcia's reply, he turned to Al and chuckled "He said that he knows his rights and that you need to show him a search warrant. He said he also wants to call an attorney."

"Tell him he can call from the book-in desk in the jail. Tell him that since his hands are cuffed, he needs to have you dial the number for him first. Do you mind taking him back for us and help him make his call? Then, go ahead and put him back in the cell. Be sure you help him dial the number." At that, Al winked at Cardenas without Garcia noticing. A slight smile crossed Cardenas' lips. He left the office with Garcia in tow.

Al then turned to me; "You think we have enough to get one of the Justice Courts to give us a search warrant?"

"Come into my office and I'll help you type up the affidavit. Let's try Judge Crocker. He seems to be a little easier than some of those other judges. The only problem I see is that since he didn't take anything out of the house on Celeste, we really can't specify that we believe that stolen property is in his apartment. I think with what we have, though, it's enough for probable cause. It doesn't hurt that there was no carpet cleaning equipment in the van when I searched it. Let's write it up and see what the judge says.

As we were starting, Officer Cardenas came through the door whispering to himself. He immediately went to my desk and wrote down a number on a yellow pad. "There!" he declared. "I've been trying to memorize that number ever since I dialed it."

"Ralph, would you go have Barbie call the phone company and find out who that number goes to?"

As Cardenas left the office, Al and I turned our attention back to the affidavit. In a few minutes, Cardenas came back in laughing. "You ain't gonna believe this, you guys, but that number is his. He had me dial his own home number."

"Did you hear any of the conversation?" Al asked, knowing what the answer will be.

"No. Since he said he was calling his lawyer, I didn't think I should listen" Cardenas replied.

"Well, you did right, Ralph." Then Al turned to me "I guess a search warrant will be waste of time. I bet that place is being cleaned right about now."

"I'll call Walter Wood over at Dallas PD and see if he will send someone over to watch the place until we get there. Let's get going." I turned to Cardenas; "Come on and go with us. We might need your translation skills. Besides, you need to learn this stuff."

Judge Crocker quickly read our affidavit and asked a few questions. It didn't take much convincing, and he handed us a signed search warrant. We drove directly to the apartment on Fish Trap and were pleased to see two DPD patrol cars in the parking lot.

One of the Dallas officers accompanied us as we climbed the stairs to the second-floor apartment. He hammered on the door and shouted "Dallas Police...open up" several times before he turned to me. "Look, before we kick it down, let me go get the manager. We know her and she's works with us when we need her. She can bring a key. It will keep her from having to replace the door."

"Anything you say, officer. I'm just glad to have your help."

Within a few minutes, he returned with the manager. She was holding a ring of keys in her hand. When she turned the lock, the Dallas officer had her stand back. We entered with guns drawn, shouting "Police, we have a search warrant!" A quick search found that we were by ourselves.

At first glance, there wasn't anything there that looked remotely like stolen property. That was until I opened a closet door in the hallway. At first I couldn't tell what I was looking at. It was a chest-high stack of multi-colored cloth. It took a few seconds for me to realize that I was looking at a stack of bedspreads. As I was flipping through, trying to get an idea of how many there were, Al came up behind me.

"There are a couple of stereo receivers and a TV in one of the bedroom closets. I don't see any identifying markings on them. Looks like the place was cleared out before…, now what in the hell are you laughing about?" Even without knowing, Al was starting to laugh along with me.

"Looky what I found," I sang, stepping aside so Al could get a good look. By now, the other officers had joined us in the narrow hallway.

"What the hell is that?" the Dallas officer asked. As he did, it was beginning to dawn on Al and he smiled broadly.

"Bedspreads! Lots of bedspreads!" I declared. I'll tell you something. I might not be able to pick out my television set among a bunch of others like it, but I can recognize my own damn bedspread from across the room. Chances are, there are probably pillows left in those burglarized homes that match these bedspreads. They may have cleared out the stolen stuff before we got here, but the dummies left the most easily identified items behind. Like I always say 'If you take crime out of the hands of criminals, it would be a profitable business. It's criminals that screw up good crime."

The Dallas officer broke into a belly-laugh. "The Great Creekwood Bedspread Caper! And to think I was here when it all happened."

Two hours later, the municipal courtroom at Creekwood looked like a quilt show at a country fair. We strung bedspreads over the seats and then started calling all of our burglary victims, asking them to come to the station and see if they could identify their bedspreads. We even had some officers from Burglary and Theft at Dallas PD sending some of their victims over.

Before anyone arrived to look through the bounty of bedspreads, I had Cardenas bring Ramon Garcia from the jail and stand him at the door of the courtroom. Under his breath, Garcia said "Ay mierda!." When I turned to Cardenas, he immediately answered; "He said, 'Oh shit."

"Oh shit's right, amigo." I said. "Oh and you wanted us to show you a search warrant? Well, here you go," I said as I hung it up in front of his face. "We have a copy for you. It will be in your personal belongings when you're released. Which may be a long time coming."

As Cardenas turned Garcia around to walk him back to the jail, Barbie came up and handed me a call note. "He said his name was Gip. He said to call him as soon as you can. He didn't leave a number."

Tuttle answered right away. "It didn't take long to re-schedule the show that was so rudely interrupted on Saturday. Gonna be next Saturday. This time, we're staying in our own damn state. Screw those Okies. Be at my place on Saturday at the same time. You game?"

"I am if you are, Gip. I'll see you on Saturday."

-

I was high from the day's excitement and was anxious to hear some "attaboys" from someone. Someone, that is, that's not a cop who's heard it all before. I wanted my triumph through the streets of Rome. Kay had always been there before to pat me on the back and tell me what a good cop I am. I decided that maybe this would be a good time to face Kay and try to get my life back on track. I turned on the familiar street where her parent's house was located. I had been coming to their house for so many years. But, as I approached, I realized that this time was different. There was a red car parked at the curb in front of the house. I recognized it immediately as the red Jaguar that Tom Warmer had so proudly showed me on New Year's Eve. It was parked directly in front of a fire hydrant. Tom always believed that laws were made for the common people and not the son of a big firm lawyer.

As I sat in my car and looked at the Carson house, I realized that I was getting exactly what I deserved. I decided that the only thing that would wash down the lump in my throat was lots of good bourbon…lots of good Weller's

Reserve. I knew just where to find it, too. I turned around and headed to Richardson.

CHAPTER 13

I woke up to the familiar sound of static and police ten-signals coming over a radio. I allowed myself to drift between sleep and wakefulness, listening to the routine business of police work as it was being broadcast over the air. Suddenly, I had the feeling that I must still be in my car. But, that couldn't be right because I could also feel that I was completely naked. If I could just wake up, all would be explained. The problem was that I was deep within a well, a well of bourbon. Well of…hum! That reminded me of Weller. Wait a minute, Weller! I rose up only to have a wave of nausea pass through me like a tsunami. As my watering eyes began to clear, I was aware that Lynne Littleton was sitting cross-legged at the foot of the bed. She was nude and was holding a cup of coffee. "See," she said. "I told you I would bring you breakfast in bed."

"Say, you didn't happen to hear anyone call for one thirty-four over that radio, did you?" My voice sounded like some cartoon frog.

"No, and I've been listening all night, too. You left it on when you went to sleep, and I was afraid to turn it off. Oh, here," she smiled as she handed me the cup.

"I'm sorry! I guess I just forgot…shit! I yelled as the coffee scalded my tongue. I fanned my mouth with my open hand, wondering if I would wind up with a speech impediment for the rest of my life. "What time is it, anyway?"

"There you go again" she laughed. "Do you always ask naked girls what time it is? If you weren't so damn cute, you would probably never get laid. You know that?"

"I've done alright so far, thank you very much," I said as I touched the tip of my tongue. It was numb.

"Come on, Cubby, and eat. I fixed eggs and bacon for you. I'm supposed to work in the leasing office today and I have to get ready to go. I'm going to have to start earning some money if I'm going to keep you in Weller bourbon. You put a pretty good dent in that bottle last night." She got up and picked up a tray of food, placing it on the bed in front of me.

146

"Did I tell you about the chase I was in yesterday?"

"Three times! I think you kept forgetting that you told me because you would tell me again later. At least the story never changed, so it must have been an accurate account."

"Well, it was pretty cool" I said, feeling a little embarrassed. "How about the bedspreads? Did I tell you about the bed…"

"Oh yea!" she interrupted. "I heard all about the bedspreads." She leaned in and gave me a kiss. "Detective Bryant, I think you are a super-cop right out of the movies. I love you! Eat while I take a shower" she said as she jumped up and bounded for the bathroom.

I wolfed down the breakfast that Lynne had made for me, wondering what the bacon and eggs were going to think when they are introduced to the bourbon that's already lurking in the depths of my stomach.

As Lynne finished her shower, I jumped in and gave myself a rinse. I soaped up my face with hand soap and used Lynne's leg razor to shave. When I finished, I realized that it left my face looking like Ramon Garcia's after he had climbed through the windshield of his Chevy van.

As I scrambled around the apartment for my clothes, finding different pieces in various places, Lynne followed behind me. "I don't have to worry that you'll go home to your wife now" she said, giving me a big grin.

"Why's that?" I asked.

"Because I hid your underwear," she laughed.

"I don't think that the absence of underwear will make a whole lot of difference now."

As I walked through the front door of the station, I could see that there was activity in the municipal courtroom. People were sorting through the bedspreads, occasionally picking out one and bringing it to Al, who was sitting behind the judge's bench. He looked like he was running a flea market booth.

I waved from the door and mouthed, "You need any help?" Al just smiled and waved me off. Good! My head was splitting and I needed another cup of coffee.

As I poured myself a cup, I felt a hand on my shoulder. "Good job yesterday" Chief Rogers said. "I tried to congratulate Al earlier, but he said you were the star of the show. It just might make you a good candidate for Officer of the Year next December." He gave me another pat on my shoulder and walked away.

My marriage was falling apart. I was sleeping with the wife of a murder victim. I was hiding a witness from the district attorney and I was concealing information about a crime…a murder in another state. Yea, some Officer of the Year! About that time, the eggs and bacon had finally decided that they were in the wrong neighborhood and were trying desperately to find the road out. I was able to get to the locker room toilets just before they made their escape.

I rinsed my mouth out in the bathroom sink, grabbed my cup of coffee and walked back to my office. I was greeted with two more call slips from Benny Rabalais. I picked up the phone receiver and dialed his number in New Orleans.

"Mr. Rabalais, this is Detective Marc Bryant. I see that you have tried to reach me over the past couple of days. Is there something new you want to discuss with me?"

"Yea!" he snarled. "I want to know exactly what you know about Ivan Delacroix and where you got your information. I want to know who your source of information is about Delacroix, and I want you to put me in touch with that person."

"Mr. Rabalais, we talked about all of this the other day. I told you that I would be happy to cooperate with New Orleans Police or the local FBI. You, Mr. Rabalais, are neither. If someone from New Orleans PD wants to provide my information to you, that's their business. I've got nothing further to share with you, sir."

"Let me tell you something, Detective. I've got some very powerful friends. In fact, you'd be surprised who my friends are. I tried to do this the right way by coming straight to you. You're not going to like it when I call in some favors from some of my friends." His words were coming out like the growl of a pit bull dog.

"Mr. Rabalais, if you're threatening me, I going to have a couple of U.S. Marshals drag your ass to Texas and have you tried in federal court. But, if you hang up now, I might just forget the whole thing." The line went dead with a loud click.

The conversation with Rabalais cleared my head enough that I decided this would be a good time to confront Kay. I dialed her parent's number. I recognized the voice of my oldest daughter, Katy, as she answered; "Carson residence."

When Katy realized it was me, she started right in; "Daddy, I miss you so much. I wish we could go home. Would you please come to see us. Mom has been crying a lot."

"Katy, I love you and this will be over soon. I miss you and Kim."

"Don't you miss mom too?" she asked. It broke my heart.

"Of course, I miss your mom. I love her. Is she there? Let me talk to her."

After some muffled conversation, Katy came back on the line. "Mom said she didn't want to talk to you right now." She was beginning to cry.

"Just hand her the receiver, Katy." I waited.

"I don't have anything to talk to you about," Kay said as she entered the call.

"Don't do that, Kay. Don't drag Katy into the middle of this."

After a few seconds of silence, Kay said "I know that you took that Lynne out to dinner, Marc…in public, in front of my friends. How could you do that?"

"Kay, it was a big mistake and all I can say is I'm sorry. I was hurt because you turned me down when I asked you to go with me and I guess I was just retaliating. It was stupid of me, I know."

"Have you been staying with her at night?"

"Have you been staying with Tom Warner at night? I saw his car parked in front of your parent's house last night."

"Marc, for Christ's sake, my parents are here. Besides, Tom is just a friend and you know it. He's our friend. I'm thinking about talking to his father, anyway."

"So you need a lawyer? Look, Kay, I'm coming over."

"No, Marc. I don't want to see you…" I hung up before she finished.

149

I drove to the Carson residence wondering how I let my life get so completely screwed up. Al was right. I was losing my family. My job was probably next.

I parked at the curb where Tom's red Jaguar has been the night before. Kay's father, Ted, met me on the porch as I walked up.

"Marc, Kay has asked me to tell you that she doesn't want to see you. I can't let you in. I'm sorry." As he spoke, Katy and Kim came outside and hugged my legs. Both were crying.

I squatted down and held them both. "Hey, you guys, I'll get this all worked out and we can go back home soon. I miss you both so bad. It will all be okay soon, I promise." I stood up and turned to Kay's father. "I understand, Ted." I could see Kay watching through a front window, tears streaking her face.

As I walked back to my car, Ted Carson followed me. "Marc, I hope you two can get this sorted out. I've liked you from the day I met you and I've always been proud that you are my son-in-law. I'll do whatever I can to help you through this. I feel like you've sort of wandered off the path a little. I've been there myself, believe me. I'm always going to take Kay's side, no matter what. I'm her father, but I like you a lot and I want you two to be together; if not for your own sakes but for those beautiful little girls in there who love you both. Well...enough said. Take care of yourself and come back when your heads in a better place." He reached out and put his hand on my arm; then, turned and walked back to his house. I drove back to the police station, feeling completely exhausted and defeated.

The rest of the week seemed to fly by. Al had managed to make several solid cases against the alphabet bandit, Ramon Garcia. I continued to spend evenings with Lynne, taking care not to stay all night. I didn't feel like pressing my luck any further. My evenings with her were happy and fun. I could feel myself falling more and more in love with her. I felt like I was the center of her universe. It was heady stuff.

-

Saturday morning found me once again on my way to Gip Tuttle's place in east Dallas County. I saw that Gip didn't have his dog trailer hooked to his car as before. I guess he hadn't been able to get his dog back from the Oklahoma authorities.

"This time, we're headed to familiar territory," he said as he walked up to my car. "Follow me and we'll drop your car off at the same place. I'll explain it to you on the way."

"We're going to a place just a little east of here. There's a dogman that has access to a barn. There's only going to be a couple of fights. They're finishing the one that was about to commence before we were interrupted the last time. Remember Rule 19? That's something we won't have to worry about this time." At that, Gip gave me a big grin.

"Okay, I'll bite…excuse the pun. Why aren't WE worried this time?"

"Because this time, we've got the law bought off ." He let that soak in. I glanced at a passing road sign and realized we were on the highway that led northeast of Dallas. It was all rural up that way and there were plenty of barns. Cops in this part of the state didn't make a whole lot of money. I'm sure that a couple of hundred bucks extra in their pocket would be hard to turn down.

We traveled in Gip's car for over an hour. The roads that he turned on were getting progressively more remote, most topped with tar and gravel. We had gone from state roads to farm-to-market roads to county roads. Now, we were stirring up dust on a caliche topped country road when Gip slowed and turned onto a dirt lane that was blocked by a closed metal gate. A man stepped from the trees and waved. When he recognized Gip, he turned and pushed gate open. As we passed him, I realized that he had a badge pinned to his shirt and a pistol on his belt.

"If there are only two fights today, then why am I here? What are the chances of Donovan showing up to a two-fight show? I don't like taking all this risk for nothing."

"It's because one of them is between two champion dogs. That's why the big crowd last week. This bout has been talked about for a long time and there's a lot of money being bet. The sire of one of them is a dog I bred and trained myself. Don't worry. There'll be a lot of dogmen here. As a matter of fact, it's the kind of show that Donovan would go to. It's private and there's big money to be made."

I began to understand what he meant by private as a farm house and adjacent barn came into sight. Cars were parked all around the little white farmhouse and I could see a large crowd milling around the barn. I immediately started to scan the group, hoping I would see Donovan. No luck.

The barn reminded me of the one at Maurice Cox's place. It gave me the creeps. This one had a square pit and the wooden walls were not as high. Like Cox's, though, the floor was sand and the walls of the pit were stained with blood.

Two rows of bleachers surrounded the pit. As my eyes adjusted to the lower light, I realized that there was a huge rattlesnake hanging on the wall across from the door. Although its head was gone, I saw that it had been a monster in its prior life, looking like it was over 5 feet in length. I wondered if it was there to invoke some kind of pagan god…maybe the god of needless bloodshed.

I watched the same two dogs that I had seen the week before again going through the ritual of weighing and washing. In no time, they were going at each other in the pit. One dog would grab the front leg of the other, shaking it like it was trying to kill a rat. Then the other would lock on to the opponent's neck and they would thrash to the sandy floor. It took about thirty minutes for one of the dogs to decide he had enough and refused to fight, standing behind his scratch line and turning his head away. The barn seemed to explode with cheers and shouts. Seeing that dog in such miserable defeat was hard to watch. I checked out the crowd again and suddenly realized that one of those cheering was none other than Otto "Sad" Sack. I quickly ducked my head and told Gip, who was on my right side, to lean a little forward to block me from being seen. As best I could with my chin tucked into my chest, I glanced around to see if his ape-like brother-in-law with him. I didn't see anyone else I recognized.

Sack closely watched the weigh-and-wash ritual of the two dogs that were going to be the upcoming championship bout . It gave me a chance to climb out of the bleachers and stand at the entrance to the barn. I then checked inside and out to make sure that neither Willard Green nor Ran Donovan was around.

When I was satisfied that they weren't, I went back inside and stood beside the upper bleacher, watching as the handlers brought the dogs into the pit. A man sitting on the end of the row asked me if I wanted to sit down. I told him that my back was acting up and that I needed to stand. I used him to block Sack's line of sight to me.

The fight between the two champion dogs lasted over an hour. Cheers rang out and bets were made back and forth. From where I was standing, I could see only about a half of the pit...but it was enough. I could see the dogs locking their teeth on each other and shaking their heads violently back and forth. The dogs seemed to instinctively go for the stifle of the other as if their atavistic calling told them how their ancestors brought down prey. Finally, one of the dogs refused to cross his scratch line and, after a twenty-second count, the fight was called.

I tried to walk ahead of Gip as I made my way back to his car. If Sack saw me and recognized me, I was hoping he would not realize I was with Gip Tuttle. Gip seemed to sense the same thing and allowed me to walk way ahead of him, stopping and talking with other dogmen along the way. As I glanced back, I could see Otto Sack standing at the edge of the barn and looking directly at me. I hoped that I was far enough away from him that he wouldn't recognize me. He looked my way for a few seconds and then turned and walked back toward the barn entrance. Gip finally arrived and unlocked the car door. I quickly climbed inside.

As we pulled away and started down the sandy road, Gip hurriedly asked; "Do you think Sack saw you?" It was the first time I had ever seen Gip show any nervousness.

"He stood and looked out at me as I was walking toward the parked cars. I was a long way from him. He turned and went inside the barn and I didn't see him after that. I made sure he didn't see which car I went to. I don't know, Gip, if he recognized me or not."

"Well, we'll know soon enough. If he did, I'll probably get a visit from Ran Donovan. It won't be pretty, that's for sure. Maybe we'd better make this one your last show for a while until we see what happens."

"Yea, I was thinking the same thing, Gip. The last thing I want is to get you and Judy hurt. You took a big chance with me and I won't forget it. I owe you big-time."

"Speaking of forgetting" Gip said "you can pay me back by forgetting everyone and everything you've seen. Such as, forgetting you saw that deputy at the gate. Our deal was for you to find Ran Donovan and nothing else. We tried. I hope you'll keep your word."

"That's a promise, Gip. I'll stay away, but I want you to let me know if you hear from Sack or Donovan after today. Okay?"

The drive back to Gip's house was mostly in silence. We both seemed to reflect on the consequences if Sack recognized me and realized that I was with Gip. I'd seen and heard enough of Donovan's vengeance. I just hope I'm not going to be responsible for getting Gip Tuttle and his wife killed.

I stopped at Lynne's apartment on my way back to Creekwood, making doubly sure this time that I wasn't being followed. I told her about seeing Otto Sack.

"Marc, if Ran finds out that Gip brought you to those fights, he'll kill him for sure. Why is it that the big-deal FBI hasn't found him yet? You know what I think? They don't want to find him. He has too many friends in high places, Marc. If he started talking, a lot of heads will roll, heads that belong to gangsters and politicians, both. God, I hope nothing happens to Gip and Judy. You have to make sure of that, Marc. You got Gip into this and he's your responsibility now."

The bad news was taking away the usual joy I felt at spending time with Lynne. I suddenly craved the quiet and solitude of my own home and my own bed. I gave her a quick hug and told her I would see her later. I was half way through her front door when I heard her say, "Please don't leave."

We lay side by side in Lynne's bed, talking about whatever was on our minds. Lynne turned on her side and asked; "If you could put yourself anywhere in the world this very second, where would it be?"

"I don't know; maybe in a little A-frame in the Colorado Rockies, sitting in front of a fire place. How about you?"

She rolled over on her back again, staring toward the ceiling as if it wasn't there. She stayed that way for a few seconds and then answered: "I would like to be sitting on the edge of the Trevi Fountain in Rome. I've always wanted to see it. I've never been to Rome. I was in Ireland once. My dad took us there because he was doing some kind of deal to import Irish whiskey. I was pretty young and I don't remember much. But it wasn't Rome. I can't think of anything more romantic than being in Rome, sitting next to the Trevi Fountain…with you. Promise me you will take me to Rome and see the Trevi Fountain one day. Do you promise?"

"You know I can't promise you something like that" I answered.

"Then, go home!" I looked to see if she was being cute but I could see the tears in her eyes. She continued to stare at the ceiling that wasn't there.

I dressed and started toward the front door. "Will you come back?" she called from the bedroom.

"Yea, you know I'll come back. Get up and turn on the alarm before you go to sleep." I drove back to Crestwood feeling more uncertain about my life than I had ever felt before.

CHAPTER 14

For the next few days, things remained the same between Kay and me. We had reached a sort of détente and found it easier to just not speak to each other. One day, Kay's mother brought the girls to the McDonald's in Creekwood to eat lunch and have some fun on the playground. I was invited. I didn't know if that was Kay's idea or her mother's. I didn't care, either. I was just glad to spend some time with my girls. I crawled through the plastic tubes in the playhouse, growling and chasing them around and around. We laughed so hard until I noticed a disapproving look from the manager, who was standing at the door with his arms folded. I suddenly realized that my coat was flying open and my pistol was clearly visible. I quickly climbed out, discretely showed my badge to the manager and joined Kay's mother at her table. The manager just rolled his eyes and went back to his counter duties. Kay's mother put her hand to her mouth and stifled back a laugh. Maybe she doesn't think I'm the terrible person after all.

The week was notable by the absence of further calls from Benny Rabalais. Ever since our last conversation, I hadn't heard anything from him. Although I wondered if he had just given up, I knew in my heart that he didn't seem the type to kiss away a half million dollars. Not without a fight, anyway.

I was making my round of calls to Walter Wood, Agent Griggs and Deputy Johnny Flynn on Thursday to see if anyone had received any further leads on Donovan. When I reached Flynn, he said that he was just about to call me.

"Hey Marc, glad you called. I told you about those DPS Intelligence guys who are working on the interstate dog fighters. They're putting together a meeting out at their headquarters building tomorrow at 10:00 am. They are anxious to hear what you know about Donovan and his connection to those fights. Can you make it?"

"I can't give up sources and I promised that I wouldn't name any names, but I don't see any harm in giving them some general information that I've picked up during this investigation. Sure, I'll be there."

"That's great, Marc. I'm sure they will be glad to have anything they can get. See you tomorrow."

The Texas Department of Public Safety has a large headquarters building on an interstate highway just northeast of Dallas. Several functions of the state police have offices there including the Texas Rangers. It was a safe place to hold a clandestine meeting of undercover and intelligence officers since entry was restricted and there were usually more than twenty or thirty uniformed officers in the building at any given time. Once I had identified myself to the officer at the front desk, I was escorted to a large training room in the center of the building. I was surprised to find that the room was almost full. I recognized officers from Dallas Police, the Sheriff's Department, the Department of Public Safety and even a couple of Texas Rangers.

Each of us was asked to stand and tell our name and our department. I was shocked as one man stood and announced that he was Clayton Tarver and that he was an investigator for the ASPCA, the American Society for the Prevention of Cruelty to Animals. Until that moment, I never realized that the ASPCA had investigators. He looked the part, as well. He had lank brown hair that was parted on the side and hung over the other side of his head. He had a rubbery face, droopy eyes and full lips. He reminded me of a basset hound. I wondered if an uncanny resemblance to an animal was a prerequisite for being an investigator for the ASPCA. Once he had introduced himself, he glanced around the room with a look of defiance, as if he was aware that his credentials didn't quite stack up to the rest of those in the room.

Officers from the DPS talked about their attempts to get undercover officers into the ranks of the dog fighters and their failures at getting any of the dogmen to provide information. All the while, Johnny Flynn kept smiling and pointing toward me. Finally, the person leading the meeting, a lieutenant with the DPS Intelligence Service, asked if I had any information that might be helpful.

I explained to everyone that my interest in dog fighting was strictly to locate a person that I suspected of committing a double murder in my city. I explained that I had a source that was able to get me into two recent fights. I explained that the fights are well organized in advance, held in remote and guarded places and, finally, that they were referred to as "shows" and not "fights." Also, I explained that the fight enthusiasts called themselves "dogmen." I explained that the fights were executed under a strict set of rules and that, contrary to what I had always heard, were not fought to the death. The rules and some of the jargon that I had picked up from Gip were of great interest to them, especially to a couple that appeared to be on undercover assignments. They were taking notes and listening to my every word.

As I talked, I realized that the ASPCA investigator Tarver was glaring at me with a scowl on his face. Finally, he waved off another question that was being asked and said; "Of course, you know that you are going to have to tell us who got you into those fights and when and where they happened." Suddenly, the whole room went quiet. All eyes were on Tarver and his eyes were on me.

The lieutenant who was chairing the meeting broke in and said "I think we all understand that Detective Bryant is here only to give us some general information and is not obligated to reveal his..." Tarver suddenly interrupted, still staring hard at me.

"Animals were being tortured! That's against the law. In some states, it's a felony. You're a witness. You have an obligation to the law to tell me right now all you know about the crimes you have witnessed." I could suddenly see that behind the droopy eyes was a fevered zealot on a mission. Those eyes were now burning into me.

"I'm under no such obligation, Mr. Tarver. It IS mister, right? I mean, you don't have a badge and a police commission, do you?"

"The ASPCA has sworn officers with the right to make arrests in New York State" he shot back at me.

"I hate to state the obvious, Mr. Tarver, but you aren't in New York."

"The ASPCA is a national organization, Detective...a very powerful one. We have many important people who support us. I can compel you to give me that information if I so choose" he was spitting his words across the table at me. The rest of the room stayed silent.

"So, what are you gonna do, sic a feral cat on me?" That seemed to break the spell and the entire room broke into a laugh. That is, with two exceptions;

me and Mr. Tarver. I was too angry to laugh, and Tarver certainly wasn't in the mood.

I turned to the lieutenant, who was now red-faced and clearly embarrassed. "I guess I've told you all I can and keep the integrity of my investigation. I'll be glad to share what additional information I come up with in the future. I'm willing to meet again with all of you, except that animal cop across the table. He'd be wise to stay out of my sight from now on." I folded up my notebook and started toward the door. The lieutenant and Johnny Flynn followed me out. I stopped in the hallway and turned to them.

"Marc, I'm sorry. I didn't realize he was going to be here. I appreciate your coming here and sharing what you could with us."

The lieutenant followed up with; "I'm with Johnny on this. I sure appreciate your help. It was my boss's idea to have that guy at the meeting. The ASPCA has done a lot of investigation into those dog fighters and we hoped he would be able to give us information that we don't have."

Johnny turned to him, "Yea, but he isn't even a sworn officer, and you have undercover people in there. That wasn't very smart."

As we talked, Tarver came out of the room and brushed past us without speaking. He disappeared around the corner of the hallway, walking toward the main lobby.

"No big deal. The dumb bastard just made me mad, threatening me like that. Look, I'll help out any way I can in the future. I appreciate the work you guys are doing on this, lieutenant. I'll do what I can to help."

As I drove away from the DPS headquarters, I noticed a car pulling out a few seconds behind me. I quickly turned into the parking lot of a café on the service road of the interstate and waited for the car to pass. Seconds later, a white 1971 Ford Fairlane passed by. Tarver was at the wheel. I turned my head and opened my door to get out. He passed by without stopping. I tried to grab the license number, but he was too far away.

I tried to sleep in on Saturday morning, but my body was used to waking with the sunrise. I missed hearing the comic voices and slapstick sounds of Saturday morning cartoons coming from the other room, as well as the smell of coffee and breakfast that Kay always had ready when I managed to crawl out of bed. I lay on the bed feeling myself sinking into another depression and decided to get up and do something. I showered, shaved and drove to the Greek bakery. I thought I would surprise Lynne with breakfast.

I went through my perfunctory ritual of checking my rearview for someone following me. At first, I wasn't sure if the car that I had seen as I was pulling out of my neighborhood was the one that was several car-lengths behind me now. I took the exit to the shopping center with the two-story parking garage that I had used to check for tails in the past. As I entered the garage, I could see the same white car turning off of the service road and moving in my direction. I pulled into the parking garage and then drove immediately to the exit on the other side. I found a parking space next to the exit and waited. In a few minutes, I could see the white car approaching the exit. The driver had just enough time to have driven through both floors of the garage in search of my car.

I waited until the car was making its exit and drove forward, blocking the way. I recognized the car immediately. It was the white Ford Fairlane that had pulled out behind me at the DPS headquarters. Clayton Tarver was behind the wheel. He frantically locked the doors of his car and, at first, would not look at me as I rapped on the window next to his face.

"You know what, Mr. Tarver? I'm going to let you go this time. But I want you to listen to me." He then turned to face me, his insolent expression made me want to break his window and drag him out by his hair.

"If I ever find you following me again, I'm going to consider you a threat to my safety. I'm going to believe that you intend to do me harm. And then, I'm going to act accordingly. At least, that's what I'm going to tell the grand jury, anyway."

"You're threatening me?" he yelled, still not willing to roll down the window.

"Well, what do you think, dumb-ass? Hell yea I'm threatening you. Now get your ass out of here."

I backed up and let him by. I watched as he drove out of the parking lot and back on to the highway. I then continued my trip to Richardson, making sure I checked the rearview all the way.

CAJUN RULES

On Monday morning, I was greeted by Captain Copeland as I walked through the lobby door. "Well, there's our local celebrity," he announced. "You do remember, don't you, that all press releases go through the chief's office?"

"What the hell are you talking about?" I asked, genuinely confused.

"You haven't seen the Times-Herald this morning?" he asked.

"I hate to keep repeating myself, Captain, but what in the hell are you talking about?" Before he could answer me, Chief Rogers walked in. "Marc, I need you in my office." I had a real bad feeling about all of this.

"Did you authorize a story in the paper about dog fighting? I don't recall you getting permission from me first." With that, he tossed a newspaper on the desk in front of me. A headline read; "Local Police Investigating Area Dog Fighting."

"Go ahead and read it" the chief said. "Take your time. I'll wait."

The news story contained several quotes from Clayton Tarver, a "Special Investigator for the American Society for the Prevention of Cruelty to Animals." It was obvious where the reporter got his information. Unfortunately, my name was also prominent in the article.

"Detective Marc Bryant with the Creekwood Police has become something of an expert on these illegal fights. During a meeting with local officers, Detective Bryant explained that these 'shows', as they are euphemistically called, are done with an adherence to strict rules and that security at these so-called shows is tight."

In the article, Tarver described how pit dogs are bred for their aggressiveness and are rigorously trained. He went on to say that part of this training is to allow the pit bull dogs to fight other dog breeds that are not as aggressive; allowing the pit bull to experience "a kill." Tarver stated that even stray cats are thrown into the pits with these dogs and allowed to be "torn apart by these dangerous animals."

I knew right away that I was going to be in big trouble with Gip Tuttle. I knew that the best thing was to go straight to Gip as soon as I could and let him know about the meeting. I honestly felt that I had not betrayed him or his confidence in me, but I knew that this would shake his trust. I also realized that if Otto Sack had recognized me and had seen me with Gip, the article would confirm that Gip was working with the police.

I explained to Chief Rogers about the meeting and about my confrontation with Tarver. I told him that I needed to get to my source right away and warn him that there may be trouble headed his way.

As I was walking past my office door, I could hear my intercom ringing. It was Deputy Johnny Flynn. "I guess you've seen the paper this morning. The sheriff has already called the DPS Director in Austin and lodged a complaint. They should have never let that guy come to an intelligence meeting in the first place. I just wanted to tell you how sorry I am that I got you into this. I hope this doesn't jeopardize you investigation or your source."

"I can tell you that my source isn't going to be happy about this, that's for sure. I'm on my way now to see if I can smooth things over with him. I'm particularly worried because I saw Otto Sack at that last dog fight. I don't know if he saw me or not. If he did and realized who I was with, it could go real bad for my informant."

"Is there anything I can do to help out, Marc? I feel real bad about this."

"No, nothing I can think of, Johnny. I'm on my way to see my source. I'll let you know. Maybe it will just blow over."

I drove to Gip's house as fast as I could, hoping I could get there before he read the morning paper. As I pulled up, I found him sitting on his front porch, drinking a cup of coffee. He looked up and down the road before he motioned for me to come up.

"Hey Gip!" I said, trying to sound as friendly as I could. "I've got something to tell you about" I said as I sat down on the steps.

"If you're talking about that story in the paper, I know all about it."

"So you've read it already?" I asked.

"No, I don't take the paper. They won't throw it here. The paperboy is scared of the dogs. But, I've been getting calls all morning about it. Whoever that guy is with the SPCA don't know shit. It's all phony-baloney. He even said that we throw stray cats in with those dogs. What a crock of crap. There ain't a dogman alive who would risk getting a good dog blinded by some damn cat. They mentioned that you are named in the article. How did you wind up in there?"

I explained to Gip about the meeting. I told him that I talked only in generalities and did not give any information that would lead back to him or to any of his friends. I felt like I was giving a closing argument to a very skeptical judge. As I spoke, Gip listened intently; then, looked over my shoulder and stared hard at something behind me.

"Did you bring them with you?"

I turned and saw a white car about a hundred yards away, sitting on the side of the road and facing our direction. I could tell immediately that it was Tarver's white Fairlane. As I hurriedly ran to my car, the Fairlane made a quick u-turn and drove away, scattering gravel as it went. By the time I got to the place where it had been sitting, it was out of sight.

When I got back to Gip's house, Judy had joined him on the porch. She held a cup of coffee out to me as I walked up. "Hi, Detective Bryant, it's so good to see you again. Was that someone you know?"

"Unfortunately it was," I answered her. "Gip, that was the ASPCA guy we were talking about. I guess he followed me here. I'm sorry."

I explained to Gip about my encounter with Tarver at the meeting and later in the shopping center parking garage. "I had told the officers in the meeting that I had been to some of these dog shows and that a source had gotten me in. Tarver demanded that I tell him who my source was and where the shows had taken place. My guess is that he was hoping I would lead him to my source or to one of the shows. With all these dogs in your yard, I'm sure he's figured out who you are. Before you go anywhere, Gip, I would make sure he's not watching. I'll see what I can do to get him off of our tails."

"Well, so far, I haven't heard anything from Otto Sack. So that's good. Maybe he didn't see you the other day. Like I told you, I'm doing this to help Lynne. I knew I was taking a risk when I let you come along. I know you'll do the right thing, Detective Bryant. I know that Lynne trusts you, so you must be a good man."

As I drove away, I thought of Gip's remark that I must be a good man. I had managed to lie to and betray everyone around me over the past few weeks. How could anyone think I was a good man?

Later that afternoon, I was catching up on my case notes when Barbie called on the intercom, "Marc, there's a guy on line two. He's the guy who has called you before and won't give me his name. He said that it's urgent."

As I answered, Gip Tuttle immediately began to speak. He sounded panicked. "Detective, Ran Donovan just left. I'm afraid he might come back. He had his toadies with him, Sack and that big dumb brother-in-law. They were asking me about the newspaper story and if I knew where you had gotten your information. Anyway, while Donovan was talking, Willard Green came in and said that the police were watching my house. I went to the window with Donovan and saw that white Ford that the animal cop was driving. It was parked in the same place as before. Donovan asked me if I knew who it was and I said I didn't. They climbed into their car and started driving toward the white Ford. I figured I'd better let you know so you can get over here."

"Go look out of the window and tell me what you see," I quickly told Gip. He was gone a few seconds and came back out of breath. "They're gone. Everyone is gone. The white Ford ain't there anymore, and I don't see the car that Donovan was in, either."

"Did Sack say anything about seeing me at that show?"

"No, he never mentioned the show" Gip answered. "But he kept staring hard at me, like he was trying to see if I was lying or something."

"Okay, Gip, I'm on my way. What was Donovan driving?"

"It was a dark blue Mercury; a new one. It had a license place from another state, but I couldn't tell which one."

"Keep watch for me. I'm going to drive by. If I seen Donovan's car, I won't slow down, but when you see me, get in your car and drive to that motel parking lot where I left my car before. I'll be waiting on you there."

I drove quickly to Gip's place, occasionally turning on the red lights in my grill to clear traffic ahead of me. I was relieved to see that the blue Mercury wasn't there. I passed by and then drove to the motel on the highway. In a few minutes, Gip drove up.

I showed him a chart from my briefcase that had color photos of all the license plates in the country. He picked out the Mississippi license plate right away. "I didn't get the number, but I think the letter on it was an "A," he said.

"I'm going to let the FBI know that Donovan was spotted with Sack and Willard Green and give them the information about the car and license plate. I'll try to keep your identity a secret so that you won't have them over here asking questions, but I really have to let them know. They want Donovan in the worst way."

"Whatever you think, Detective Bryant. He really didn't seem like he was mad about anything and was asking about a dog he was interesting in buying. He thought that I knew about the blood-line. We were just talking about that news story when Willard Green came in and told him about that white car. I don't think he was there to hurt me, but you never know about him. He's like a rattlesnake that doesn't rattle first."

As I started my car, Gip added; "Oh, I almost forgot. Donovan asked me if I had heard from Lynne and if I knew where she was now. I told him that I thought she was back in Ohio. He didn't ask anything else about her."

When we left the motel parking lot, I drove back to the place where I had seen Tarver's Fairlane that morning. There were pieces of glass on the side of the road. It was car window glass. I got out and examined the pieces and saw three or four dark spots on the gravel among the broken glass. I stooped down and pressed my finger into one of them. When I pulled my finger back and looked at it, I saw that it was unmistakably blood. I was pretty sure whose blood it was, too. Tarver's remarks in the newspaper were prophecy. A less aggressive breed had just been thrown in with three highly aggressive pit bulls. I picked up as much of the glass as I could find and put it in one of the paper evidence bags that I kept in my car. Carefully, I scooped up some of the blood-splattered gravel and bag it up, as well. I then drove back to my office to call Agent Griggs and fill him in on the latest developments.

Griggs told me that the information about the Mississippi license plate tracked with some recent information that he had received. A source had told the FBI that Donovan had been recently spotted in Gulfport, Mississippi. That part of Mississippi was a well-recognized enclave for the Dixie Mafia. He would be right at home there. Griggs thanked me for the update and said that once all of this was over, he would like to talk to my source of information. For the time being, he was going to stay clear so it wouldn't put him or my investigation in jeopardy.

My next call was to Johnny Flynn. I told Flynn that I had a bad feeling about Clayton Tarver. He said that he would get Tarver's license plate number from the state and then have his people in the field keep an eye out for the white Fairlane. He asked me to keep the evidence I had collected on the side of the road in case things turn out bad for Tarver. For the time being, there wasn't much else I could do.

I drove to Lynne's apartment to let her know that Donovan was in town and asking about her. I told her to be particularly cautious. That was how I justified the visit in my own mind, anyway. The truth was I just wanted to be with her. She was the only person in my life whom I hadn't disappointed lately, at least, so far, anyway.

CHAPTER 15

The following week started out like most others at Creekwood PD. An armed robbery of a convenience store in town had all the area merchants on edge and I was working with other departments to see if the description that I had gotten from my victim matched any that had occurred in other cities around me. I was hoping that someone had a lead or a suspect that might help me jump-start my investigation. I had just come in on Tuesday morning and was headed to my office with cup of coffee when I ran into Barbie Morris in the hall.

"Marc, I was just coming to find you. I thought I saw you drive in. Deputy Johnny Flynn is on the phone and said he needed to talk to you right away."

I sat down at my desk and punched the blinking light on the telephone. "Johnny, what's up this morning?"

"We found Clayton Tarver. He's dead. Here's the weird thing, though. It looks like he was chewed up by wild animals…like a bear attack or something."

"You mean it could have been an accidental death?"

"Well, not unless after he was attacked, he wrapped himself up in three plastic drop-cloths and rolled himself into a ditch over in the east side of the county."

"I was afraid that his encounter with Donovan wasn't going to end well. You got any leads at all?"

"The body's over at the medical examiner's office. Our ID people are all over that ditch. Would you meet me at the ME's office and have a look at the body? Maybe see if you can come up with any ideas?"

"Sure. If you're ready, I can leave now" I told him.

"Great, Marc, thanks! I'll see you there."

I always hoped that each trip to the autopsy room at the medical examiner's office would be my last, knowing however that as long as this was my profession, there would be many more. As I stepped off of the elevator on the basement floor, I saw Field Agent Tony Simms walking toward his office with a cup of coffee.

"Hey Tony" I called to him. "Have you seen Johnny Flynn from the sheriff's department this morning?"

"He's in there with Doctor Pittman right now. Boy, what a strange case. That guy looks like he was killed by a werewolf or something. Go ahead on in. Flynn told me to look for you."

As I approached the autopsy table, I could see Doctor Pittman pointing something out to Johnny Flynn. On the table before them was the brutally torn and savaged body of Clayton Tarver. I walked up just as Pittman was telling Flynn that the damage appeared to be from a canine, probably two or more dogs or wolves. "And" Doctor Pittman continued; "since there hasn't been a confirmed wolf sighting in Dallas County since the 19th century, my money's on a dog attack." As they talked, I noticed that Tarver's hands were covered in clear plastic bags. Hopefully there was evidence under his fingernails and that it had been properly preserved.

Johnny turned to me and said, "Well, you don't have to be Alfred Hitchcock to know where this plot is headed, do you? We really are now going to have to talk with your source. He's the only lead we've got that can connect Tarver here with Donovan and his cronies"

"Sure, Johnny, I'll set it up with him. It will be in his best interests to get them off the street, anyway. Hopefully, he'll see it that way.

"Oh, by the way, Marc, do you have that glass and the blood evidence that you picked up on the road last week? Doctor Pittman said that they found a few pieces of car window glass in Tarver's clothes."

"It's still in my briefcase out in the parking lot. I'll go get it and bring it in to you. Anything else on the body that might give you a lead?"

"Yea," Johnny replied. "We checked his hands, and he has what looks like wood and blood under his fingernails. We bagged his hands to preserve it. Also, he had sand on his clothes. It looks like when he was attacked, he was in sand. It's all matted in his blood."

Being in that hated autopsy room had me so distracted that it kept my brain synapses from firing like they should, but something at the back of my mind

168

kept telling me that the sand and wood was important. I pushed the thought aside as I went to my car and retrieved the bags of evidence. When I passed them to Johnny Flynn, I told him to call me when he learned anything further. I took a deep breath of fresh air when I got back to the parking lot.

It was just after I had arrived back to my office and had a chance to think about the situation with Tarver that my brain cells finally began to percolate. Wood and blood! I suddenly thought about the wood-walled pit in Maurice Cox's barn. He had told me that Ran Donovan used the barn occasionally for private fights. There was sand on the floor of the pit. I called the sheriff's department dispatcher and asked him to have Johnny Flynn call me as soon as they could get in touch with him. It wasn't long before he called.

"Johnny, do you remember me telling you about Maurice Cox's barn with the cockfighting pit? He told me that Ran Donovan used the pit sometimes for private fights. The walls are wood and there is sand on the floor. You think that might be the scene of your crime?"

"I'd be willing to bet a year's salary on it, Marc. Good job! Hey, can you meet us there? First, I've got to write up a search warrant and find a judge who would be willing to sign off on it. Then, I need to gather up my identification guys and, last, I need to stop by and tell your dad what a brilliant cop his son has turned out to be." A compliment like that from the famous Johnny Flynn was as good a praise as I could ever expect in this life. "Give me a couple of hours and I'll be there" he finished.

"See you there."

I arrived at Cox's place ahead of everyone else and waited in my car. In a few minutes, several cars arrived, a couple carrying uniformed deputies. As Flynn climbed out of his car, he waved me over. "I just got another piece of the puzzle that, for sure, makes this place the scene of the crime. One of our patrol officers found Tarver's white Ford in a parking lot less than a mile from here. He's sitting on it until we finish up here."

The uniformed deputies went to the front and back doors of Cox's house and forced them open. The rest of us went back to the barn. The padlock that was unlocked during my last visit was now locked and in place. One of the deputies went back to his car and returned with a pair of bolt cutters. With a snap, the lock sprang away from the hasp. A deputy picked it up with a gloved hand and put it in an evidence bag. Then, we carefully opened one side of the double doors and peered inside. The barn seemed to be exactly like it had been when I was here before. This time, however, there was a different odor in the air. It was strong and hinted of blood and excrement. The sandy floor of the pit was freshly disturbed and dark stains were evident on both the sand and the wooden sides of the pit. I stood back and allowed the identification technicians to enter. They immediately began taking photos, their flashes in the darkened barn causing the scene to freeze in my eyes and then slowly fade out.

One of the technicians held the beam of his flashlight over something on the floor of the pit and called Flynn over to have a look. When he came back to where I was standing, I asked him what he had seen.

"Looks like hunk of flesh and a human tooth. Your hunch was right on, Marc. I need to get with that FBI agent, Griggs, and kick this search for Ran Donovan up a notch. I hope your source will cooperate with us."

"I'll talk to him, Johnny. He's scared of Ran Donovan; and, from the looks of things, he has a right to be."

I returned to the station and went straight to my phone. I dialed Gip's number and told him about the discovery of Clayton Tarver's body. I told him that his testimony was essential and connecting Donovan with Tarver. My conversation didn't go as well as I had hoped, but went about as well as I had expected. Gip Tuttle was one of those types who, when they get scared, they get belligerent. He was both right now.

"If anyone sets foot on my property, 'poe-leese' or not, I'm turning my dogs loose on 'um. I gotta twelve-gauge that's loaded with double-aught. What the dogs don't get, I will." I let this flash of anger run its course and waited until he wound down.

"Gip, listen to me. They aren't coming to your place. You can just drive away from your house and meet me somewhere. I'll take you to the deputy. All you have to do is give them a statement about what happened when Donovan saw Tarver's car. It's a murder rap for all three of those cockroaches. You won't have to worry about them after that." I knew that there would be a lot more than that to it, and I hoped Gip hadn't thought that far ahead.

"Ah, hell! Let me know where you want to meet. Damn, I wish I never got myself involved in this shit."

"I'll let you know as soon as I talk to the deputy and find out when and where." Gip made no reply as he hung up the phone.

I called and left a message with Flynn's dispatcher to have him call me as soon as he could. The dispatcher said that he was still out at Cox's barn. It wasn't until later in the afternoon before Flynn called me back. He sounded harried and out of breath.

"Marc, things are really starting to jump. I just found out that one of our uniformed deputies stopped Otto Sack and Willard Green in Sack's car last night around eleven just off of Dowdy Ferry Road. The deputy said that they were driving in the dark with their lights off. Sack said that he had forgotten to turn them on. The deputy said that they were both sweating bullets. He looked around inside their car and didn't see anything suspicious. He had nothing to hold them for and had to let them go. He filled out a field interview form because they acted so suspicious. Turns out, they were around a mile from where Tarver's body was found. Hell, he may have even been in their trunk when the deputy stopped them. I just ran this all by the DA's office and they said I had enough to get warrants for Sack and Green. I tried to talk them into giving me one for Donovan. The assistant DA said that I didn't have enough probable cause to arrest Donovan. Somehow, that doesn't surprise me. Anyway, I sure hope your guy comes through for us. He's the key to getting Donovan."

"I talked to him, Johnny. He's not real happy about it, but he did agree. Just tell me when and where to bring him and I'll get it done."

"First, we need to go ahead and get Sack and Green out of the way" Flynn replied. "In fact, we're getting a team together to go out now and get them. We'll wait until you get here if you want to come along. We might find something that will tie them to your murders."

"Okay, Johnny. I'm on the way." Finally, things were beginning to move on the Littleton-Ryan case. I reached for the phone to call Lynne and let her know what was happening. Then, I thought about that organized crime investigator with the DA's office and decided not to trust the phones. I'd go to her place once everything was over. I filled Captain Copeland in on what had transpired so far and that I was on my way to meet Flynn. On my way out, I stopped at Al's office to tell him what was going on and see if he wanted to go with me. His light was off and his office was empty.

Once I arrived at the sheriff's department, I fell in behind a long caravan of cars, including plain and marked Sheriff's Patrol units. We move quickly out Highway 77 into the southern part of Dallas County. Eventually, the parade of cars turned on to a gravel topped road and finally to a white frame house that sat on a couple of acres of fenced land. Immediately, I recognized several small shelters in the front that housed pit bull dogs. Three or four were chained to stakes in front of these shelters. There were two cars parked in front. Neither was the blue Mercury with the Mississippi license plate.

Uniformed deputies deployed both in front and behind the house, taking care to stay out of reach of the dogs. As the deputies in back waved to the men in front, Johnny Flynn stepped from his car and called out to Sack and Green.

"Otto…Willard, this is Deputy Johnny Flynn. We have warrants for your arrest. Step out on the front porch with your hands where we can see them. You've got one minute before we come in after you." I stood at Johnny's side, my pistol in my hand.

Suddenly, the front door flew open and everyone raised their guns and aimed them at the front porch. Sack's wife, Ethelene, ran from the front door, her hands raised high above her head. She was screaming, "Don't shoot me, don't shoot me!" as she ran.

"Come toward me, ma'am" Flynn called to her from behind his car. "Just keep moving toward me. We won't hurt you."

Ethelene Sack was shaking and crying as she reached out and grabbed Johnny's arm. "Don't kill them, please! They'll give up. They're just scared" she sobbed.

"Who all is in there?" Johnny asked.

"My husband, Otto and my brother, Willard Green. That's all."

"How about Ran Donovan, Mrs. Sack. Is he in there?"

"No, I swear. It's just Otto and Willard. I promise. I haven't seen Donovan."

Flynn then turned his attention back to the house. "Okay, your time is up. We're fixing to bring this place down around your ears. You'd better get your asses out on the front porch pronto."

The front door opened and a pair of hands emerged. "Don't shoot." It was Otto Sack. He stepped out on the porch, holding hands high above his head. "Don't shoot me. I ain't done nothin."

"Okay, Otto, keep your hands above your head and walk straight toward my car," Johnny told him. As Otto started to step down from the porch, his hands still raised high above his head, he called out to Flynn, "I'll make a deal with you, Deputy Flynn. It was…" The explosion behind him propelled Otto off of the porch and on to the sidewalk below. He fell hard, face down, a large shot pattern showing on his back. Suddenly, two of the deputies fired shots into the front of the house.

"Cease fire, cease fire!" Flynn yelled. "Willard, you dumb son-of-a-bitch, toss that shotgun out and then come out behind it with your hands raised."

"Fuck you, you fuckers!." Good ol' Willard. He could always be depended on to turn a clever phrase. Another shot was fired inside the house, but since we were all crouched behind our cars, I couldn't tell which direction it went.

Flynn restrained Ethelene, holding her down behind the car as she tried to run to Otto, who was now bleeding profusely on the sidewalk. From where I was, crouched behind my car, I could see that Otto's color was fast draining from his face. The bleeding was slowing down, as well. He was dying.

"Please go get him," Ethelene pleaded with Flynn. "You can save him. Please!"

"I can't risk it, Mrs. Sack" Johnny said. I could hear the anguish in his voice. "Other than that shotgun, are there any other guns in the house?"

"There are some pistols and a twenty-two rifle!" Ethelene cried. She then rose up and shouted, "Willard, let these men save Otto. Please! He's dying. Please don't shoot. Let them come and get him." There was only silence from inside the house.

Suddenly, one of the sheriff's patrol cars started moving forward into the yard and toward the porch. I could barely see the top of the deputy's head as he guided the car. As he pulled up beside Otto, the front door opened and the deputy reached out and grabbed Sack by his arm and dragged him into the front seat of the car, using the open door to screen him from the porch. With Otto still hanging slightly out of the car, the deputy backed up and turned the car to the side, using it as a barricade. I rushed over as he pulled Sack out and on to the gravel road in front. It was a brave thing to do, but useless. Otto was obviously dead.

Flynn called over to a uniformed lieutenant who was squatted behind his car, "Get on the radio and get Dallas SWAT out here. We're going to have to do a forced entry. They've got the equipment. Get an ambulance started, as well."

The deputy loaded Otto's body into the back seat of the car. Ethelene climbed in with Otto. The deputy then started down the road, no doubt to meet the ambulance when it arrived. Then, we waited. Flynn would call out to Willard Green every few minutes, telling him to come out with his hands up. Still nothing from inside. We continued to wait.

After what seemed like hours, the Dallas Police SWAT van arrived. The officers were dressed in military style camo with black vests and helmets. They took positions around the edge of the property with rifles aimed at the house. Flynn and the SWAT supervisor had a quick conference. Then, one of the SWAT officers removed a short barreled gun from the van. I recognized it immediately as a grenade launcher, what we called in Vietnam a "thumper" because of the sound it made when it was fired. It was now being used to propel teargas cartridges. From behind one of the cars, the officer began firing teargas rounds through the windows of the house. In a few seconds, the white smoke began to pour from the broken windows and fill the yard around the house. Even from where I was still crouched behind my car, I could already feel the effects in my eyes and nose.

Almost at the instant that the smoke began to pour out, several of the SWAT officers, now wearing gas-masks, began storming through the front door. I could hear them also hitting the back door. There was shouting coming from inside and through the thick, acrid smoke. After a few minutes, one of the SWAT officers came to the porch and drew his finger across his neck in the classic cut-throat gesture. I took it to mean that Willard Green was dead.

We allowed the teargas to dissipate and then walked to the porch. The SWAT supervisor told Flynn that they had found Green's body lying on the floor of a bedroom. He had apparently put the barrel of the shotgun into his mouth and pulled the trigger. As Flynn and several other deputies went inside, I decided to just return to my car and wait. I had seen enough carnage for one day. All of this was for nothing because Ran Donovan was still out there, somewhere, and was still a lethal threat.

It was getting late in the evening as we finally finished searching through the house. The guns were all bagged up as evidence. I asked Johnny Flynn to put a hold on a sawed-off .410 shotgun that was lying on a kitchen counter. I didn't see how it could be tied directly to the shooting of Rick Littleton, but I would see if the ballistics examiner Dan James could do something with it. We did not locate a .38 revolver, as I had hoped.

I was tired and my clothes reeked of teargas. I wanted to take a shower and drink enough bourbon to put me to sleep. I also didn't feel like being alone. I promised Johnny Flynn that I would meet with him the next day and help him put this all together. I then started my drive to Richardson and to Lynne's apartment. I knew it was late, but I didn't feel like going home to an empty house.

I parked my car next to Lynne's yellow Volkswagen in the parking lot and got out. It was a cool, still night. The fresh air felt good. I saw that most of the windows in the apartment complex were dark. I hoped that I wouldn't scare Lynne by showing up this late. As I approached her apartment, I could hear a slight sound that I had never noticed before. It was familiar, but I just couldn't place it. As I got closer I realized that I was hearing the bell on the photo-eye alarm system that I had put in Lynne's apartment. I pulled my pistol from its holster and rushed to her door. It was slightly ajar and I cautiously pushed it open. The apartment was dark. All I could hear was the loud ringing of the bell. I started toward her bedroom, my pistol out in front of me. As I got to her bedroom door, I called out to her.

"Marc, look out, he's got a gun!" I could barely make out the form of Lynne as she was backed into a corner of the bedroom, next to the patio door. I could see the form of a man in the center of the bedroom. His back was to me.

"Drop the gun, Donovan. Throw it down or I'll kill you."

As the man turned toward me, I saw an expression on his face that seemed more questioning than resolute; almost as if he was confused. I could clearly see that he was holding a small automatic pistol and that pistol was swinging around toward me. It was clear that he didn't intend to drop it. I felt the recoil jerk my hand back and upward as I fired a shot into the man. He dropped like a puppet that suddenly had its strings cut. I held my gun on him as I approached and kicked the automatic out of his hand. As my ears began to clear from the loud explosion of my shot, I became aware of the ringing bell and Lynne shouting from across the room.

"It's not him, Marc!. It's not him!"

"What?" I asked, trying to grasp what had just happened.

"It's not Donovan, Marc. It's not him."

I got on my knees and rolled the man over on his back and felt for a pulse in his neck. "Who is he, Lynne?"

"I don't know, Marc." She was beginning to cry. "He kept asking me about Ivan Delacroix. He kept saying that he wanted me to come to New Orleans and help him get his money back. He was going to make me go with him. He had a gun. He was, like, crazy or something."

I could tell that his pulse was light and rapid. He was trying to speak, but I couldn't understand what he was saying. I leaned into his face and finally understood one word "Rabalais." I carefully slipped his wallet out of his coat pocket and opened it. I could see a Louisiana driver's license with the name "Benjamin Rabalais." Outside, I could hear sirens approaching. I stood up and walked back into the living room. I could see that a crowd had formed outside, anxiously trying to see through the opened front door.

"Would someone call an ambulance, please?" I asked. Someone shouted back to me that they had already called the police. At that same time, I saw a Richardson Police patrol car stop in the street next to the parking lot. The officer ran toward the crowd, the beam from his flashlight bouncing on the ground as we went. He cautiously approached the door, one hand on his side-arm and the other holding the flashlight away from his body. The beam was directed at me. The crowd parted to let him by. I held my badge out in front of me. He hesitated for a second and then approached the door.

"Are you okay?" he asked as he squinted to examine my badge.

"Yea, I'm okay, I guess. There is a guy lying on the bedroom floor in there that isn't doing okay, though. He's going to need medical attention right away."

The officer's eyes left my badge and he then focused on my face. "What happened to him?" he asked.

"I shot him."

The officer's eyes, now wide with excitement, dropped to the pistol that was still in my hand. "Hey, no offense, detective who-ever-you-are, but would you please lay that gun down on the coffee table?" As I place the pistol on the table, two other officers arrived. One stayed with me while the other two went into the bedroom. I heard one of them say, "Excuse me, ma'am" as Lynne came into the living room, wrapping herself in her robe.

The first officer then came back into the living room and said; "This guy is going to need paramedics like…fast."

"Ambulance is pulling up now" a newly arrived officer said as he came through the front door. He turned to the crowd in front and said; "I'm going to need everyone to get back and let the paramedics through." As he turned back to the room, I could see that he was a lieutenant, probably the beat supervisor. "Sir" he said as he walked toward me, "would you and the lady please go sit down at that dining table and not talk to each other until the detectives get here? I'd appreciate it."

In just a few seconds, the paramedics had Benny Rabalais loaded on a gurney and were rolling him through the living room. His color was the same as Otto Sack's had been just a few hours before. Lynne and I sat in silence. She faced me, her eyes pleading as if she was silently asking for help. I gave her a quick smile and then rolled my eyes and shrugged as if to say, "Oh well, what can you do?"

As I heard the ambulance start its run to the hospital, a tired looking man in a shirt and slacks came through the front door. I recognized the all-too familiar look of a detective who has been rousted out of his bed and into the middle of a frantic crime scene. He came over, pulled out one of Lynne's dining chairs and sat down hard, expelling a deep sigh.

"I recognize you," he said as he turned toward me. I've seen you around for a couple of years. You're a detective at Creekwood PD, right? I'm Detective Harold Alvarez." He then leaned forward, pulled a small spiral notebook from his back pocket and flopped it down on the table. With a flourish, he pulled a ballpoint pen from his shirt pocket and then said, "Go ahead. I'm all ears."

I repeated the same story that I had given Agent Jim Griggs and everyone else about how Lynne had overheard a conversation between Ran Donovan and her husband that mentioned a murder and the name Ivan Delacroix. I explained that Lynne was a protected witness and widow of one of the two victims whose murders I was investigating. When I mentioned Randall Donovan, Alvarez whistled between his teeth. "Ran Donovan! Damn, I thought that old gangster was dead. Maybe it was just wishful thinking. Anyway, go on."

I told him about the deaths of Otto Sack and Willard Green earlier, and that since I had expected to find Donovan with them and he wasn't, I decided to stop and check on Lynne before I went home. "I honestly thought it was Donovan when I came into the room. He turned toward me with that automatic and wouldn't drop it when I told him to. So, I shot him."

Alvarez stared off for a few seconds, then turned back to me and said; "Sounds reasonable to me. Do you need to notify your supervisor in Creekwood?"

"Yea, I'd better call and see what my chief is going to want to do." I picked up Lynne's phone and called the chief's home number. When he answered, he sounded like bear coming out of hibernation.

I started through the long explanation, being periodically interrupted by Chief Rogers exclaiming, "Oh, shit!" When I finished, there was silence. I was beginning to think that the line had gone dead before he finally asked, "So you were at Lynne Littleton's apartment? Wait a minute. Never mind. We'll get into that later. Is there an investigator there with Richardson?" I handed Alvarez the telephone receiver.

After a brief conversation Alvarez ended by telling Chief Rogers, "I think I have all I need right now. I don't see any reason to have Detective Bryant and Miss Littleton to come to my office tonight. What do you say if we all meet at your office tomorrow morning?" He then handed the receiver back to me.

"Marc, go home right now" the chief ordered. "Stay home until you hear from me. You might ask the Richardson officers to keep an eye on Lynne Littleton's apartment for a while, but you need to stay away from there. Am I making myself clear to you?"

"Yes sir! I'm on my way home now." As I hung up the phone, the apartment manager pushed through the officers and walked into the apartment saying, "I'm the property manager, I'm the property manager." She then ran to Lynne and hugged her.

"Oh honey, the officer told me what happened. Did someone try to rape you? Are you okay?" Then she turned to me, "Did you shoot the son-of-bitch? I'm so glad she's okay." She then turned hear head toward the bedroom door and asked in a panic, "Is there blood on the carpet in there?"

Lynne explained to the manager that she didn't want to spend the night in the apartment. At first the manager offered to have Lynne stay with her. They finally decided that Lynne would to go an unoccupied apartment in the complex until they could decide what to do. She helped Lynne gather up some sheets and pillows. As she walked toward the front door, she turned to me, her blue eyes flooding over with tears. I stepped forward and hugged her.

"Everything's going to be okay, Lynne. I'll be back once we get things sorted out tomorrow. The Richardson officers will be close. Call me if you need anything. I'll see you later." She pulled her head back and looked into my eyes. She held her gaze for a few seconds, then turned and walked out with the manager. I walked back to my car and drove home.

When I got home, I stumbled into the shower and turned on the hot water. I began thinking back on the events of the past weeks. I thought about all the destruction that Ran Donovan had left in his wake, all the deaths that had followed him, starting with Rick Littleton and Terry Don Ryan. Then there was Maurice Cox and Clayton Tarver. Tonight it was Otto Sack and Willard Green. Then, there was Benny Rabalais, possibly dead by my own hands. As I stared at the tile wall and recounted everything that has transpired in my life, the water began to turn cool. I realized that I had stood in the shower so long that I had run out all the hot water in the heater. I crawled into my bed and closed my eyes, not realizing that this tragic drama had not yet ended.

CHAPTER 16

"Come over here, Detective Bryant. Let me show you something interesting." It was Dan James, standing over a ghostly pale body on a metal table in the autopsy room. With one hand, Dan was motioning me over to him. With the other, he was pointing out a large bullet wound on the chest of the man who was lying there. Blood was pouring out of the wound like an open faucet. From a distance I could see that the man was Benny Rabalais. As I came closer, the body began to morph into Lynne Littleton; then, the flesh started to fall away and it became the torn body of Clayton Tarver. "We might get lucky here. The bullet may still be in the body," Dan said, a huge unnatural grin spreading across his face. I bolted awake to the sound of someone screaming. I realized after a few heart-pounding seconds that it was me. Sweat had soaked through my pillow. As I tried to pull myself out of this deep sleep, I became aware that the phone had been ringing the entire time.

"Marc, this is Captain Copeland. The chief wanted me to tell you that the Richardson officers have pushed back the meeting this morning to three this afternoon. He wanted you to stay home and be near the phone. He will call you when he wants you to come in. Okay?"

"Yea, sure, Cap. I've got no place to go."

"Are you doing okay, Marc? Do you need anything or do you want me to come over and wait with you?"

"No, thanks! As a matter of fact, I think I would like to just be alone for a while. I'll be ready when the chief calls."

I stood at the kitchen window and stared at the back yard while the coffee pot steamed and bumped. I poured a cup before the pot had quit its rumbling and watched as coffee grounds rose to the top of my cup. I dipped out as many of them as I could with a paper towel and went outside to sit at the patio table. The morning was crisp and fresh. I looked across at the playhouse where I had spent so many days watching my daughters serving make-believe tea and cleaning house with a small broom, practicing at being grown up. "It's all a lie," I wanted to tell them. "Don't do it. Stay where you are. Being grown up is no fun." Again, the telephone intruded into my thoughts.

"Marc, I heard about the shooting this morning when I got to the office." It was my father. "Are you okay?"

"Yea, dad, I'm fine. There's a meeting this afternoon with my chief and the investigating officers from Richardson. I wish it hadn't happened, but it could have easily gone the other way. I did what I was trained to do."

"Do you feel like you need a lawyer to represent you at this meeting today? If you do, I'll arrange to have someone there."

No, dad, I don't need one. It was a clean shooting. There shouldn't be any question about it. If I think I do later, I'll let you know."

After I got the usual father pep-talk about how he and my mother were behind me all the way and would be there if I needed them, he hung up. I had no sooner put the receiver down when the phone rang again. This time it was Kay.

"Marc, have you seen the news this morning on Channel Five? They say that you shot a man who was assaulting a woman in an apartment in Richardson. Are you okay? Thank God you answered the phone. I called the station and Barbie told me you were at home."

"I wasn't hurt, Kay. I'm fine. I wish it hadn't happened, but there was just nothing else I could do. I'm glad you called. I miss you."

"Marc, was the lady in the news story Lynne Littleton? Were you at her apartment? Was the man you shot Randall Donovan?"

"Look, Kay, first of all, the man I shot was not Donovan. Yes, the lady was Lynne Littleton and, yes, I was at her apartment. I had stopped by last night because there had been a shooting earlier involving two of Donovan's guys. I was worried...look, it would be so much easier to explain all of this in person. Can you come over here or can I come there. I miss you."

"Marc, that's not a good idea now. I didn't want to talk about this now but I've met with an attorney. He suggested that I not see you until I decide if I want to go ahead with a divorce. I still can't decide what I want to do."

"I love you, Kay!"

"I love you too, Marc. That's the hard part." She hung up.

CAJUN RULES

I poured another cup of coffee and turned on the television. I found a local news program and waited to see if they would report the shooting in Richardson. In a few minutes, the commentator said, "There was a shooting overnight in Richardson. Our sources on the ground reported that a man, armed with a pistol, broke into the apartment of a single woman on the south side of town. Shortly after the break-in, a Creekwood Police detective came on the scene and shot the man. Evidently, the police detective and the woman victim are acquainted, but the nature of that acquaintance is unclear at this time. The name of the man who was shot has not been released by Richardson Police, but they have confirmed that he later died at a local hospital. Just in the past hour, we have learned that the Creekwood detective, who was identified as Officer Marc Bryant, had been involved in an earlier shooting incident in east Dallas County that resulted in two deaths. Details about that shooting have not been released by the Dallas County Sheriff's Department. We have also been unable to determine if the two incidents involving Detective Bryant are connected. When we know more, we'll pass it along to you." The commentator finished with a glib smile.

The newsman had confirmed what I had feared was already true. Benny Rabalais was dead. I went to the phone and called Lynne's number. Things were out in the open now and calling her from my phone didn't seem like much of a threat. I let the phone ring several times before I convinced myself that I had dialed it wrong. I hung up and tried again. Still no answer.

I then called the apartment complex and got the manager on the phone. "No, Detective, I haven't seen Lynne yet this morning, which is odd. I let her stay in one of the empty apartments last night and thought I would have heard from her before now. She probably just slept in. She had a horrible experience…well, both of you did. As soon as I see her, I'll have her call you. Give me your number."

As the morning passed into afternoon, I had called Lynne's number repeatedly with the same results. She did not answer. I was becoming more and more concerned about her. Again, I called the manager.

"I just went to check and she is not in that apartment. Her own apartment door is locked and she didn't answer when I knocked. I then looked out at the

183

parking lot and her car is gone. All I can think is that she has gone out somewhere. When she comes back, I'll tell her that you are worried about her."

Just before three, the phone rang. I lunged at it, hoping to hear Lynne's voice on the line. It was Captain Copeland. "Marc, the chief wants you to come on in and go directly to his office. They are waiting on you."

"I'm on my way, Captain" I answered. Before I walked out, I tried Lynne's number one more time. There was still no answer.

As I walked through the back door of the station, I was met by Captain Copeland. He faced me and put his hand on my shoulder. "Are you okay, Marc? It ain't easy to take a life, even though you were right in doing it." He stood and looked into my face as if he wanted to say more. He finally turned and led the way to Chief Roger's office. The door was closed. Copeland knocked twice and then opened the door. Chief Rogers was at his desk. Seated in front of him was Richardson detective, Harold Alvarez. Sitting next to Alvarez was a man I recognized as one of the Texas Rangers that I have seen over the years. Both men stood up as I walked in.

"Marc, you know Detective Alvarez," Chief Rogers said. "This is Ranger Tad Arnold. I'll let Detective Alvarez explain why he's part of this." After I shook hands with Alvarez and Ranger Arnold, everyone sat down. Captain Copeland closed the door and sat in a chair next to it.

"Detective Bryant," Alvarez started out; "the reason we pushed this meeting back a few hours was because something has come up that I needed to explore a little more carefully before I talked to you. As a matter of fact, we were going to stop by and have Mrs. Littleton join us. Seems that the lady has vanished."

"Are you sure she hasn't just gone out for a while and is coming back?" I asked as sick feeling started to creep into my stomach.

"No, I don't think so. Evidently, sometime during the night, she packed up some of her clothes and a few other items from her apartment. Our patrol officers were keeping a watch on the complex but it was a busy night. The officer in that district told me that he checked by a few times but didn't see her. To me, it looks like she doesn't intend to come back. Can't say I blame

184

her, though. Randall Donovan is a nasty character. If I thought he was after me, I'd keep moving too."

"We really don't have any reason to go after her," the Ranger interrupted. "She hasn't broken any laws. In fact, she's the victim here. I would like to know more about her relationship with Benjamin Rabalais, but I think you can give us all we need on that subject. As I understand it, she told Detective Alvarez here that she didn't even know the man. Strange how he just showed up at her apartment."

"She didn't know him" I explained. I related once again the story I had told so many times; the lie I had told so many times. "All she knew was that she had overheard a conversation between Ran Donovan and her husband, Rick Littleton where Ivan Delacroix's name was mentioned, along with talk about a murder."

"Did you tell Lynne Littleton about Rabalais? Did you tell her that he had been calling you, wanting to know who your source was?" The Ranger sat forward in his chair, leaning toward me as he spoke. His gray eyes never blinked as he stared into my face.

"I don't think I ever told her his name. I did tell her that I had given her information to FBI Agent Jim Griggs and that he had passed it along to the FBI office in New Orleans. I told her that the New Orleans agents didn't seem all that interested. Someone there must have tipped Rabalais off."

"Then, how did he know that your source was Lynne Littleton?" he asked, sitting back in his chair.

"I have no idea" I replied, looking from the Ranger to Chief Rogers. As I spoke, Alvarez reached into his notebook and removed a clear plastic sheet protector with a piece of a page from a yellow pad pressed down inside. He handed it to Ranger Arnold. The Ranger held it up so that I could see it. I immediately recognized it as the note I had given to Al with Lynne's address on it.

"This was in Rabalais' coat pocket. Obviously, it's Mrs. Littleton's address. The address you were at last night when you shot Rabalais. Chief Rogers here tells me that he recognizes that as your handwriting. Any idea how that got into Rabalais' pocket?"

I was thunderstruck! My mind was swirling. I could feel my mouth opening and closing but I was unable to speak. I finally was able to say; "I gave that to Al West. I wanted him to know where Lynne was living in case something happened to me. How Rabalais came by it, I have no idea."

"Then, maybe that will explain what else we found in his pocket," the Ranger continued as Alvarez pulled another sheet protector form his notebook and handed it to the Ranger. When he held it up to me, I could see that it was an envelope with a return name and address printed in the upper left corner. The printing read; "Rabalais Bail Bonds. 615 Camp Street; New Orleans, LA." On the bottom of the envelope was a telephone number that had been written with a pen. I knew it as soon as I saw it.

"That's Al's home phone number" I said. Even after I had seen it, I still couldn't believe it. "Why would he have Al's number in his pocket?" I asked, knowing the answer even as I asked the question.

"Well, we were wondering the same thing Detective Bryant. Maybe we should ask Detective West to come in and see if he can shed some light on this." The Ranger then turned to Chief Rogers, who picked up his receiver and punched in a number. "Al, would you please come to my office. We need to talk to you."

Captain Copeland opened the chief's office door and waited for Al. In a few seconds, he walked in and looked around the room. When his eyes fell on me, I could see from his expression that he knew what was about to happen. He sat down, cross his legs and turned to Chief Rogers. "You wanted to see me?"

"Al, this is Detective Harold Alvarez from the Richardson Police Department."

"I know Harold," Al said as he turned and smiled at Alvarez.

"And," Chief Rogers continued, "this is Ranger Tad Arnold."

"Pleasure," Al replied coolly, reaching out and shaking hands with the Ranger.

"Detective West," the Ranger began, "do you know Benjamin Rabalais from New Orleans, or should I ask DID you know him since Detective Bryant here has put him in the past tense?"

Al looked the Ranger straight in the face and calmly said; "Yea, I knew Rabalais. I knew him back when I was a cop in Louisiana."

"Have you spoken to him lately, Detective? The Ranger then asked. The two men stared directly into each other's faces like they were trying to see which one would blink first.

"He called me at home one night about a week ago and said he was coming to Dallas and wanted to meet with me when he got here. He told me that he was out a half-million on a bond for a guy named Delacroix who didn't show up for a hearing. He said that someone at New Orleans PD told him that Marc had a source who could testify that this Delacroix was dead and couldn't come to court. He said he tried to get Marc to give him the source but Marc wouldn't return his calls. He asked me if I knew who it was. I told him that I did. Then, he called me early yesterday morning and said he was in town. He wanted me to meet him at a coffee shop on Mockingbird Lane over by the airport."

"Did you meet with him?" the Ranger asked.

"Yea, I did" Al answered back, never changing his expression. "I told him who the source was and gave him her address. Marc had written it on a piece of paper and gave it to me once. I gave it to Rabalais."

"Did Rabalais tell you what he intended to do? Did he tell you that he had a gun and was going to break in and assault Mrs. Littleton?" The Ranger was now shouting at Al. Al then turned away from Arnold and faced me; his flint-hard expression was now soft. Tears welled up in his eyes.

"Marc, I told you that I worked for a police department in Louisiana before I came here. It was in a little town between Baton Rouge and New Orleans. It was where my family had lived for years. There was a gambling joint at the edge of town that we were paid to protect. It was owned by the Maricones in New Orleans. We knew it. The police pay was lousy, but we made good money protecting that place. It was the only way we could make ends meet. You know what I mean?" All I could do was nod in agreement.

"One night some kid, the son of a state politician in Baton Rouge, grabbed one of the hostesses in the club and tried to get her to leave with him. Me and another officer threw him out. He waited in his car until the place closed and then tried again to grab the girl as she walked to her car in the parking lot. She

187

managed to break his hold, pulled a gun out of her bag and shot him. When his politician father found out, he had the State Police come down on the place hard. The other officer and I were arrested and charged with accepting bribes from the Maricone Family. The other officer knew Benny Rabalais and had him get us out of jail. Later on, Rabalais pulled some strings with the Maricones and the charges disappeared. I wasn't going to wait for something like that to happen to me again. I decided to move out of Louisiana and find a police job in another state. That's how I came to Creekwood PD."

"How did Rabalais know you were here?"

"Lots of those officers back there knew that I had gotten the job here at Creekwood. I figured that Rabalais must have mentioned his problem in Creekwood and it got back to someone who knew I was here. That's all I can think of. Rabalais didn't say how when I talked to him."

"Did he threaten you, Al?" I was hoping to salvage some goodness out of him.

"He said that he would leak it to the city leaders here that I was once connected with an organized crime family in New Orleans. I knew that just to have my name associated with the Maricones would get my job. Rabalais said that he was just going to talk to Lynne and get her to fly back to New Orleans with him. He said he would pay her expenses."

"Come on, Al! You knew why I was keeping Lynne's whereabouts a secret. You know what a threat Donovan is. Hell, people are dying all around that guy. You know how mobbed up Rabalais was. How long do think it will take for this go get back to Donovan? Now, Lynne Littleton is on the run out there by herself and there's no one around to help her." Alvarez and Arnold seemed content to let our little drama play itself out, neither saying a word.

"And that's partly why I did it too, Marc. You were throwing your life away on that woman. Hell, she was nothing but a gangster's wife. Your own wife and kids have already left you over this. I knew it was only going to be a matter of time before she got your job, as well. I kept trying to warn you, and you would just ignore me. Now, it's all blown up and she's gone. In a way, I'm glad I did it. I like you, Marc. You're probably my best friend. You have such a beautiful wife and family. I just hated to see you piss it all away over that damn hippy chick." Al seemed spent and fell back in his chair, looking at the floor.

After a long pause, Chief Rogers finally spoke up. "Gentlemen, do either of you anticipate filing any criminal charges here?" Detective Alvarez and Ranger Arnold both shook their heads. "Then I think these needs to be handled by me and my department."

"We agree, Chief," Arnold said as he got out of his chair. "Do you have anything to add, Harold?"

"No, nothing. Chief Rogers, if there is anything you need from me, let me know. Thanks for your help." With that, Alvarez and Arnold walked out of the office. Captain Copeland again closed the door.

"Marc, I want you to go home and wait until we decide what we're going to do. Keep your badge and pistol. I'll get back to you as soon as I can sort this all out."

He then turned to Al, who was still staring at the floor, his shoulders slumped forward. "Al, I am suspending your from duty pending a decision by Captain Copeland and I, in consultation with the Mayor and City Attorney. I need you to give me your badge and pistol. Don't touch anything in your office. In fact, Captain, would you please go and close up Al's office? Al, you can wait in the lobby. I'll have one of the patrol supervisors drive you home."

As Al pulled out his badge case and removed his badge and ID card, Chief Rogers again spoke, "Gentlemen, I have completely lost confidence in both of you. Marc, you were repeatedly told by both me and Captain Copeland not to get romantically involved with Lynne Littleton. You betrayed my trust in you. And, Al, regardless of your motives, what you did placed a witness in jeopardy and provided confidential information to a person who is a known associate of organized crime. Because of your actions, a man is dead. I can't believe I just lost my entire detective division in one fell swoop. Both of you get the hell out of here. I'll let you know when to come back." With that, he sat down hard and gave a deep sigh.

As I walked back to my office, Barbie Morris called my intercom. "Deputy Johnny Flynn has called a couple of times. I told him you were in a meeting. He asked me to have you call him as soon as you came out."

"Hey Marc, are you doing okay?" Flynn asked as he answered my call.

"Yea, I met with the Richardson detective and a Texas Ranger a while ago. They aren't taking any further action. I've been put on leave until the chief decides what he wants to do."

"The reason I called is that we've found enough evidence to positively hook Sack and Green to Tarver's killing. The medical examiner called a little while ago. That tooth and the piece of flesh we found in Cox's barn was positively identified as coming from Tarver. Plus, when we searched those cars in Sack's yard early this morning, we found a bloody plastic drop cloth in the trunk of one of them. It was the same car that Sack and Green were in when the deputy stopped them."

"What did Ethelene tell you?" I asked.

"We couldn't get her to talk to us. We came close, though. When I told her that I knew Sack, Green and probably Donovan had taken Tarver to that pit and had dogs tear him up. She said "He ain't the only one." When we tried to get her to tell us more, guess who showed up in all his slick-haired eminence?"

"Lawyer Lincoln Treadwell," I answered.

"Give that man a Cupie Doll!" Flynn laughed. "I tried to convince her that Donovan was going to be tying up loose ends and she was one of them. She looked scared when she left with Treadwell, but I don't expect to hear anything else out of her. I really don't have enough to charge her with anything. So, anyway, I guess that girl in the apartment last night was Littleton's wife, huh?"

"Yea and she's in the wind now too, right along with Donovan," I said.

As I hung up the phone, I sat at my desk forming and weighing an idea in my mind. When I felt that I had made the right decision, I walked back to Chief Roger's office and knocked on the door.

"Come in!" he shouted.

"Chief" I said as I sat down. "I have an idea I want to run past you. What Al did was wrong, but I can't help but think he did it for a reason he felt was good for me and the department. He's a damn good cop, Chief. Through all of this, he has always had my interests at heart. Obviously he and I can't continue to work together. I think you've come to that decision already." The chief nodded his head.

"Go on" he said

"If I voluntarily resigned, gave you a letter of resignation today, would you reinstate Al? You don't need to lose him, Chief. He's too valuable an officer. I have some other places I can go. First, I want to get my wife and kids back. I'm not sure I can do that as long as I'm still a cop. Then, I want to find something to do that will never put a strain on my marriage again. What do you think?"

"Marc, let me consider this. If I say no, will you quit anyway?"

"Probably" I replied.

"Go home and let me sleep on it. I agree about Al. We would be losing a damn good cop. And we would also be losing a damn good cop with your departure. I'll let you and Al know something in the morning."

As I returned to my office, I pulled the telephone directory out of my desk drawer and looked through it until I found the number I wanted. I then turned to the phone and punched the number into the keypad. In a few seconds a cheerful voice answered, "Wellington's International. How may I direct your call?"

"Dan Tyson, please. Tell him it's Detective Marc Bryant at Creekwood Police."

"Hey Detective Bryant, good to hear from you. I hope this isn't an official call."

"Does your offer still stand?"

"Oh, hell yea it does!" he answered. "Come by my office Monday morning. Let's talk."

After I finished with Dan Tyson, I drove to Gip Tuttle's house to tell him about Otto Sack and Willard Green. I was also holding out hope that Lynne might be staying there. As usual, I found Gip sitting on his front porch. The dogs in his yard were all facing him as if he was holding court.

"Detective Bryant, I was expecting a visit from you. I heard about Otto and his dumb-ass brother-in-law. Couldn't have happened to a nicer pair of assholes. Any idea where Donovan is now?"

I sat down on a porch step and started going over the events of yesterday. As I spoke, Judy came outside and handed me a cold beer. "Surely you're not on duty this late in the day, right?" she asked. The cold yeasty beer was just what I needed. When I started to tell Gip and Judy about the shooting at Lynne's apartment, Gip broke in: "Yea, we know all about that. Do you think Donovan sent that guy to grab Lynne?"

"I don't know, Gip. I don't think so. I think it was something altogether different. Lynne has disappeared. I guess she's scared now that her location has been revealed. Have you heard from her?"

Gip turned his head and stared off, not making a reply. Judy got up and went into the house. She returned in a few seconds with an envelope in her hand.

"Yes, Detective Bryant, we've seen her. She stopped by yesterday morning. She said that you would probably be coming by and asked me to give you this." She handed me the envelope. As I opened it and removed the note inside, I could faintly detect the soft vanilla scent of her on the paper.

Marc;

I'm sorry I had to leave like this. I trust you with my life but but I just don't trust the people around you. Please don't look for me. I'll be fine. I have enough money to go someplace and stay. Once I feel safe, I'll get in touch. I don't want to lose you. I love you. We'll be back together soon, I promise. Take care of yourself and be careful. Please keep Gip and Judy safe.

L

"She wants me to keep you two safe. I'm not sure how long I can do that. I was suspended from the department today. It's a long story that I don't have the energy to tell you. Once I know more, I'll make sure you know. By the way, Gip, Johnny Flynn with the sheriff's department still wants to get an affidavit from you about Donovan and Tarver. Sack and Green may be out of the way now, but Donovan's still out there."

192

CAJUN RULES

I finished my beer and walked back to my car. For some reason, I felt myself wanting to drive back to Richardson on my way home. "Muscle memory" is what the firing range instructor called it as he taught us to draw and fire our side-arms by reflex. I realized that there were a lot of memories I was about to leave behind. Once again, I came home to a dark and cold house.

CHAPTER 17

And so began my life as Assistant Director of Corporate Security for Wellington's International (Central Region). It was an impressive title for a less than impressive job. My main function was to keep the hands of the managers and cashiers out of the company profits and make sure that high-dollar steaks weren't going out through the back door. The job came with a company car; a nice Buick Regal with a vinyl top, a salary that would make even Chief Rogers envious and a private office with a view of the parking lot. Whenever I wondered if I had made the right decision, I could always gaze out at my Buick that was sitting below my window. It was reassuring.

I had been on the job for three months and already I was beginning to see how vastly different corporate life was from public service: Theft was now called "shrinkage"; police tradition was replaced with "corporate culture," and justice was found on the bottom line of a ledger. There were still "captains" and "chiefs" who were now called "vice presidents" and "regional directors." They weren't much different than their counterparts in the police department. Each one jealously guarded their little fiefdoms like feudal lords.

Chief Rogers and Captain Copeland had taken my advice and kept Al West on the department. He got two week suspension without pay. His wife, Joann, had a good job so I'm sure he didn't suffer much. Chief Rogers had also taken my advice and brought Office Ralph Cardenas in to replace me as detective.

My marriage was at an impasse. Kay and the girls were still living with her parents. Up to now, Kay had not moved forward with the divorce. Dan Tyson had offered the services of the law firm that handled all of Wellington's legal work. I told him that I would let him know if things began to move forward. Kay's mother brought the girls over on weekends and picked them up on Sunday nights. She refused to say much about our situation whenever I tried to engage her in conversation as she dropped the girls off. Once, when I was particular persistent, she said that Kay still loved me and that she thought things might eventually work out for us. She said that Kay had been hurt deeply and required a lot of healing. She assured me that she and Kay's father were putting some gentle pressure on her. She also confided that my girls were outright begging to come home. I just needed to be patient, she finally said.

I was looking through some material that was sent by an alarm company that was trying to get Wellington's business. I was familiar with them and knew their alarm systems to be reliable. As I turned the pages of the slick brochure they had sent, my secretary, Dixie Winters, came to the door. Every time I looked up at Ms. Winters, as she preferred to be called, I missed the bright pretty face of Barbie Morris and her quick wit. Ms. Winters had an urgent expression on her face and I wondered why she hadn't bothered to just call my intercom.

"Mr. Bryant, there's an Agent James Griggs on the phone. He said he was with the FBI. What should I do?"

"Quick, Ms. Winters. Go to the safe and burn all the documents. Then join the rest of us in the parking lot. If we all run at the same time, they can't possibly get all of us." Her lips began to form a large "O" and she looked like a guppy that had flopped out of its bowl.

"It's a joke, Ms. Winters. Put Agent Griggs through to my phone." As she turned back toward her desk, her mouth still looked like the grill of a '58 Edsel. Gee, did I miss Barbie!

"How's the life of the pork chop cop?" Griggs started right in. "Finding any malfeasance amongst the fresh greens in the salad bars?"

"Do you FBI guys write your own material or do you have a staff of comedians on the payroll?"

"Touchy...touchy! I come bearing news," he laughed.

"Good news or bad news? It'd better be good news. If it ain't, I'm hanging up."

"Well...maybe a little of both," he replied. "We got Randall Donovan."

"When...where?" I gasped. I couldn't believe what I was hearing.

"Truth be told, Marc, we've had him for a while. I've just now been given the clearance to call you. The Justice Department has been trying to deport old man Vincent Maricone for a long time. He's been here most of his life, but he never applied for citizenship. His deportation has been tied up in the courts for years. Recently, the case was assigned to new judge who swore he was going to get it done and send Maricone back home to Italy. Old Maricone, using the Mafia calculus that you can cancel the message by getting rid of the messenger, decided to have the judge hit. He was going to have Donovan do it."

"Holy shit!" was all I could say.

"We had managed to put one of our agents into the Maricone family ranks a couple of years ago. He was just starting to move up, too. He found out about the hit and that Donovan had been tapped to do it by Vincent Maricone, himself. He was able to let us know where we could find Donovan, but that's all he could find out. We put an around-the-clock surveillance on Donovan. Washington took charge and brought in a bunch of extra agents and techs. It finally paid off. We followed Donovan as he placed plastic explosives and a motion sensing detonator under the Judge's Mercedes. It was a Donovan special, for sure."

"Jim, that's amazing!"

"You haven't heard the best part yet. Donovan knew he was looking at spending the rest of his life in a federal prison, which wouldn't be long once the Maricones had someone in the prison yard take him out. He wasn't really part of the Maricone Family, which was why old man Maricone picked him to start with. Using Donovan would put some distance between them and the dirty deed. Anyway, Donovan didn't feel any particular loyalty to the Maricones, so he cut a deal."

"You got him to talk?" This was getting more and more incredible.

"Talk? He sang like Ella Fitzgerald. We've got indictments on old man Vincent, himself, along with two of his capos and several of his soldiers. He's even given us cases against the family in Tampa. He's a walking encyclopedia of organized crime in the south."

"How about your witness in Bossier City? Did he give that up?" I asked, getting ready to ask the big question.

"Yep, said he used the same kind of explosive device on him that he was going to use on the judge."

I finally had to ask; "Did he talk about my case?"

196

"Yea, that's why I called, Marc. I got to go to the safe-house where he's being kept and spend all the time I needed with him. He admitted the murders of Rick Littleton and Terry Don Ryan. He said that he, Otto Sack and Willard Green, took them to the river bottoms and shot them."

"Did he say why?"

"He said it was just a matter of family honor. Sack was family. After Littleton and Ryan beat up Sack and his wife, Donovan kept getting pressure from them to get revenge. He said that's why he made Sack and Green fire shots into Littleton. Since they wanted revenge, he made sure they were part of the deal."

"How about that ASPCA guy, Clayton Tarver? Did you ask him about that?"

"Yep. Donovan was convinced that Tarver must have been following him around when they caught him watching them from his car on the road. When they stopped him and wanted to know who he was, he refused to tell them anything. He said they took him to Cox's barn and tried to get him to talk. They threatened him with a couple of pit bulls that Sack brought in. Donovan said that Tarver kept telling him that he was going to send them all to the pen. You can probably guess what happened then."

Finally, I asked; "What about Lynne Littleton? Did he say that he was trying to find her?"

"I asked him about her. He said that he never intended to hurt Lynne. He said that she was like the daughter he always wanted. He never could understand how she wound up with a loser like Rick Littleton. I think he really cared a lot for her. Anyway, he told me that he didn't know where she was and hoped that where ever she is that she was safe and happy."

I felt like my heart was pounding out of my chest. "You mean all of this was for nothing?"

"Yea, Marc. That's the bad news. You had no way of knowing, though. You did what you had to do and you did a damn good job."

I searched for something else to say. I stared at my desktop with a thousand thoughts running through my mind at once. After a long silence, Griggs spoke up;

"There was another reason I called you. I've got a friend that I went through the academy with. He left the FBI a few years ago and joined a company in DC that specializes in filling foreign contracts."

"What kind of contracts?" I asked.

"Anything from soup to nuts. If the Shah of Iran wants a fleet of helicopters, my friend and his company can fix him up. Here's the deal; they are looking for American cops to help train the Saudi police force, sort of their version of the highway patrol. I told him all about you and he is real interested in talking to you. You can make a fortune on a two-year contract over there. There's no alcohol and you will have to live in the American compound, but you can make more in two years than you can in five years chasing steak thieves."

"Let me think about it, Jim. It almost sounds too good to pass up. I've been trying to get Kay and the kids back. Anyway, let me give it some thought and I'll let you know."

"He's got a couple of months to recruit, Marc. So, there's no big hurry. Let me know. Sorry to have bummed out your day. No matter what you decide, let's stay in touch."

I walked by Ms. Winter's desk and told her that I would be out for the rest of the afternoon. "In case Mr. Tyson should ask, what should I tell him?"

"Tell him that I'm going to get a demonstration of a new alarm system that I'm considering. The brochure is on my desk." I was glad to find that my ability to lie on the spot was still just as good.

I pulled up in front of Gip Tuttle's house and felt some comfort in seeing him sitting on his porch, as usual, looking out at his dogs. He gave me a smile and a wave.

"Gip, I've got some good news for you." As I sat down on the front steps, Judy came out, drying her hands on an apron. "I'm so glad to see you, Detective Bryant. It's been such a long time. Can I get you some…"

"Judy, would you please hush up a minute. Detective Bryant has some good news to tell us. Go ahead, Detective."

"Well first, since I'm no longer a detective, just call me Marc." As both Gip and Judy began to speak, I held up my hand to interrupt. "It's a long story, but what I want to tell you is that you don't have to worry about Randall Donovan anymore. He's in custody and he's going to be for a long time...probably forever."

"How did that happen?" Gip asked.

"I can't go into the details, but the feds got him and they've got him good."

"Well, Detective...I mean Marc, it's a better world now that that mean son-of-a-bitch isn't out there anymore, pardon my French" Judy inserted.

"I'm not saying that you do, but if you happen to know how to get a hold of Lynne and let her know, I would appreciate it. Where ever she is, I'm sure she will be relieved to know that Donovan isn't out there anymore."

I caught Gip and Judy exchanging furtive glances. Then, Judy nodded her head to Gip. He cleared his throat and said; "Marc, we, uh, didn't tell you the whole story about Lynne when you were here before. In fact, she told us not to tell you, but I feel..." Judy interrupted him, "We know how you feel about her. We love her too, Marc. She's like our own daughter. I know that you only have her best interests in your heart."

"What are you two talking about?" I looked back and forth at them.

"Well," Gip began, "do you remember me telling you that I offered to put her and Rick in touch with a dogman I know who is a jeweler down in Miami, back when I thought they had that stolen necklace?" I knew what was coming next.

"Well, when she was here, she asked me to put her in touch with him. I did."

I stared at the faces of Gip and Judy, searching for something to say. They both lowered their heads as if they had just admitted to a horrible crime. Then, I started to feel something that I hadn't felt in a long, long time. I felt a good old-fashioned belly laugh boiling up inside me. It burst forth from me in a loud guffaw that sounded like the braying of a donkey. In a few seconds, Gip and Judy joined in and the three of us were laughing and howling out on the porch like lunatics. I'm sure Gip's pit bull dogs must have looked up at us marveled at what a strange species we humans are.

Finally, Gip's laugh became a bout of coughing and I just ran out of breath. Judy grabbed her sides and said, "I think I just wet my pants!" This brought on a whole new round of hysterical laughter. It felt great! Months of tension pour out of me. With a wave, I walked to my car, still laughing. This was truly a day of discovery. As I drove back to my office, I kept thinking of a verse that I learned in Bible School when I was kid, "Nothing is covered up that will not be revealed; that will not be known."

The days and weeks began to speed past me. I no longer felt that I was still tethered to my old life as a police officer with all the recent revelations and I was able to just move on. I kept weighing the idea of going to Saudi Arabia and training new cops. On top of being very lucrative, it would be a once-in-a-lifetime adventure, one I could tell my grandkids about. It was a tough decision to make and one that suddenly became infinitely more complicated with a single phone call.

"Mr. Bryant, there is an international call for you on line four. It may be from one of our restaurants in Europe. The caller didn't give their name to the overseas operator."

"Thanks, Ms. Winters," I said as I reached for the phone. Wellington's had been building restaurants in the UK, Germany and Italy over the past year. I wondered if one of them was already having security problems.

"This is Marc Bryant" I said. The line was silent except for the faint static that you'd expect from a long-distance call. Then, finally,

"Hi, Cubby, bet you never expected to hear from me again, did you?" Suddenly those old feelings came back to me in a rush; the same feelings I used to get when I would gaze into her electric blue eyes or catch that vanilla scent or hear her voice, as I was hearing it now.

"Lynne, are you okay? Are you safe? I've worried about you so much." My words were pouring out of me and I felt my heart pounding in my throat. "How did you find me?" I finally managed to ask.

"I called the police station and talked to Barbie. She told me that you weren't a cop anymore and gave me your number. Why did you leave the police department, Marc? You loved that job. Was it because of me?"

"It's a long story, Lynne, but no, it wasn't your fault. It was Al who told Rabalais where to find you. He was threatening Al with some bad stuff from

Al's past. Anyway, I just decided to move on, Lynne. Oh, and Lynne, Ran Donovan has been caught by the feds and is no longer a threat to anyone. You don't have anything to worry about from him any longer."

"Oh, Marc, that all seems like such a long time ago. Are you and your wife back together?"

"No, we haven't gotten back together. I'm not sure if we ever will." I waited for her reply, but she was silent.

"So, you had that necklace all along, huh? Where was it? I think I saw just about everything you moved from that house to your apartment. Where did you have it hidden?"

"It was in a bank box all that time, Marc. Rick and I rented it under my mother's maiden name. We had to find some place to keep it safe."

"I keep remembering the day we went to your house to get your things. You rushed over to your dresser and seemed relieved at what you saw. I've always wondered about that, Lynne. Was the bank box key laying there? I don't remember seeing it."

"Sort of, Cubby. It was in a jar of face cream. I knew it was okay when I saw that the jar was still there. I tried to throw you off by going to the money under the floorboards. I guess that didn't work, huh? Can't get nothing past you."

"So Gip's friend was able to help you out?" I asked.

"Yea. It took him a little time to make the right contacts, but he treated me good on it; better than I expected. Of course, he got the biggest share, but I did okay. That's why I'm calling you."

"What do you mean?"

"Do you remember that fountain that I wanted us to sit beside one day? Don't say it if you do. Just, do you remember?"

"Yea, Lynne, of course I do. Why?"

"Because I want you to meet me there. I love you, Marc. I miss you so bad. I want to spend my life with you. I have enough now that we can live good lives together with practically anything we want. I want to share that with you. It's beautiful here and we can have so much fun."

"Lynne, I don't know…"

"You love me, don't you Marc? I know you do. As much as I love you, you just have to love me that much back."

"Of course, I love you, Lynne. You know that. It's just that I'm finally getting my life back together…"

"Okay, Cubby, listen up. You have one month to think about it and, you know, get your affairs in order, as they say. On the thirtieth of next month, at high noon, I will be sitting on the edge of that fountain. If I see you, then I will know that you are mine forever. If I don't, then I guess you never were. Please, Marc! Don't make everything that's happened to us all for nothing."

As I hung up the phone, Ms. Winters came to my door. "Is there a problem over in Europe?" she asked.

"Yea, you might say that. Nothing I can't handle though." I turned and stared out of my window, thinking of all the directions my life could go with one simple decision. It was a decision that I finally made late in the afternoon. I drove straight to the Carson house. As usual, Tom Warner's red Jaguar was parked at the curb, and, as usual, it was parked next to the fire hydrant.

When I knocked on the front door, Kay's father opened it. "Sorry, but I really need to talk to Kay" I said as I tried to walk past him. He reached out and grabbed my arm.

"Marc, she's out by the pool with the girls…and Tom Warner. Would you please go out there and get rid of that arrogant smarmy bastard and then get your family back?"

As I walked out of to the pool, I could see Kay lying on a lounge chair. Tom had a chair pulled up next to her. I could hear the girls splashing in the pool.

"Kay, I need to talk to you" I said as I walked toward them. Immediately, Tom got up and approached me, his hands held in front of him with his palms out.

"No, Marc, you aren't going to talk to her. My father's firm represents her and you will have to go through them. I am going to have to ask you to leave right now." By now, he was a couple of feet from me.

"Tom, do you remember what happened to you a few years ago, almost right on this very spot?"

"Yea" he snarled. You hit me without any warning. It you hit me again, my father's firm will sue you for every cent you have, provided you have anything left now. You're not a cop any more, Marc. In fact, I happen to know that you are no longer held in very high esteem with Creekwood Police."

"Oh, I don't know, Tom" I said, giving him my best smile. "I can still call in a few favors. In fact, I just called one a few minutes ago."

"Oh yea?" he said, getting up in my face now.

"Yea! I told them to send out a wrecker and tow that red Jaguar that's blocking the fire hydrant out front."

Tom's mouth made the same shape as Ms. Winter's and his head began to swivel between me and the door leading into the house. Finally, he ran for the door, brushing past Kay's father who gave him a little wave as he passed. He then turned to me and winked.

When I turned back to Kay, I could see that she had her chin tucked into her chest and her hand over her mouth. I realized she was laughing. She then threw her head back and laughed out loud, reminding me of Gip and Judy a few weeks earlier. It had been a long time since I had seen Kay laugh like that. It was beautiful.

"Poor ol' Tom," she laughed. "He was never very lucky in this yard, was he?"

"Kay, I want to talk to you about something" I said as I sat down on the chair that Tom had so graciously left for me. "I'm thinking that a change of scenery would be good. I'm thinking about traveling."

"Where are you thinking about traveling to?" Kay asked.

"I was thinking about Orlando, Florida. You know, they have that Disneyworld Park out there now. Then, maybe over to Cape Kennedy, to the NASA Space Museum."

"You want to go to Disneyworld? Why?"

"I think the girls would love it, Kay." As I said this, Katy and Kim ran over to me and wrapped their little wet arms around my legs. "Oh boy," Katy shouted. You're taking us to Disneyworld?"

"I'm taking all of us to Disneyworld." I turned and looked into Kay's eyes. "I want my family back, Kay. I want you back. I did some stupid things. I'm so sorry I hurt you."

Kay looked off to her right and I followed her eyes. She was looking at her parents, who were standing under their awning with their arms around each other. They were smiling. Kay turned back to me and, again, our eyes met.

"Maybe it would be good for the girls…and for us, I guess. I'm not going to tell you that I'll come back to you. I won't commit to that now. But, maybe the trip will help me decide."

"You'll see, Kay. Things have changed. Give me a chance to prove to you that things are different now and prove how much I love you."

As Kay looked deep into my eyes, she said, "Then, can I ask you a question?"

"Anything," I answered.

"Since you're working for Wellington's now, do you still get the free dinner passes?"

"You bet! They give me four every month."

"Well…," Kay smiled and kissed me on the cheek, "that's a start."

THE END

ABOUT THE AUTHOR

Martin Brown is a native of Dallas, Texas. He was a patrol officer and detective with the police department in Garland, Texas, leaving in the early 1980's to form a private detective agency in downtown Dallas. He retired to a small ranch in Glen Rose, Texas where he lives today.

THANK YOU FOR READING!

If you enjoyed this book, we would appreciate your customer review on your book seller's website or on Goodreads.

Also, we would like for you to know that you can find more great books like this one from Cold West at www.ColdWest.com

COLD WEST PUBLSHING

An Imprint of Creative Texts Publishers, LLC

www.ingramcontent.com/pod-product-compliance
Lightning Source LLC
Chambersburg PA
CBHW072354020726
47506CB00004B/1114